Tales of fire

....

Madison Sullivan

Contents

To Slay a Dragon

I smelled the copper tang of death before I saw a carcass. The trail of blood on the path started as nothing but a light spotting. A few feet further, it grew into a thick streak of reddish brown which led to the remains of a deer that was missing its body from the waist down. Sharp teeth had cleaved skin, fat, and bone, leaving the animal's entrails oozing freely into the snow. There was no stench of decay in the biting cold, but I still felt the urge to squeeze my nose shut while my guide, Endris, crouched to study the carcass.

"The dragon's nest shouldn't be far now." Endris' braided dark hair slipped around the curve of his shoulder to his back as he turned to look at me. "The tracks are fresh, and the deer died no longer than a few hours ago."

"Ah, good," I said, nudging the half-eaten carcass with my boot. "If I ask the dragon nicely, you think it will make me a fire? I'm freezing."

Endris groaned as he rose to his feet. "We part ways now," he said. "Finally."

"Aw, I'll miss you too, Endris."

I looked up at the steep path ahead of me. It'd lead further up the mountains and to a dragon's nest, where I would have to face the beast alone. Such were the rules. Man versus dragon, with no interruptions and no help. Endris was only here to act as my guide through the mountain passages.

The Serpentine Mountains could easily be mistaken for a serene place. Ice crystals growing on sheer cliffs sparkled in the sunlight. Pine trees reached higher than the queen's castle to the heavens, and at the summit, one could overlook valleys of green, stretching into the distance as far as the eye could see. Wind whistled along the slopes of looming mountains, eager to engulf trespassers and fling them off the crumbling paths. It was a long way down from here.

For all his moodiness, I was still grateful I took Endris with me. Some refused to 'waste' the coin. Many of those people never returned, or so the innkeeper at the Last Stop had claimed. There was some ulterior motive there, given that she also received a share when she recommended guides like Endris to travellers.

"This is your last chance to change your mind, Laurence," Endris said. "You don't need to do this. You can leave the beast in peace."

I turned to Endris. His dark brown eyes bored into mine, solemn and pleading. "You know, you keep saying that," I said. "But if you don't want people to slay dragons, consider stop guiding them up these mountains and finding them dragons."

Endris sighed. "You're right. I don't believe in these hunts. The beasts never leave this mountain. They keep to themselves, and we should offer them the same courtesy. But lofty morals do not put coin in my pocket. So, if you're certain of this..." Endris pointed at the path up ahead. "The wind is in your favour; it won't be able to smell you coming. You will have one surprise shot if you're quiet."

I tapped my chin. "I don't know, Endris. Being quiet is going to be a challenge."

"Right, I don't know what I was thinking. Maybe you can crack jokes until the dragon loses its will to live."

"Sounds good. I'll do that. Maybe the dragon does like my jokes and it will give me one of its teeth willingly."

Endris shot me a tight-lipped smile. "I know this is all fun to you, but a dragon is not a joke. Be careful and don't be long — I think commander Ytel may try to leave without you. He was muttering about wanting a quiet ride home last time I saw him."

"I'll try not to make the fight drag on. Get it? Drag on?"

"... I hope the dragon eats you." Endris ducked deeper into his leather coat and turned away from me.

"At least it will be warm in there," I joked at his retreating back.

Nerves clawed at my insides, however, as Endris nimbly climbed down and disappeared from sight. I knew he was right. Much as I wanted to, I wouldn't be able to joke or charm my way out of a fight with a dragon.

Before moving on, I checked all my equipment one last time. My quiver was full of arrows made of wood with copper heads to bolster my storm-touched powers. My trusted yew longbow was slung over my shoulder. I had named her Stormbringer.

Satisfied with the state of my arrows and bow, I resumed my climb on the winding road. The higher I went, the more intense the cold became. I grew up in a town near the Thundercoast, but even in stormy weather at sea, I had never felt such biting cold. The wind sawed at my throat. My fingertips, which were not covered by gloves, had long gone numb.

The cold wasn't the only danger one faced in the Serpentine mountains. Aside from the obvious dragons living here, many had told me cautionary tales of scarps and crumbling stone. Brilliant scholars and dragon hunters plummeted to their death before ever reaching a dragon's nest. Poor sods.

I could not let that happen to me. I had to reach the nest, kill a dragon, and be knighted by the queen. It was that, or facing much more dangerous dragons at home; disappointed parents. I'd take my chances with the one in the mountains.

"You carry the hopes and dreams of house Montbow, Laurence," I mockingly imitated my mother's voice. Then I lowered my voice to imitate my father. "You were storm-touched after generations of no magical abilities in our family. Every single moment of your life has been leading up to you shooting that one arrow between the eyes of the dragon. Then you will charm the queen and ask for money for our house. And while you're at it, also fix our old trading contracts, secure your sisters and brothers good marriages, have the Thundercoast rebuilt, jump higher. No pressure, though."

I sighed and walked on. For a while, snow crunching under my boots and the wind was all I heard. Then a deep rumbling blended into the howling. The breathing of a beast, and a testament to its sheer size. I came to an abrupt halt. That would have to be the dragon. My fingers trembled on the grip of my bow as I sneaked further. I drew an arrow from my quiver and stayed low.

I wasn't Endris, who possessed a wealth of knowledge on dragons (even if I'd never admit he had good traits to his face), but I knew instinctively that I could not face this beast head on. The dragon's fiery breath was its most dangerous weapon, aside from its teeth and tail. If I got caught in its fire before it died, I would be a pile of ash. My eyes darted to the right. There was a natural opening in the rock with a path leading upward.

Deciding to take my chances with more cover, I stepped onto the path. It was dark, but shafts of light slipped through cracks in the stone overhead. I heard water running somewhere behind the tunnel, and the ground was slimy. I had to shuffle forward slowly to prevent myself from losing my balance on wet rocks, but my gambit paid off. Light shone from the other side of the tunnel. I sidled forward, back pressed firmly against the bumpy rock wall. Once I reached the edge, I peeked around the corner.

There, I saw it. The dragon.

I sucked in a shuddering breath and held it. I couldn't help but marvel at the sight. The beast was pitch-black, like charcoal in a fireplace, with webbed wings I estimated could stretch as far as the pine trees were tall. Its eyes were closed as it appeared to be sleeping, but its mere presence emanated raw power.

I understood, for a moment, what Endris meant. Part of me didn't want to kill a magnificent creature like this. It deserved to be free and soar through the skies. Unfortunately, like Endris, I couldn't afford to have lofty morals. Morals were reserved for nobles who weren't of an all but decrepit house and on the brink of losing their title and their crumbling estate.

I would have one surprise shot. One chance. Taking a deep breath, I touched the copper tip of my arrow with an ungloved finger and charged it with my storm magic until the copper glowed green. I attached the arrow to my bow and took aim.

Between the eyes. No suffering. Nice and clean.

I breathed in and out and released the arrow.

I realised the direction was off immediately. I'd missed. Shit, shit, the wind. I'd hadn't accounted for the wind; it was stronger outside of the tunnel where I was standing. Such a foolish mistake.

The arrow swished past the dragon's head and buried in its left wing. A deafening screech echoed through the mountain range and vibrated throughout my entire body. The dragon's emerald eyes settled on me, and my heart stopped.

In a wave of panic, I balled my right hand into a fist and unleashed the magic in the copper head of the arrow. The dragon shrieked in pain as thunder rippled through its flesh. I had torn holes in the membrane of its wing — it would not be able to catch wind. If the dragon couldn't fly, I still stood a chance.

I drew a second arrow, but the dragon didn't give me the chance to take another shot. It opened its mouth. Hot flames burst forth, and

I dove into cover, groaning as my elbows caught the brunt of my fall. Even while hidden behind solid rock, I felt the scorching heat of its fiery breath. One touch of that and I'd be cooked like a boar on a spit.

My breathing came shallow and fast as I tried to come up with a new plan. I had relied on finishing the fight with one arrow, maybe two. I wasn't prepared for a long battle, nor did the dragon seem to want a long battle.

Heavy thumping moved my way, and the ground shook as the dragon charged the tunnel and slammed its body against the entrance. I nearly lost my footing. The stone wall crackled dangerously, and I got pelted with dust and small pieces of rock. One more slam like that and I feared the tunnel would collapse on top of me.

"Oh, shit," I swore.

I did not sign up for this. I couldn't stay here — I had to run to the other side and pray the dragon lost my trail. I fought to keep myself from slipping on uneven, wet stone while I made a run for it.

I made it halfway before the ground rocked again, and I fell. A shadow cast overhead, and I realised the dragon had climbed on top of the tunnel trying to pursue me. But the stone could not carry its weight for long. The crackling noise grew louder.

When I looked up, I saw the wall on my left rupturing in front of my eyes. Cursing, I threw myself against the opposite wall, right before the tunnel partially collapsed. Light poured into my face as rock broke off and hurdled down the slope with an ear-splitting noise. The dragon, unable to fly, got swept along in the landslide and disappeared from sight in an enormous cloud of dust. I heard it crash into the valley below, and then the mountains grew silent again.

The ground under my feet was stable. I slumped down, trying to gain control of my breathing and my drumming heart. The dragon fell down into the frozen valley, but our battle had not ended yet. Not until I confirmed it was dead, and I took its scales and teeth as proof.

"Come on, Laurence," I told myself. "At least you're not cold anymore. And they're counting on you. You are the hopes and dreams of your house."

I grinned despite my dire situation. Saying the words 'hopes and dreams' out loud made me snort every time. I allowed myself one more moment to catch my breath, then forced myself to my feet.

Thankfully, most of the paths Endris and I had taken to travel up were left intact. On trembling legs, going down took an eternity, but eventually I arrived at the foot of the mountains.

Following the destruction the landslide had left was easy. All I needed to do was pursue the trail of snapped pine trees, boulders, and rubble. The trail led all the way to the lake... and there it ended. No more rocks, no more snapped trees, but also no dragon.

All I saw was water, snow, and pines swaying in the wind. I didn't understand. How could the dragon have gotten away? It couldn't fly, and it was too large to move in this dense forest without leaving traces of where it went.

I looked left and right, looking for clues regarding my missing dragon, and that was when I spotted a strange shape near the edge of the water. It almost looked like a... I squinted as I walked closer, and then my eyes grew wide once I realised the form I saw was a young man.

A naked young man laying with his face down and his legs dangling in the water.

***

A /N
Hey, so sometimes I enjoy making maps for some visual support when I write. It's just for fun and to get an idea of how I picture things. Don't expect geographically 100% correct maps haha. Whenever I make a map of a location, I'll leave it for you all at the end of the chapter. c:

Location: Serpentine Mountains

Eternally in winter's grasp, this beautiful but inhospitable mountain range houses beasts of legends: dragons. The only people willing to risk traversing the steep slopes are dragon hunters hoping to become a knight, and scholars interested in how these mountains, which play outside of nature's laws, came to be. Many travellers have met their unfortunate demise trying to navigate the winding paths.

The Last Stop is a village located west of the Serpentine Mountains. Its inhabitants are mostly guides and shopkeepers making their living from accommodating travellers journeying to the east, or seeking to travel up the mountains.

Oleander

I was convinced I'd roll the man over and find a stiff, frozen corpse.

The only corpse I'd wanted to handle today was a dragon's, but unfortunately, we couldn't always get what we wanted. This poor bastard in the snow sure didn't.

During our trek up the mountains, Endris had told me of a peculiar phenomenon that made victims of the cold take off their clothes in their confusion, believing they were burning instead of freezing. This wouldn't be the first person found stark naked in the snowy valley if I could believe Endris. Obviously, I hadn't believed him. I'd laughed at him. Should've known he was serious because he always was.

I trudged through the snow towards the man. When I reached his side, I hooked my arms under his armpits and pulled until his legs were out of the lake. The man wasn't stiff yet, but his skin was icy-cold to the touch. When I pressed my fingers to his neck, I felt a faint pulse.

I raised a brow. "Really? You're not dead?"

Well, shit. This highly complicated matters. If he was dead, that'd be it. I'd done everything I could by dragging him out of the water, and I'd be free to hunt my dragon and fetch the body after. Now, I was in a moral predicament. Depending on who you asked, either risking letting the dragon go or not helping this man was the wrong choice.

I stared off into the distance. No dragon in sight. Perhaps I'd been wrong and it could fly even with tears in its wing's membrane. I could try to find my way back to its nest and wait for it to return there.

I was obligated to try. If I lost my dragon now, it could be months before I had saved enough coin for another attempt. I'd make my entire family homeless if my sisters twirling their hair and batting their eyelashes was no longer enough to keep debt collectors patient. A lot to risk for one stranger who was likely to die.

I stood and turned away from all-but-corpse in the snow. I took exactly two steps before guilt, as if tethering me to this man, made me stop. With a deep sigh, I turned back.

"Guess the dragon's long gone now, and all the other people I have to save are far away. You're in luck."

The man wasn't heavy, so I hoisted him on to my shoulder. His arms flopped against my back, while I made an eye sweep of the rock walls. There were plenty of caves embedded in the weather-worn stone. I picked one at random. I could only hope the one I chose wasn't owned by wild animals whose mother had never taught them to share.

The cave I entered smelled musty, but not animal-musty. I noticed ash scars on the stone from past fires, which meant I wasn't the first one here. It looked good enough. I unclasped my cloak and carefully wrapped it around the man. When I lifted his head to put the hood on, his long hair shifted to the side. I dropped him when I saw his ears.

Pointed ears.

I reached for my bow and readied an arrow. With a drumming heart, I aimed the arrowhead at the man's forehead.

I had read books about the war between humans and elves.

Ages ago, the Starcross woods, far north of the Serpentine mountains, were the largest and bloodiest battlefield known to humankind. Elves were monsters who had started attacking travellers unprovoked, using them as blood sacrifices in their rituals. They relished in leading lost human children into the swamp with pretty lights and watching them drown. King Bertram the third picked up his sword, gathered his soldiers, and put an end to their reign of terror. Ever since the war ended and humans won, the elves had vanished like nightmares of an age long past. They only existed in cautionary tales of a weary father to his children now: 'quiet or the elves will find you and carve your heart out'

I'd always imagined they were taller and scarier. The history books would have me believe elves were hideous with horns and scales and smelling like rotting eggs. But this one wasn't like a creature from nightmares. He looked like... a person, but thinner and smaller.

We weren't that different. The bridge of his nose was less deep and more in one line with his forehead, and his ears were obviously pointy. He also had no beard and longer hair than most human women. Still, if he walked in our streets and people didn't know he was an elf, he'd receive admiring stares. He was far from ugly.

I'd already given up a lot of hunting time for this supposed 'monster' wrapped in my cloak. If I wanted him to tell me his story, he needed to survive... And as a hated enemy of the palace, he could also be worth a reward if I turned him in at the palace. I'd get desperately needed coin and they could decide his fate. I put the arrow away.

"You have to survive for now anyway," I told the elf. "My family will never believe this otherwise, and I need a really good reason I delayed chasing that dragon, should I not find it again."

The elf needed to warm up, so I needed a fire. Thankfully, the dragon had been most helpful by providing me with a lot of snapped branches with its unfortunate plummet into the valley. I hurried outside to collect firewood and returned to the cave with my arms full of branches. With a small crackle of thunder from my fingertips, I had a fire going within moments.

With a fire started and without the icy wind battering us, it was rapidly growing warmer inside the cave. I finally had a moment to think on what the hell I was supposed to do with this situation.

I didn't have rope to tie the elf up. My 'captive' was skinny and naked, however. If he woke, I presumed I'd be able to handle him even without a weapon, but I kept my bow and knives close.

I glanced at the elf's ears. Mother had once told me the tip of an elf's ear hurt to touch, like the tip of a blade. It sounded like moonshine on the water; there was no way skin could cut other skin. But I'd thought the same about Endris' story regarding naked men in the snow, which turned out to be very true.

I couldn't resist poking one ear tip. Just one. Scooting closer to the elf, I reached out slowly.

The elf didn't stir or make a sound as my finger inched closer and closer to his ear, but the moment my finger touched pallid skin, the elf spread his eyes open. He blinked blearily, and then his gaze settled on me. I quickly retracted my finger and placed my hand on the handle of my knife.

"Uh, hi there," I tried with a sheepish smile. "I wasn't poking you, I swe—"

The elf screamed.

On hands and feet, he scrambled to a dark corner. While I pulled my knife, he pulled my cloak up to cover most of his face, leaving only his wide, terrified eyes and crown visible. When his gaze darted to the knife in my hand, he pressed himself against the wall with a whimper. I saw his chest heave underneath my cloak in his panic, and tears welled up in his eyes.

"Hey, you're not supposed to cry," I protested. "You're supposed to try and cut my heart out. Didn't you read the stories?"

I lowered my knife, but I definitely didn't lower my guard. The elf followed my movements closely. He uncovered his nose and lips in response to my act of goodwill so I could see his entire face, but he didn't leave his safe corner. He looked like a scared prey animal that was trying to hide from the hunter. The sight tugged at my heartstrings.

I pressed a hand to my forehead. "Great, now I feel like a monster while you're supposed to be one."

I kept prattling on, but I had no clue whether he even understood what I was saying. I'd never seen an elf. I didn't know what tongues they spoke.

"Uh, back. To. Fire. Warmth. Good," I said, exaggerating every word, while gesturing at the fire. "I know Endris would disagree, but sitting closer to me isn't worse than freezing. Don't try anything funny, though. I'll stab you."

Whether the elf understood the meaning of my words, I still didn't know. He seemed to at least understand my gestures and body language. Keeping my cloak tightly wrapped around him, he crawled back to the fire. He sat as far away from me as possible, hugging his knees to his chest. His eyes kept darting my way nervously.

I didn't know much, but it was clear to me that this man was no warrior. He wasn't a hideous monster from nightmares, either. He looked regal with prominent cheekbones, green eyes veiled by impossibly long lashes, freckles on his nose, and silky, silvery hair that fell perfectly around his oval face despite nearly freezing to death.

I narrowed my eyes at the elf. "So, speak," I ordered. "... If you even can. Anyway, why are you here?"

The elf shrunk back in fear at my harsh tone. He swallowed thickly and glanced at the cave opening. "Where... where is here?" he asked.

The elf spoke in a thick accent, with rolling r's and odd intonations, but at least he spoke.

"So you can understand me?" I asked. "Good. We're in the Serpentine mountains. Well, we're in the valley below the mountains if we want to be precise."

"... The Serpentine mountains," the elf repeated softly.

"Yep. So, why you're here and where did you came from?"

"I..." The elf looked into the flames licking at the branches. His bottom lip started trembling again. Eyes filled with unshed tears. "I don't remember."

I awkwardly scratched the back of my head. It was hard to remain stern when the enemy you were interrogating kept almost crying. "Like nothing? You don't know who you are?"

"No, I know my name. I'm..." The elf's eyebrows knitted, as if he had to dig deep for the answer. "Oleander."

I swallowed my remark about that being a strange name. Oleander looked at me with a hint of curiosity, though fear still had the upper hand. "And what is your name?" he dared to ask after a brief hesitation.

"I'll be asking the questions," I replied curtly. "Not you."

Oleander flinched like I'd slapped him in the face, and I immediately felt like a monster again. I knew appearances could deceive, but by the creators, this elf was making it difficult to behave the way I should with an enemy of the palace. It was like kicking a puppy.

"Laurence," I reluctantly gave him my name.

I already regretted it when Oleander offered me a shy smile. It broke my heart a little. He was supposed to be a coldblooded killer, but so far, I had seen no signs of him wanting to sacrifice me in some sort of dark ritual. Everything this man did was making it harder to do what I needed to do; fire a warning signal to Endris and get him here so we could dress this elf, tie him up, and deliver him to the queen.

Cursing under my breath, I rose to my feet. I had to do it. I couldn't return home empty-handed.

"Stay here," I told Oleander.

"Are you going to find others?" Oleander asked. I heard a tremor in his voice. "I can't go to a human settlement. They will hurt me."

I grimaced. I liked it much better when I thought he couldn't understand me, and he couldn't ask such tough questions. I breathed in and out deeply before spinning around to face the elf. I wouldn't lie, but I wouldn't tell him the entire truth, either.

"You need clothes," I said. "I'm going to call my friend here, and I will stay with you until he gets here. He's grumpy, but won't harm you. Got it?"

Oleander hesitated, but then he nodded.

"Good. Just... sit by the fire. Drink something."

I pulled my waterskin from my belt and handed it to Oleander. Then I swiftly exited the cave before the elf could ask more confronting questions.

I grabbed my bow and pulled an arrow from the quiver at my hip as I walked out into the valley. With my fingertip, I charged the copper arrowhead, aimed for the heavens, and released the arrow. When I clenched my palm, the arrowhead crackled. I made it explode with branches of green light spreading like a tree in the sky.

Oleander poked his head out of the cave. His eyes were big and round again, but this time I saw a small sparkle in them. "You roar!"

I let out a surprised laugh before I could stifle it. "What? I 'roar'?"

"Yes."

He pointed at the sky.

I almost looked at where he was pointing, but I couldn't lose sight of the elf. "Oh, you mean my storm magic? Is that what you call it, roaring?"

Oleander nodded. "It suits you."

"Why?" I snorted. "Because it's very, very noisy, just like me?"

"Because those who roar are courageous. Most humans would kill an elf rather than giving him a chance... And most elves would kill a human rather than giving him a chance."

Oleander was dead serious from what I could tell, and an utterly unwelcome flush crept up my neck. I was giving the elf false hope. He thought I was a good person, while he was only going to be a bag of coin to me and I told him half-truths to keep him calm for the time being. I had no choice. I had to protect my family; I couldn't protect a stranger too. Not even one as intriguing as Oleander.

I cleared my throat and walked past Oleander back into the cave. "Endris will find us soon," I said. I plopped down in front of the flames. "And now we wait."

Enemy of the Palace

Endris arrived in the valley before I had finished gathering new branches for the fire. Despite his tall stature, Endris was quiet as a cat. I didn't hear my guide approaching until the crunch of pine needles right behind me gave me a start. I whirled around, dagger clenched in my hand, only to find Endris standing there with one raised eyebrow, wind-swept hair, and berry-red cheeks. He had clearly run the entire way.

I clutched my chest as I put my dagger away. "You scared me. Has nobody taught you sneaking up on people is rude?"

Endris didn't reply. His gaze swept over me and then settled on my face. "You fired a crackling arrow, yet you're completely fine?"

"And you ran all the way here for me," I replied with a wink. "Sorry, I just missed your grumpy face so much I had to summon you here."

The vein on Endris' forehead popped out. "You better have a good reason for this, or I'm doubling my pay."

I had learned from past encounters Endris was always serious. I raised my hands in surrender. "I have a good reason. How shall I say this..." I glanced at the downed trees and rubble left by the dragon, then at the cave embedded in the sheared-off rock face where the elf was waiting. I pressed my finger to my lips and continued in a hushed tone, "There's an elf in the cave."

Endris stared at me. "Certainly. And I have the fey queen living in the inn's basement."

"I hope she enjoys her stay then, because this one time I'm not kidding." I pointed to the cave, which had smoke escaping through the opening. "There's an elf in there. If you don't believe me, go see for yourself."

Doubt flickered in Endris' dark eyes. His eyebrows squished together. "If this is a joke, I'm charging triple," he threatened. Then he started crossing the valley with long strides. I picked up my stash of branches and hastily followed him.

Oleander was wrapped up in my cloak near the fire just the way I had left him, but he jumped to his feet when Endris burst into the cave.

Their eyes met. Endris' posture stiffened, while Oleander simply observed Endris with quiet curiosity. It was a good sign that my guide wasn't reaching for his sword, but I hadn't a clue what he was thinking.

I cleared my throat. "Oleander, Endris. Endris, Oleander."

Both men ignored me in favour of staring at each other. How rude.

Unlike he'd been with me, Oleander seemed calm with Endris. A slow smile spread on his lips, his eyes lit with an inner glow. "Hello," he said.

"You need clothes, elf," Endris replied curtly. He shook the bulky pack he had strapped to his shoulders off and handed it to Oleander. "Take what you need from this."

When Endris turned to me, he looked like a nervous horse about to bolt. "Outside," he barked before grabbing my arm and pulling.

I allowed Endris to drag me outside, but protested loudly all the way. "Ow! Stop! There's a reason I became a bowman, you know. I bruise like a peach. Let me walk on my own!"

Endris finally released me several feet away from the cave. "How, by the creators, did you find an elf?" he hissed, shooting me an intense, icy stare like I was to blame for his presence here. Then he gestured at the rubble. "And what happened here?"

"Both excellent questions, I said. "The dragon caused a landslide and plummeted into the valley after I shot its wing, leaving the trail of destruction you see here. When I tracked it down to the valley, the elf was in the water and when I pulled him out, he was alive. Says he doesn't remember how he got here, though."

"Did you finish the hunt, then?"

I blew my cheeks out and released the air. "Nope."

"You chose to save the elf over chasing the dragon?" For the first time ever, I saw the tiniest spark of admiration in Endris' eyes. I had to snuff it immediately.

"Not — not exactly," I said. "Look, the dragon was gone. It left no tracks in the valley, but the elf was right here and I knew I couldn't return home empty-handed."

Endris was back to his grumpy self. His lips pressed together in a slight grimace. "Naturally. It's still fortunate you found him when you did, I suppose."

"Sure." I said. "Hey, why did that elf seem so happy to see you?"

"I don't know."

Endris' words slipped out a little too fast. He talked to me sideways rather than head on. How well did I know my guide, really? I'd trusted him enough to let him lead me up the mountains because he was well known and trusted in the palace. Endris brought many hopeful young men and women eager to prove themselves and become knights to the mountains. But word in the street was that he had spoken with the queen, pleading against the dragon slaying tradition.

"So, did you bring a rope in that rescue bag of yours?" I asked. "We have to tie the elf up. I'm going to hand him over to the queen."

"I have a rope, yes," Endris replied. I felt the reluctance in his words, and I understood. I'd felt the exact same reluctance.

"Look, I know Ole- the elf, looks..." I swallowed my last word because I couldn't say I thought he looked beautiful. That was a dangerous word to use for an elven man. "Innocent," I settled on. "But he's an enemy of the palace. The war never officially ended. We only stopped fighting because the elves vanished. You remember that, right?"

Endris' eyebrows drew in. "Yes, I know that."

"Does human children's blood soaking the ground of Starcross woods mean anything to you?" I pushed harder. "To not agree with the dragon hunts decreed by the queen is one thing. To be reluctant to capture an enemy of the palace is another. I don't like it either, but we have to turn him in."

"I know." Endris ground his teeth. I'd never seen him shaken by anything, but this elf seemed to bring it out in him. "Yet, you're right. I think we shouldn't kill him."

"Good thing I only want to capture him, then. I'm bringing him to the palace and the queen can decide."

"Yes, you let the palace decide. Your hands are clean." Endris snorted. "Handing him over is killing him, but the cowardly way because you aren't able to raise the sword yourself. Just like you nobles gladly eat the meat, but call skinning the rabbit barbaric and insist it happens outside of your sight."

Endris looked genuinely angry at me. We played around a lot, but I always thought we were jesting and liked each other underneath all that. Now, I wasn't so sure.

"What's going on, Endris?" I asked. "Why do you care so much for an elf?"

Endris turned away from me, rubbing a hand through his hair. "I don't care. But I think he isn't a part of this war, Laurence."

"We're all part of this war."

"You can honestly be so—" Endris made an exasperated sound. "What has this elf done to us? Look at him. He's no threat, and we were never personally at war. Our ancestors were." Endris shook his head. "No, not even our ancestors. The king who picked up his weapon and made knights follow was at war."

"Yes, because the elves were slaying innocents and sacrificing them to whatever demented gods they worship!" I protested. "For all we know, they still do that, just not to humans because we drove them out!"

"Should I also blame you then, for what your uncle did to your family and your servants, driving you all to ruin?"

I froze. He did not just go there.

For a moment, Endris seemed unsure of himself, too. Even if my family was no longer wealthy, I still had my title, and he did not. When we got back to the inn, I could have commander Ytel cut his tongue cut out for the insolence and we both knew it.

Endris regained his confidence when I stayed silent. His hands curled into fists then straightened. "I'm meaning to say: will we blame every human for every single mistake made by a human? For every killer, do you shoot all other men, too? If so, we could never speak with anyone because everyone would be dead."

"That sounds like a brilliant plan," I said lightly. "I will shoot everyone and never speak to anyone again. What a nice and peaceful life."

Endris stared at me. He waited for my decision, not my jokes, as usual. He silently pleaded with his eyes, like he did for the dragons, but stronger.

I groaned and looked away. "I can't deal with both you and the elf giving me the puppy eyes. But I won't go home empty-handed. You know that."

I needed a source of coin or a dragon for knighthood, or I might as well climb this mountain and jump to my death after the dragon.

Mother and father tried to keep up appearances, but nobody was fooled. People only needed to look at the cracks in the walls of our estate, or hear a debt collector complain in a tavern, and they would know.

Endris looked like he was biting back more unfriendly words about nobles and greed. Then he nodded. "I understand. I will give you free guidance up the Serpentine mountains for a second dragon hunt attempt, and I will return home with you to your parents and offer my services, and all coin I make guiding people up the mountains, to the Montbow family for two months."

My jaw went slack. "I'm pretty sure I heard that wrong. You want to work for the Montbow family for free over this? Why does this matter so much to you? This elf is a stranger and a monster. Allegedly, according to the stories."

"Stories written by the victor," Endris countered. "Does he seem like a monster to you?"

"... No," I reluctantly admitted. I had found myself thinking quite the opposite, too. Oleander had been on the verge of tears when threatened. He was scared, alone, and cold. I already dreaded the moment I'd arrive at the palace and turned him in. The look on his face when I betrayed him and tied him up would leave a sour taste in my mouth.

I growled in frustration. "What would you have me do? If I don't bring him in, someone else who sees him will. The moment we arrive at the inn, the elf will have all blades and arrows pointed his way. Commander Ytel will have my head if he finds out, too."

"Unless... we don't go to the inn," Endris suggested. "The elf needs to travel back to his people through the Starcross woods. If we travel west and restock once at your parents' estate, he can reach the woods safely."

"Are you out of your mind?" I bit. "You can't seriously be suggesting I take him to my mother and father? My brothers and sisters? Hey everyone, this is my new friend. Yes, I know I make questionable decisions, but I swear this one is not a blood-loving monster who will eat my siblings while we sleep."

"I will keep an eye on him," Endris promptly offered. "We don't have to enter the estate, and I will take full responsibility for him. He won't attack you or your family."

Just when I thought I couldn't be more confused, I was. "You truly feel strongly about this."

"Yes," Endris simply replied.

"I'm going to find out why."

"No, you will not."

Turning on his heels, Endris started walking back to the cave. I walked with him.

"So, we're not taking him to the inn?" I asked.

"No. I suggest you let commander Ytel know the hunt failed because of a landslide, and that he needs to report to the palace. We will travel to your estate to prepare for a swift second attempt. It's the truth, aside from not mentioning the elf."

"By the storm god's breath. I can't believe I'm agreeing to this." Dragging a hand up my forehead, I entered the cave after Endris.

Oleander had put on the clothes from Endris' pack. The sleeves were too long and that belt was working hard to keep the pants from dropping. My lips twitched at the sight. "Well, they're a little large for you, but better this than too small."

"Yes." Oleander smiled shyly. "Thank you for the clothes, sir."

"You're welcome," Endris said, before turning to me and shooting me a look as if saying 'yes, such a monster.'

"Are we leaving now?" Oleander asked.

I crossed my arms and looked at Endris. He insisted we bring him along so he could fill him in.

"Yes, we are going to Laurence's house," Endris told Oleander.

Oleander's eyes grew wide. "Will they be alright with me being there?"

"Yes," Endris replied for me, before I could open my mouth to say definitely not. "Because you will cover your ears." Endris reached into his pocket and pulled out a ribbon. "Tie your hair and make sure your ears stay covered."

Oleander accepted the ribbon and tried to reach back to tie his hair. When he lifted his arms above his head, he winced and lowered them. "I think I have hurt my arm. Could you tie it for me?"

Oleander addressed me. There was so much trust in his gaze now.

He trusted the wrong people. I'd been ready to hand him over to the palace if Endris hadn't interfered. I still wasn't sure if I wouldn't after reaching our estate, and no other noble would take kindly to an elf asking them to tie their hair. I only knew how to handle long hair because I had to help my sisters since we had dismissed all our maids.

With a sigh, I took the ribbon. "Alright, turn around then."

I tied Oleander's soft, silvery hair into a ponytail and stepped back. Oleander patted his ears, noted they were perfectly covered, and smiled at me over his shoulder in gratitude. I couldn't smile back. As long as he had memory loss, this elf wouldn't survive a day on his own. Anyone who pretended to be kind to him would gain his trust. If we let him out of our sight and he wandered off, he'd die. And so would Endris and I for harbouring an enemy.

How did I let them talk me into this?

Tread Lightly

O leander moved nimbly despite almost freezing to death in Serpentine's lake. He still looked like he could use a hot bath and a hairbrush, but he didn't have trouble keeping up with me and Endris while crossing the lush fields that lay below the mountains.

It was much easier to breathe here. With the warm sun on my face and life blooming in the fields, the Serpentine mountains already felt like nothing but a bad memory. We'd shed our jackets and scarves and I would gladly stay away from the death trap cliffs behind us forever if I could.

Perhaps Oleander was only relieved to be away from the biting cold as well, but I swore he almost seemed comfortable with me and Endris now. Had it been me in his stead, I would've been far less gracious about traveling with elves. Knowing I was heading for an elven settlement, I might've even tried to escape.

To prevent Oleander from running off, I walked behind him. I watched how he crossed the winding river that lay between us and the road leading to the Last Stop. With unearthly grace, the elf swooped from stone to stone until he reached the other side. He was quicker on his feet than Endris. It almost made me self-conscious of the slurping and splashing of my boots in the water since I wouldn't risk jumping on the slippery stones.

After reaching the shore, I walked beside Oleander. "Aren't you fatigued or stiff or something?"

Oleander blinked and looked up at me in question.

"I've never seen a man thaw this fast."

Oleander's jaw went slack in surprise, then his face lit up. "Likewise. You pointed a knife at me when we met, and now you have invited me to find shelter in your home with your family."

My ears grew hot. "That's not what I meant!"

Endris snorted from in front of us, adding insult to injury. "He got you there," he said, like he wasn't the reason the elf was going to my family's estate.

I ignored Endris. "What I meant is: nearly freezing isn't an affliction one just walks off moments later."

"Oh, well..." Oleander carefully rolled his shoulders and winced. "I don't know how I got in the lake, but I really am unharmed. Only my shoulder hurts a little. But thank you very much for your concern, Laurence."

A warm smile accompanied Oleander's words. We held each other's gaze for a moment, and then Oleander's foot caught on a loose rock. He staggered, and I stretched my arms and caught him.

"Whoa there, careful."

I should tell myself that too. Careful. I couldn't get close to an elf, and in my arms was definitely too close. With shafts of golden sun lighting them up, Oleander's eyes looked different from a human's. I saw iridescent green, like flares of magic, in the elf's irises. I was very aware of the silvery strands of his hair touching my arm, and of Endris' gaze prickling on me.

I quickly released Oleander and retreated. "There are loose rocks hidden in the grass," I said. "Eyes on the ground, elf, not on me."

"Sorry, I will keep my eyes to myself," Oleander apologised, his voice soft.

I looked ahead to hide my embarrassment. Tall, swaying pines lined the borders of the stone road leading to the Last Stop. Once we climbed the hill, we would see the village in midths of a green landscape dappled with rocks on one side and a forest on the other side.

Endris patted my shoulder. "Don't forget to ask knight commander Ytel for extra supplies when you arrive in town."

"And to tell him the hunt failed." I threw my head back and sighed at the sky. "Need I remind you this was your idea, Endris? Why don't you grovel for more supplies?"

"No," Endris said. "Commander Ytel will be obligated to obey you without question while he is free to question me. Throw your weight around. It's the easiest and quickest way."

"Yes, all this weight of empty pockets and cob-webbed coffers."

I walked on alone, regardless, allowing Endris and Oleander to wait at a safe distance away from the village.

On the other side of the hill, the road expanded, and I found myself at the outskirts of a riotous assemblage of houses made of pine wood; the Last Stop. I had found it a pleasant place to be, so long as you didn't mistake the innkeeper, or anyone who kept pouring you more drinks, for a friend. Their hospitality lasted until the bill came and it turned out they charged an arm and a leg for any extra service.

Before I reached the first house, the clopping of hooves on stone disturbed the peace. A russet horse galloped my way. Seated on the horse was a figure with a pale blue eyes, wearing green robes.

Knight commander Ytel was a short man who only reached to my shoulders, but insisted on riding an absolute monster of a horse. He said the bulky ones usually seen ploughing the field were less jittery than their wasp-waisted cousins and that was why he preferred them. I'd always had a feeling he wanted a large horse so he would tower over people for once. It didn't seem to matter to him he almost had to sit in a split in the saddle.

"Laurence!" Ytel called out when he saw me looking his way. The horse whinnied when Ytel pulled on the reins and it slid to a halt in front of me. "I heard there was a landslide in the mountains, and a crackling arrow was fired. I was on my way to see what was going on with his lordship."

"To see if you could find me buried below the rubble and laugh, I'm sure," I joked.

Ytel smirked. "Perhaps, but I wouldn't admit that to your face, my lord."

"I'm surprised you'd head for the mountains. I heard some rumors of you wanting to ride off without me for a quiet journey home."

Ytel pressed a hand to his chest like he was scandalised. "That was Endris' idea. I said no such thing."

I was certain he did say such things.

"The hunt failed, Ytel," I said, getting the bad news out of the way first. "I lost the dragon in the landslide."

"Ah, that's a shame, my lord," Ytel said with a smile a little too broad for convincingly feigned disappointment. "I was hoping you'd have become a man today."

"Alas, I'm still just a lord," I said with an equally feigned smile.

Conversations I had nowadays were always like this: circling one another, striking and parrying. Exhausting. There was an ever-present mockery clinging to the word 'lord' on Ytel's tongue beneath forced obedience because I had a title and he did not.

"You'll have your quiet ride home, Ytel. I'm only here for supplies," I said. "Endris agreed to take me for a second dragon hunt in a month. You can return home to Denuran in the meantime, if you so please."

Ytel dipped his head. "Certainly. Say, where did you hide Endris? I would like to say goodbye to him, too."

"He's not here," I said.

A mocking simper curled up Ytel's lips. "I see that, your lordship."

"You know how he is. He's up ahead, still forag-"

"Excellent."

Ytel dug his heels into his horse's flanks and sped down the path without awaiting the rest of my answer.

"Ytel!" Cursing under my breath, I ran after the horse.

This was exactly what I meant with my words not holding the weight Endris thought they did anymore. I sped down the stone road, but couldn't possibly overtake a horse to warn Endris. Ytel would see Oleander, and I could only pray to the storm god he wouldn't recognise him as an elf with his ears hidden.

Once I'd climbed the hill, I found Ytel standing with Endris and Oleander up ahead. Ytel had dismounted, but at least our cover wasn't blown, since he wasn't trying to behead Oleander. Endris regarded me with a raised brow as I approached, quietly asking me what the hell had happened to the plan.

"So our good lord Montbow found you and rescued you." Ytel turned to me when I joined the group. "How noble of him! Looks like he's your knight in shining armour without being a knight because you blocked him from becoming one."

Oleander's face fell. Ytel truly had a way of slipping accusatory stings into jovial words.

"He ruined nothing," I defended Oleander between heavy breaths. "I made a choice."

"You chose him over the dragon." Ytel's eyes traveled down Oleander's form. "Are you going to sell him, your lordship? Finding a dragon for knighthood is a better investment than a servant, even a pretty one that will fetch a good price."

"This man will be a guest in my hometown," I emphasised.

Oleander seemed to take Ytel's words in stride, even to disregard them entirely. He only looked at me. "...Why do you need a dragon for knighthood?"

"To slay it," Ytel replied before I could open my mouth.

Oleander's eyes grew wide. "Why?" he asked.

"There is no why. It's meaningless bloodshed," Endris said.

Ytel furled his brow. "It's tradition! What better way to prove yourself than going on this arduous journey up a mountain where weather, rock, and dragon alike try to kill you and bring glory to your family?"

Ytel reached into his shirt and pulled out a black necklace with a shard of a tooth on it. Endris sighed deeply as Ytel showed the necklace to Oleander.

"Ten winters ago now, I travelled up those winding mountains and cleaved a dragon's head in half with my sword. The blood splatter and crater where it crashed can still be seen today. It was a red dragon. Nasty ones."

Oleander stared at the shard of dragon tooth. He looked even paler than when he was freezing, while Ytel was about to fall into his hundredth retelling of his epic fight with a red dragon. Each iteration of the tale it lengthened and became more unbelievable. The only small kernel of truth left was that he slew a dragon.

"That's enough of that story, Ytel," I stopped the knight commander with a smile. "You're going to make me jealous with all your manly prowess. Save the tales for your friends at the tavern."

In response to me cutting the story short, Oleander scooted closer to me. Don't come to me for protection, I wanted to tell him. Go to Endris.

Ytel guffawed at my joke. "One day you will understand the glory of battling a dragon, my lord. If you're lucky."

"Of course," I said. "Why don't you fetch my horse from the stables? And extra supplies for my new friend."

Ytel raised an arm above his head and, while rotating his wrist in a continuous, flourishing wave, he stooped into a low bow. "As you say."

While Ytel mounted his horse, I turned to Endris. The cat was out of the bag now, so there was no reason he couldn't go in my stead. If I could avoid going to the Last Stop and repeating fifty times over to every villager that the hunt failed, I would.

"You can go with Ytel to help," I said. "I'll wait here with our guest."

Endris narrowed his eyes, but then walked after Ytel without protesting.

Dealing with Ytel was tiresome, but sitting in the grass with the elf wasn't any less awkward. Oleander still sat too close for an enemy and he certainly didn't keep his eyes to himself like he had promised.

"Laurence?" the elf asked after a few moments of silence.

"Hm?"

"What is your home like?"

"It's... large," I said, which was the truth, albeit vague. "Lots of boats and water."

"Will they be cruel to me?"

I was quiet for a moment. "If they see your ears, yes," I told him honestly. "But as long as you keep your hair in that ponytail, they won't be."

"Alright."

The silence returned. I enjoyed the sound of the wind blowing across the field and absentmindedly plucked blades of grass and wildflowers.

"Laurence?" Oleander asked.

I hummed.

"Why do you want to be a knight?"

"Because I'm a blood-thirsty monster, of course."

Oleander just stared at me.

I exhaled. "Never mind. It's necessary. I roar, as you say it, and that means I can kill a dragon. That means I become a knight, and that means I will earn a lot of coin for my family."

Mother and father would have my head for failing. A stone sunk into the pit of my stomach at the realisation I'd have to go home and tell them.

"Is there no other way to become a knight?" Oleander asked.

"No," I replied. "It's a tradition set up by king Bertram. He decided that this was the way we could prove ourselves. It's seen as more fair than making knight a title to inherit, because anyone who is born with magic or with significant strength can travel up those mountains and slay a dragon. This way, we get knights who are truly powerful and deserve to be part of the queen's personal guard."

Oleander pursed his lips in disapproval. "There are many ways to be powerful. You have words. Why are they not enough?"

I laughed. "I don't exactly have words. Many would agree that I would be much easier to tolerate if I shut up."

"But I prefer it when you speak," Oleander replied. "I like your voice."

I looked at the elf. His eyes shone with absolute, unjustified faith in me. He needed to stop complimenting me. He needed to stop seeing me as his saviour.

"Oleander," I started slowly, "I don't know what you're used to beyond the Starcross woods. But here, you can't talk like that to another man. Or to someone you're not courting. Or to a lord. There are so many reasons you can't talk to me like that. You will stop."

Promptly, I got up from the grass and walked away from Oleander. I heard a muttered sorry behind me and closed my eyes with a sigh. It didn't matter that Oleander had flares of magic in his eyes and glass hair. I already had many problems. I couldn't add an elf who was overly attached to me to the list.

Child of the Storm

In the afternoon, on our third day of travel, I saw the bright sparkling of sunlight reflecting on waves in the distance. The briny sea air of the Thundercoast stung my nose. I was home.

The wilderness had its downsides, like brigands, bears, and other beasts that wanted to make my innards become outards. Being at the Thundercoast, however, brought on an abundance of other problems that couldn't be solved with a bow and arrow. I supposed nothing stopped me from letting thunder rain down on the debt collectors and unmannerly townsfolk, but I best not take uncle Harold's route of 'handling the situation.' We had all seen where that led.

Endris wanted to take a detour to the coast and see the ocean, and I happily obliged. Frankly, I'd agree to anything that slowed our journey so it would take longer to deliver the bad news about the dragon hunt.

Resting on the beach was no punishment, either. The ocean was the thunder god's domain, and I felt at peace in the golden sand, listening to the crashing of waves rolling inland and the fizzling of foam. Rocky bits and shells were scattered all across the shoreline. While Endris and Oleander took off their shoes and waded in the salty water, I looked for seashells and picked up the prettiest ones. Then I chose a nice spot near the water, crouched, and aligned the seashells in a branch shape. Artistic endeavours didn't come naturally to me, so it took a while and plenty of rearranging before I was satisfied.

A shadow casting overhead made me look over my shoulder. Oleander stood behind me, craning his neck to see my work of art in the sand. It surprised me the elf would even come near me. Oleander had taken my warning to heart. Ever since our talk in the grass, he hadn't spoken to me much. He rode with Endris and stayed out of my way. Now, he smiled at me like I had never snapped at him at all.

"Why are you drawing a Y in the sand?"

I smirked. "Why do you think?"

"Oh..." Oleander blinked. His smile lingered on his lips. I didn't know if he actually caught my wordplay or kept smiling because he didn't know how to respond. I supposed it didn't matter.

"Whenever I'm at the beach, I recreate the thunder god's mark to thank them for blessing me with a touch of their power," I explained.

I stood and tugged on the collar of my shirt, revealing a small part of the mark etched into my skin, chest to hip. It looked like a lighting scar, but was not quite a scar. The lines were a dark shade of greenish brown like a tattoo, but it wasn't a tattoo either.

The thunder god had visited me when I was five. My sisters and I were playing robbers in the woods. One moment I was running through a clearing, the next there were whispers filling my mind and a hot searing pain flaring up from my abdomen to my chest. I blacked out. When I came by, the mark was carved into my flesh and storms obeyed me. My parents had wept tears of joy, hugged me tight, and threw a feast at our mansion.

I'd been a simple child, happy with the hugs and the attention and not realising how much had changed. I stuffed my face with cake at the banquet while my parents bumped me, the nondescript middle child, to the top of the inheritance line. I'd played tag with the girls visiting our estate, unaware their parents were discussing arranged marriages with my parents.

Oleander studied the shells in the sand, then my chest. I could almost feel his eyes caressing the mark, and my skin felt hot. I let go of my shirt so the fabric sprung back up and hid my chest.

Oleander's gaze shifted to my face. "Are you going to make the entire mark in the sand?"

I groaned. "No. Look, I know it's tradition, but it's not fair, alright? I got a whole damn lightning bolt, branches and all, covering my entire upper body, while some people only get a small mark."

"The markings continue much further down then?" Oleander's gaze slowly travelled from my chest down to my belt.

A flush crept up my neck. Endris stepped beside Oleander and shot me a stern look, warning me to not joke inappropriately. He needn't be concerned. I might've taken this remark as flirting had it been coming from anyone other than the elf. Oleander didn't seem capable of innuendos. If I wasn't allowed to joke, however, all I had to offer was awkward bumbling.

"Yes, it continues further down," I pressed out of my throat.

Oleander nodded, a twinkle in his eye. "The thunder god sounds benevolent for sharing their power. I am certain it's your intent that matters to them, not how elaborate the gesture is."

I shrugged. "Hey, if they wanted grand gestures, they should've chosen an artist."

"Are elves ever storm-touched?" Endris asked Oleander.

Oleander hummed. "Roaring, uh, I mean storm-touched exists, yes. Elves also sing or bleed."

I froze, and so did Endris. We exchanged a glance.

"Bleed?" Endris repeated stiffly.

"Yes. Bleeders take a knife and draw extraordinary power from the lifeblood of themselves or others."

"Yeah," I said, elongating the word. "Don't mention lifeblood magic in town. It's sensitive, we shall say." I dragged a hand up my forehead. "What are we even doing, bringing an elven man to the Thundercoast?"

Oleander's eyes grew wide. "I'm sorry!" he stammered. "I promise I won't speak of magic."

Endris glared at me, then turned to Oleander. "Laurence is not saying this to be cruel. Human towns and rules make little sense if you didn't grow up there."

I snorted. "They make little sense if you did grow up there. Anyway, come to me or Endris with questions. Nobody else."

"For once, I agree with you," Endris said. He lowered himself to the ground and started brushing sand off of his feet to put his shoes back on.

The elf hung his head and followed Endris' example. I couldn't help feeling a pang of sympathy. Oleander was a hated stranger here. It wasn't his fault he didn't know the customs and rules, but I couldn't make it my problem either. I already had telling my parents and siblings I'd failed them to look forward to. A lump formed in my throat at the thought of facing them within the next hour.

Soon, we'd reach the village. If I squinted, I already saw the weather-worn Montbow mansion sitting quietly on the highest cliff. Once a beacon of hope, the building was now reduced to a crumbling, mildew-ridden, and overgrown ruin. Scarred by sieges, stripped by vultures.

I thought we'd at least have a peaceful ride along the shore before we arrived, but then I spotted movement up ahead. We weren't alone on the beach; there were a few figures on horseback. I counted three horses.

At first I simply thought they were townsfolk out fishing. The fishermen dragged giant nets behind them, catching shrimp while on horseback. As we rode closer, however, Endris suddenly raised his hand.

I halted my horse, and so did Endris.

"They are moving our way," Endris curtly informed me.

I shrugged. "But they're just townsfolk, aren't they?"

"We shouldn't take risks."

I grimaced. "Point taken."

Overseas, there was a new meaning to the word Montbow: traitor. People there spat on our flag. If these fishers weren't townsfolk, but sailors from the port of Richris overseas, they wouldn't show me any mercy.

I breathed in and out deeply a few times. "If they're enemies, leave and find a way to the mansion to warn my family," I told Endris.

From the corner of my eye, I saw Oleander digging his nails into the leather saddle, while Endris nodded. "...Understood."

I drew my bow and charged an arrowhead with thunder. Soon, however, it was proven unnecessary for me to draw my weapon. The figure at the front rode a spotted horse with a yellow saddle pad—the colour of my family—and I recognised her as my mother. The other two figures were my sister Valda, and my brother Conrad. My relief about not having to fight enemies was short-lived, however.

"Shit," I swore. "Can we never just arrive somewhere inconspicuously as planned? This is worse than Richris sailors."

The elf needed to stay quiet. If he already complimented me, he would absolutely try to compliment Valda and Conrad.

Conrad towered over pretty much everyone, and made for a striking man with two different coloured eyes - dark brown and amber - light brown skin, and a stoic mentality. Valda's biggest appeal was in her dimpled smile, cleverness, and infectious laughter. Traits she'd inherited from my mother, though mother was not smiling a lot lately. My sole selling point was storm-touched powers. I had wondered if the thunder god had chosen me because he took pity on me for being surrounded by near flawless siblings.

"Speak as little as you can," I warned Oleander.

Oleander bit his lip. "I understand."

There was a tremor in his voice. Oleander had calmed down around me and Endris the past few days, but now he reminded me of the cowering, tearful mess he'd been when we first met. Granted, I had pointed a knife at him.

"They don't know who you are. They will not hurt you," Endris tried to soothe Oleander while I dismounted.

My sister Valda was the first to call out, "Laurence!" Waving enthusiastically, she jumped off her horse and ran towards me.

"Valda!" I laughed and caught my sister in a hug. I lifted her and spun her around, while Conrad and mother also got down from their horse.

Mother greeted me after Valda with a kiss on my cheek. It would forever be strange to see my noble-born mother wearing worker's pants. While mother had never done rough handwork a day in her life, she'd immediately started learning how to fish, hunt, and fight with a sword when it became necessary for the survival of our family. I'd always believed Etta Montbow would endure hardship longer than any of us. The walls of our mansion would crumble before she would.

Conrad didn't greet me as warmly as Valda and my mother. He stayed at an arm's length and only offered me a brief handshake with lips pressed to a thin line. In order for me to become the heir of the

Montbow family, Conrad, as the eldest, lost his title. I was used to our exchanges feeling like being submerged in a cold bath, but it still stung every time.

Warm greeting or cold greeting, all three of my family members looked at my neck, searching for a dragon's tooth on the necklace Gisela, my other sister, had made for me. But the necklace I'd purposefully hidden below my shirt lacked any hunting trophies.

A stone settled in my stomach, and I stalled for a little while longer. I gestured at Endris and Oleander, who were waiting behind me. "You already know Endris, and this is Oleander. Oleander, this is my mother, Lady Montbow, my sister Valda, and my brother Conrad."

Oleander only smiled nervously, because I had told him not to speak. When Endris bowed, Oleander also made an awkward bow. Valda beamed. She was melting into a puddle at the sight of Oleander trying to be courteous, and I couldn't blame her.

"A pleasure," my mother spoke, but she wouldn't let herself get distracted by my ruse of pleasantries. She focused on me and asked that one dreadful question: "How did the hunt go?"

I didn't need to answer; everyone could read my silence. Conrad didn't visibly react. Valda's eyebrows squished together, and my mother tried to keep her composure, but I saw the flash of panic in her expression before she could conceal it.

"It's alright, Laurence," she said, brushing her fingers through my hair. "I'd rather have you home alive than buried on that mountain."

Mother's voice said: it's alright. Her body language said: what will we do if the debt collectors come back and we don't have the source of coin we promised them? What if they send mercenaries to rough us up again, and another one of us loses use of our sword arm or worse in the scuffle like your father?

I breathed in and out deeply. "The dragon escaped in a landslide. But Endris here offered a second hunt for free within a month's time."

Endris dipped his head. "If you would allow me, I'll bring Oleander to the Starcross woods where he lives, and then I would stay at the Montbow mansion until it's time for Lord Laurence's second attempt at the dragon hunt. Lord Laurence bravely rescued Oleander's life, and I would also like to repay the Montbow family by offering my services for free for two months."

"That's very generous, Endris. We gladly accept," Mother replied.

Valda could no longer contain herself and went over to Oleander. "Hello, my name is Valda," she introduced herself again. "Oleander, you simply must tell me: what do you use to make your hair silky like that?"

"My hair? Oh, I use a blend of herbal oils," Oleander replied softly.

"Splendid! Can I touch it?"

Oleander tensed like a cornered prey animal. "Uh, yes," he said, because nobody said no to Valda.

With a giggle, Valda stroked Oleander's long, silvery ponytail. I flinched with every touch and I was sure Endris did as well. After a few nerve-wrecking moments, I grabbed my sister's arm and gave it a little tug to make her stop touching Oleander's hair.

"That's quite enough. Oleander's not a doll, and he's fragile. He lost his memory."

Valda gaped at me. "He lost his memory?"

"We found him in the valley, Lady Montbow," Endris explained. "He would have died, but Lord Laurence saved him."

"Let's not let that gift go to waste then," Mother said. "We'll talk further in the mansi—"

"Oh no, I really don't think that's a good idea," I hastily interjected. "Endris and Oleander can stay in town at the inn."

Mother raised a brow. "You said Endris will work for our family. That means he stays at the mansion. His friend can too, if he can earn his keep." Her eyes shifted to Oleander. "And I do have a small job in mind that will earn you a night at the mansion and supplies for the road, Oleander."

Dismissal

I had to tell them.

I couldn't allow an elf to stay within the walls of the Montbow mansion without my family knowing who was sleeping across the hallway. Endris had promised to keep an eye on Oleander, but he was only one man—a partisan man—who had clearly taken a liking to his charge.

As usual, my mother led the way home and everyone else followed, with Conrad and Valda riding side by side, and me riding beside Endris and Oleander. Guilt picked at my conscience as we climbed the rugged ridge leading to our mansion, but I pushed it away. I couldn't speak up about the elf in front of Endris. I still needed the grouchy guide to take me on a dragon hunt, and I needed him to do so for free.

Once we reached the mansion, I dismounted my horse with deliberate slowness to ensure I was near the end of the line, behind Oleander. We walked to the stables out back, and a rush of shame heated up my face as the elf's gaze gliding over the walls of our home. Salt and slime had corroded stone over time, and veins of climbing plants swarmed upward. The embarrassment at Oleander noticing the pitiful state of the mansion only grew after we had brought the horses to the stables and went inside.

Entering the foyer, it was immediately clear vultures had feasted here while I was away. I searched the double-flight staircases, the walls, and the high ceiling, and eventually realised the relief carvings of ships decorating the upper reaches were now visible. The family banners, which used to proudly adorn the walls, were gone. Our footsteps on stone echoed as we all stepped inside.

Mother turned to Valda. "Valda, show Endris and Oleander their lodgings. They can take the free rooms on the left side of the first floor."

Mother shot Valda a stern look when the latter hesitated. I agreed with my mother. The previous occupants of the rooms were gone and wouldn't return.

After a brief silence, Valda offered us a closed-mouthed smile. "Yes, naturally. On my way," she said, gesturing for Oleander and Endris to follow her.

Endris narrowed his eyes at me over his shoulder. Then my mother took me and Conrad aside and guided us into the dining room so we could speak in private. I steeled myself for the conversation that was coming. I had to decide what to do: tell them or not.

˙ was the last to enter the room and closed the door behind me. A

˙ smell clung to the heavy red carpets, and rose to fill the entire room. Mother perched on a bench beside the large, ashen table while Conrad casually leaned against the wall. I took a seat on the bench opposite my mother and Conrad.

Light of the oil lamp overhead cast shadows on my mother's cheeks, accentuating her high cheekbones as she turned to me. "Oleander lost his memory, but he knows he needs to travel to the Starcross woods?" she asked.

The words 'he's an elf' burned on my lips. I was obligated to them if Oleander was going to stay in this house, but I couldn't tell them if it meant I estranged Endris by breaking our agreement to keep this secret.

Conrad crossed his arms. "Oleander has a strange accent and a highly unusual name," he drawled. "From what hole did you say you dug him up again?"

"I found him in the valley of the Serpentine mountains," I said.

"Huh." Conrad narrowed his mismatched eyes at me. "If he's really from the Starcross woods, he's a long way from home."

"He's not sure he's from there," I corrected Conrad, slightly irritated. "But it's an educated guess Endris and I made from the way he talks and looks."

Mother nodded slowly. "But he's not sure where he is from," she said. "And he's in your debt. Perhaps you can convince him to stay here while he recovers, rather than leaving tomorrow."

"I really don't think that's wise," I protested. "His family probably misses him. Besides, whatever skills he had before he lost his memory, he doesn't have them now. He was unable to help Endris or me with anything besides simple chores even a child could do during our journey here."

"Thankfully, I only need him for simple chores even a child could do," Mother replied lightly. "I need him to run some errands. Places where we best not show our faces as Montbows. We need all the help we can get, now that you have returned all but empty-handed."

Grimacing, I averted my gaze to my hands.

"And what does Father think of this?" Conrad added.

"He's not well today. We best leave him be."

"I see." I fell quiet for a moment, choosing my next words carefully while I gathered the courage to meet my mother's eyes. "We don't know Oleander. He could be working with enemies of our family. We kind of have a lot of those, you know. Why take the risk and keep a stranger here?"

Conrad raised a brow. "Surely even you know better, Laurence," he berated me. "The enemies we have don't go through the trouble of feigning amnesia and an accent. They go through the front gates armed with the law."

"There are easier ways to harm us, Laurence," my mother agreed.

"I suppose," I sputtered. I was running out of arguments. Mother and Conrad would get suspicious if I stumbled through words any longer. I needed more time to think, so I caved and stood. "Fine. I will talk to him about staying a little longer."

I'd especially talk to Endris, however. Leaving Oleander here while he and I went back to the Serpentine mountains was an even worse idea than making me heir of this family merely because of a god's unrelated-to-politics blessing. The elf couldn't survive without us helping him stay hidden.

As I walked through the corridor, my mind far away at the Serpentine mountains, Valda emerged from the shadows as I entered the foyer. I'd almost pulled my knife, but caught a flash of yellow and black, the bow in her hair, just in time.

"Valda, don't do that," I scolded her. "Don't jump me."

"Me?" Valda pointed at herself indignantly, her brows almost disappearing into her hairline. "I was simply waiting for you, and I wouldn't have had to if our mother just let me in on this secret conversation, too. What did you speak about?"

I sighed. "Keeping Oleander here. Mother has plans, it seems, to send him places where we can't show our face. Perhaps she will even have him open the door for 'visitors' and charm them with a smile."

"Please, no." Valda wrinkled her nose. "He's too adorable for that. I wouldn't wish that on my worst enemy. I don't know how Gisela stands it."

"You help her too."

Valda snorted loudly. "Hardly! It's mostly Gisela. I'll only bat my eyelashes for a suitor with money. He needs to have money—that's the most important part. I already have a list of potential husbands, so hurry and get knighted already. I need an invitation for the palace's autumn ball."

"Money is the most important part?" I smiled, forever amused at my sister's cunning outlook beneath her cute, dimpled smile. "You realise you have to live with the man for the rest of your life too, right? You better love, or at least like, him, too."

"Optional." Valda waved away my concerns. "I'll choose someone who is away most of the year. Perhaps a merchant who only looks for a reliable wife to overlook his land while he is away. I can't wait to have my own mansion."

"I will gladly give you this one after I become the head of this family," I joked. "If we looked at suitability rather than anomalous skin marks, the heir should've been you or Conrad."

"Believe me, I've spent many nights looking for marks of the thunder god on my body after playing in the woods, but alas." Valda shrugged. "The thunder god doesn't favour me like you."

"Yeah yeah, god it," I joked. "The mark is everything."

Valda giggled as she punched my arm. "I don't know, though. You think it would be between me and Conrad? I wouldn't count Gisela out."

I looked around the foyer. "Where is Gisela, anyway? And Fynn?"

"At the old Marchpass ruins, practicing archery. Start them young, right?"

"So young, Fynn probably isn't even strong enough yet to draw the bow."

Valda shrugged. "Doesn't stop Gisela."

"Pretty much nothing stops Gisela. I remember from when we trained together."

"I'm surprised you remember your training." Valda giggled. "She kicked your ass so hard I thought you'd have a concussion. And Gisela will kick your ass again once she hears you let a dragon escape."

I groaned. "Go away, pest. I have important heir things to do."

A grin lingered on Valda's face. "You're going to our guest to charm him into staying here?"

I laughed awkwardly. I didn't want the word charm and Oleander near each other, just like I didn't want to be near Oleander. "Mother wants it," I said. "So if I say no and she says yes..."

"It's still a yes," Valda finished my sentence sing-song. "Good luck! I brought Oleander to the room on the far left."

"Yeah. Thanks."

Leaving Valda in the foyer, I ran up the long flight of steps leading to the first floor, thinking to myself that I didn't need luck; I needed a damn miracle. I marched to what I hoped was Oleander's room because Valda sometimes liked to play little practical jokes. I knocked, half expecting to find Endris glaring at me.

After a curt knock, I opened the door.

Unlike many other spaces in the mansion, this room looked exactly the same as when I'd last seen it. The walls of the bedchamber were covered with yellow cloth drapes with more illustrations of ships, thunder, and water depicted on them. Books and papers were haphazardly stored away in an old bookcase tucked in the corner, and the bed was placed against the back wall.

At first, I didn't see Oleander and though he wasn't in the room, but when I walked inside, the little lump below the sheets in the bed stirred. Upon closer look, a small tuft of silvery hair poked out above the covers. Oleander appeared to be asleep. He trashed and moaned, muttering words in a language I didn't understand.

If he was resting, I couldn't talk to him. Too bad. I was happy to tip-toe back to the door and leave. When I reached the entrance, however, Oleander suddenly woke with a start. He shot upright in the bed, panting. Pearls of sweat glistened on his forehead as his bewildered eyes darted around the room before settling on me. He visibly tried to pull himself together, taking deeper breaths to calm himself.

"I can come back later," I quickly offered, already retreating into the hall.

"No, I'm sorry," Oleander breathed, his shoulders rising and falling fast. "I had a nightmare about..." he trailed off with a frown.

"Do you remember something?" I asked, trying not to sound too eager. If he remembered, he'd likely want to leave. I tentatively stepped back into the room and closed the door.

Oleander brushed aside some strands of hair clinging to his forehead. "I'm not...sure. I saw a landslide and dragons."

All my hope deflated. "That is what actually happened. Interesting it's so clear. I would've expected if you're so confused you take your clothes off in the frost, you'd have some delusions."

Oleander grabbed the sheets and clutched them to his chest. "No, I saw dragons," he murmured. His Adam's apple bobbed as he swallowed thickly. "Have any of you ever killed a dragon? Your family? Are you all knights?"

I laughed. "No, no. We were merchants. Gold, gems, and cloth, mostly. I'm the first one in the family attempting knighthood. Most storm-touched like me went on voyages by ship as her guardian, or stayed here as fearsome protectors of the coast."

"Why are you not doing that?"

"Because... it's no longer an option," I curtly replied. There were no trading posts overseas anymore thanks to dear uncle Harold who burned bridges with our contacts for a larger profit. Now, we only had knighthood and favourable marriages left.

Oleander's grip on the sheets loosened. "I apologise for the sudden questions barrage. You must've come here to speak with me about something. How can I help you?"

I cleared my throat. "Mother told me to ask you if you wanted to stay here while you recover, and you're going to say no."

Oleander face fell. "Do you want me to leave that badly?"

"Well, I..." I opened and closed my mouth. A silence fell.

The truthful answer was yes, I did. Not because Oleander had been such a pain in the ass, but he would run into so much trouble here. I would also run into so much trouble with my family if it ever came out that I didn't tell them immediately he was an elf, even if I told them now.

"It's truly best if you leave and head for the Starcross woods tomorrow," I finally pressed out. The hurt look on Oleander's face brought a sharp twinge to my heart, but I didn't take my words back.

"Because I'm...?" Oleander reaching up to his hair to feel if his ears were still hidden.

They were covered, but if a few more strands of hair had escaped his ponytail, the tips of his ears would've been visible. What if Valda, on another day, decided she wanted to wake Oleander and offer him breakfast? What if he had been trashing all night? What if the wind tugged on his hair a little too hard, or someone insisted he loosened it up and he got oddly defensive about saying no?

This would end in disaster.

"Yes," I admitted. "It's because of that."

Oleander bit his lip and turned his head away from me. "Oh," he said. "Since you didn't hurt me, I thought you weren't like them."

"Hey, my family isn't bad, and the town isn't bad," I defended them. "It's—it's complicated. You are just much safer with your own people."

"What if they are no longer alive, and that is why I was wandering in the valley alone and nobody else came for me?"

Oleander's voice cracked. I scratched my chin, an uneasy feeling washing over me.

"...Well, shit," I said. "You have me there."

Oleander looked up and met my eyes. "What would I have to do to change your mind about me? I would very much want to change your mind."

The sincerity of the question and the sudden determination caught me off guard. At a loss for words, I studied the headboard and the flowers painted on in them to stall. "Listen," I started slowly, "I don't think you're bad. You haven't tried to drink my blood or sacrifice me to a tree god or something. I don't need to be convinced."

"Then why tell me I can't speak to you and that I should leave the mansion without meeting my eyes?"

My cheeks grew hot. "That's not what I said!" I protested. "Just tell my mother no when she asks, and leave tomorrow. As planned."

I turned on my heels and made for the door.

"Wait," Oleander said. "I fear my hair will loosen too much if I sleep with a ponytail instead of a braid. Can you braid my hair for me?"

The thought of sitting on the bed as I touched Oleander's silky hair made my throat dry up.

"I have told you before: stop. That is inappropriate now that we're in the mansion," I crisply told the elf. "Ask Endris."

I shut the door before Oleander could respond and resisted the urge to zap one of the few remaining vases in the corridor to smithereens.

I marched to the next door and knocked. "Endris!" I called. "Outside, now."

Stay or Go

W hen I sped to the staircase with Endris right behind me, Valda was already on the steps. Her dark curls bounced as she descended towards the ground floor, and despite her casual way of walking, I knew she'd been eavesdropping. It was a bad habit she'd picked up ever since I came of age and our parents started involving me in 'secret meetings' but not her. It didn't seem to matter I told her what we'd discussed afterward, if she asked, most of the time.

I ignored my sister for now and passed her without saying a word. The stables would have to make do as a safe place to talk. They were too open to provide good hiding spots for furtive family members, and the horses wouldn't gossip.

As I entered the stables, the scent of sweet hay and manure filled my nose. Like any other Montbow building, the stables were picked clean of anything that had value on the market. All that was left were hooks to hold reins and saddles mounted on the wall in an orderly row, and dust floating in the sunlight.

"No, we're not going for a ride, love," I told the speckled mare, which came up to the fence and tickled my cheek with her hairy nose. I patted her neck and turned to Endris. "You need to leave tomorrow," I ordered. "I don't want to lie to my family about what he is."

Endris arched a brow at my urgent tone. "Is that why you dragged me outside? Aside from Lady Montbow insisting we stay in the mansion overnight and have Oleander perform a small task for her, I see no reason we would've changed plans."

"Great to hear," I replied through gritted teeth. "And does everyone understand this plan? Because your good friend, Oleander, doesn't seem to want to go."

Endris blinked. He didn't seem surprised at my words, and I wondered if Oleander had said the same to Endris as to me. I wasn't so arrogant as to assume the only reason Oleander didn't want to leave the mansion was to win my favour. After all, what did he stand to gain from that? It was likely the other way around: he wanted my favour because he felt alone and wanted a roof over his head.

I sighed. "I suppose I understand his fear of traveling to the Star-cross woods. What if there are no others like him out there anymore? If he had a loving family, he wouldn't have been wandering around in human territory alone and left for dead in the vall—"

"He's not the only one left," Endris stated firmly. "There are others."

"How do you know?"

Endris' eyes narrowed, and he frowned. "All Oleander needs to do is cross the Starcross woods so he is no longer in the queen's domain," he said eventually. "He'll be safe there."

I didn't like how Endris stalled and kept sidestepping questions, but that was a minor concern compared to getting the elf out of here. At least we still seemed to be on the same page regarding that.

I raised and dropped my arms. "Oleander knows how dangerous it is for him to be here. I know he knows. Why would he not be eager to leave the Thundercoast?"

"Because he's taken a liking to you and wishes to stay at your side."

I opened and closed my mouth. "... What?"

Endris crossed his arms and glared at me, showing me there was no way he would reiterate his words. I'm glad he didn't. I felt embarrassment burning in my cheeks.

"Why?"

Endris shrugged. "Your guess is as good as mine."

"He told you that?"

"Yes."

"Literally, in those words?"

"I will not repeat myself," Endris bit.

I was at a loss for words. No jokes came to me like normal when I found myself in awkward situations, and it wasn't like I could've delivered them regardless with my tongue tied in knots.

It wasn't like two men together never happened, or couldn't happen. Heirs didn't pair up for love, however. We chose partners for political gain. Oleander would only have a future being sneered at by my arranged marriage wife. To be at the Thundercoast, he would have to hide who he really was and fear for his life constantly.

I was taking this too far.

Staying at my side didn't mean he wanted to be in my bed, I sternly reminded myself. I shouldn't have perverted thoughts about an innocent man who was in a vulnerable position. An elf without memories who clearly didn't know what he was asking for, and desperately clamped to any ties he had left in this world.

I was dragged out of my thoughts by a horse's hooves clopping on the ground outside. That had to be Gisela and Fynn coming home. I glanced over my shoulder and grimaced as dread tightened my chest.

"Make him leave tomorrow," I gritted out to Endris. "I don't care if you have to tie him up and drag him out of here. I'll arrange things with my mother."

Without awaiting Endris' response, I walked outside to greet my other sister and brother. Gisela had already dismounted and had her hands on little Fynn's waist to lift him off the horse.

"Hello, I called out, making Gisela look up as she put our little brother on the ground. Her eyes had a honey-brown soft color, but otherwise, nothing was soft about Gisela. From her prominent bone structure to her dark brown hair tied in a tight ponytail and taut muscles, she was all sharp edges.

"Laurence," she greeted me with a nod.

"Laurence!" Fynn called out. Spreading his arms, he shot past Gisela towards me, swift as an arrow. Unlike Gisela, my little brother had a friendly, round face and messy, dark hair.

I chuckled at the sight of Fynn's rosy cheeks and the sparkle dancing in his eye as he leapt into my arms. "Hey, there little man," I said, before groaning exaggeratedly as I scooped him up. "Not that little anymore. You've been gaining weight."

Fynn grinned like I didn't tell him that joke every time I picked him up. He reached into my shirt, grabbing at my necklace with his chubby fingers. "Laurence, Laurence, did you kill the dragon?" he called out.

Gisela's gaze burned on my neck as Fynn pulled out the black chain, which was painfully lacking a dragon's tooth.

"Yeah, I didn't quite get to the killing part," I pressed out. "I found the dragon, I took a shot, a landslide happened, and I lost the dragon."

The corners of Gisela's mouth turned down. She briefly covered her face with her hand. "How did you lose the dragon if you only had to fire one arrow between the eyes to kill it?"

"I had hoped you wouldn't ask that," I sheepishly replied. "I missed. It was the wind."

"That's alright," Fynn said, tugging on my necklace. "I'll play in the woods and get a mark from the thunder god just like you, and then I will kill the dragon for you."

"You don't want to go to those mountains, kid," I muttered as I lowered Fynn down. "Trust me."

"Yes, I do!" Fynn protested. "I shot an arrow, and it hit the target today. I can kill a dragon. Tell him, Gisela!"

Gisela didn't respond to Fynn. Her accusing eyes stayed fixed on my face. "You missed your shot because of the wind?" she repeated incredulously.

"And I will practice on the windy cliffs to remedy that mistake before my next attempt," I offered. "But not right now. Now, it's getting late, and we need to prepare dinner."

I forced a smile for my little brother. "Race to the kitchen!" I told him. "The one who peels the least potatoes loses!"

Fynn squealed with joy and started running, almost tripping over his own feet in his haste to reach the kitchen first.

"I will practice more in windy weather," I promised Gisela one more time. Then I spun around and ran after Fynn, eager to be away from the disappointed faces and accusative glares, which I knew I wouldn't find in the kitchen.

After the servants left, we had divided the tasks in the mansion. When we made dinner, everyone did their part—some with more reluctance than others. Conrad and Gisela wouldn't be found dead peeling potatoes or other root vegetables, but I didn't mind. Every once in a while, Mother peeked into the kitchen and lamented the heir of the Montbow family performing a servant's task. I always countered by saying she shouldn't be out fishing or learning how to fight with a sword as the Lady of the house, either.

Our kitchen was elaborate and large; a whole tower devoted to storing a variety of metal and clay pans, a giant stone hearth, and countless of herbs and spices stored in pots. I entered through the double doors, expecting to find Valda cursing at the stone hearth while trying to light a fire all alone, despite knowing I could do it with a snap of my fingers (I didn't—she didn't want me to help), and Fynn running out of the pantry with a pile of potatoes in his little arms.

I was almost right. Valda was standing at the hearth, fanning the starting flames. Fynn had carried a pile of potatoes out of the pantry and was already peeling them as if his life depended on it, the tip of his tongue sticking out.

What I didn't expect, however, was Oleander sitting beside him with a small knife in his one hand, and a potato in the other. Seeing my younger brother sitting next to the elf who had a weapon made the blood drain from my face. I crossed the room in a couple of hasty strides and wedged myself between Oleander and Fynn, taking a seat on a barrel.

Oleander smiled brightly at me. Endris' words fresh in mind. My cheeks tingled, and I turned away.

"Laurence! You're slow!" Fynn complained. "It's no fun winning if you don't make it a challenge!"

"I know, my bad," I replied stiffly, while staunchly avoiding looking at Oleander.

I fetched a potato from the pile. I'd only made a small incision when I spotted Oleander trying to follow my example, but poorly. He had the knife aimed at himself, slicing dangerously close to his face.

"Wait, not like that!" I warned him.

Being used to Fynn and his impulsive ways, I reached out without thinking and clasped my fingers around the hand holding the knife, pushing the sharp edge away from Oleander's face. Oleander looked up at me, flares of magic dancing in his green eyes. For a brief moment, time stopped. Then I yanked my hand away like he'd burned me, despite his hand being cold.

Oleander's gaze darted to the floor. "Uh, not like what, lord Montbow?" he asked quietly.

Lord Montbow. 'That is my father,' I wanted to say. But I had told Oleander to call me that, and I should be glad he had listened to me.

"Just look at Fynn. Cut away from yourself, not towards yourself," I replied curtly.

Fynn preened himself. He sat up straighter, feet drumming against the barrel he was perched on in glee. He put even more effort into his cutting work, visibly proud at being named the paragon of potato peeling.

Oleander did as I asked, studied Fynn, and mimicked his movements. I kept an eye on the elf and his clumsy movements for a little while longer, but then returned to my own work.

"Mother wasted no time putting you to work too, did she, Oleander?" Valda called out from the other side of the room.

"Not at all, Lady Montbow. I'm very grateful you will have me here, and happy to help," Oleander replied kindly.

I swore Valda was melting a little in front of us. If Oleander didn't leave soon, I'd have two of the Montbows pleading for me to consider keeping him. Three if Fynn joined in too because his mother and sister did.

"I think I'm not a good peeler, however," Oleander apologised. "But I seem to know about herbs and spices. I recognised a few in the pantry, and it seems to help me with my memory. May I be so bold to suggest I make a blend for the potatoes?"

"Yes," I immediately replied. Anything to increase the distance between us. "Go on."

Oleander stood and actually curtsied for us before leaving. I had no idea where he'd picked that up, but he made the gesture look more graceful and natural than even our most experienced servants. Did Endris teach him?

I stared at the door through which Oleander had disappeared until I felt eyes on me. Valda had gone back to tending to the fire, but Fynn was staring at me, a twinkle of curiosity in his gaze. He'd even stopped peeling potatoes, while he usually let nothing distract him from winning our competition.

"Laurence," he whisper-shouted. "Who is that man?"

"He is a guest," I said, purposely keeping my answer vague. "He'll be gone in the morning."

Fynn bobbed his head, seemingly accepting that response. But if I thought that meant he was done asking questions, I'd be sorely mistaken.

Fynn's brow furrowed. "Why does he have long hair like a woman?"

"Because that's part of his culture, I suppose. It's not that strange, is it?"

I would've named Endris as an example of another man with long hair, but before I could open my mouth, Fynn had leaned forward, resting his palms on my knees to whisper in my ear. "Is his long hair why you held his hand and looked at him like he was a woman you wanted to court?"

I nearly choked on my own spit. "I did not!"

"Yes, you did!"

Catching a hold of Fynn's wrists, I playfully wrestled him to the kitchen floor. "No, I didn't, and I'm stronger and older than you, so I'm right. You, shush!"

Fynn squealed and wiggled as I tickled his sides. I gladly took advantage of his short attention span, knowing for certain that Fynn's thoughts about Oleander and the way I had looked at him were long forgotten when I pressed a potato peel to my lip and called myself Lord Peeler Potatokins. But while Fynn easily forgot, I swore under my breath, wishing I could forget just as easily.

Under the Moonlight

We finished all the preparations and arrived at the dining room with limbs and fingers intact, carrying large pans with food that smelled amazing. That was already a noteworthy accomplishment. I remembered the first nights cooking after the last of the servants had left. Valda had set wooden utensils on fire, the fishing nets my brother had cast came up from the sea empty, and I'd cut multiple fingers while peeling vegetables.

Father's seat at the table was empty. Conrad shovelled a generous portion of potato and fish onto a plate and retreated into the hall. In an unspoken family agreement, none of us said a word about it, so neither did Endris and Oleander. Mother, who had swapped her work clothing for fine weaved fabrics, had already politely directed our guests to the far end of the table. All the Montbow family members had a designated seat, and we clung to old traditions. I often wondered why because that old life didn't exist anymore. It was beneficial for me in this case, however, because guests being placed in the far back meant Oleander wasn't near me, and none could glimpse what Fynn had already noticed.

Fynn's curious and observant nature was a curse, but while we waited for Conrad to return, his presence was a blessing. My little brother insisted I turned his mashed potatoes into a potato volcano on his plate. Sometimes he asked for a witch's hut or a castle, but the volcano was the favourite. Mostly because of the grand finale: its eruption.

Fynn bounced in his seat as I built. "Make it explode, make it explode!" he demanded, while I skilfully smoothed out the curves of the potato volcano with the back of my spoon.

With a grin, I pointed at Fynn's plate and released the tiniest spark from my fingertip. The 'volcano' erupted, splattering all over the plate. A few chunks landed on the table.

"Oops," I said, laughing as I wiped the wood clean with my sleeve while Fynn clapped.

A soft chuckle sounded from the back, and I couldn't help but dart a glance Oleander's way. He smiled when he saw me looking, and my heart jolted. I quickly averted my gaze again. Across the table, Gisela sighed. Mother's expression remained pleasant, but her unblinking eyes rested on mine, silently telling me 'enough.'

"How elegant, Laurence," Valda remarked with a lopsided grin. "Will you perform those tricks with your future betrothed at the table as well?"

"Yes, she'll just have to accept that side of me," I said. "If potato volcanos aren't welcome at the dinner table, I don't want to be a part of it."

Fynn nodded solemnly.

"Ariane Seydal will put up with anything Laurence, or we, do if he ever becomes a knight," Gisela added with a shrug.

Despite her light tone, I felt the resentment smouldering behind my sister's words. The truth remained that I hadn't accomplished my task, even if everyone stayed quiet out of fear I would leave them behind. But even when not spoken out loud, their silent disappointment was still stifling. I felt eyes on me, awaiting my reaction to my sister's pinpricks. I didn't offer any.

Conrad returned to the dining room a few moments later, and we all started eating. The herb and spice blends for the meat and potatoes garnered Oleander compliments from everyone but Conrad, who didn't tend to praise unless someone held a knife to his throat. Oleander accepted the praise shyly with flushed cheeks.

After we finished eating, Conrad, Endris, and Oleander retreated to their respective rooms. The rest of the family stayed in the living quarters, with Valda and Gisela knitting by the fireplace, Fynn bolting across the room playing with his spinning-top, and Mother and I reading.

Correction: Mother read. I pretended to read. All the enjoyment I may have gotten out of reading once upon a time got sucked out of it when fairytale books were ripped out of my tiny five-year-old hands and replaced with dry as bones material about court etiquette, war tactics, and family history.

When I spotted movement in the corridor, I grabbed the distraction from my book with both hands and turned my attention to the moving shadows. I figured it would be Conrad skulking around. He went to taverns at night to do gods know what. I never asked, my parents never asked, and I didn't want to know. It wasn't Conrad this time, however. A slim figure passed, and I realised it was Oleander moving to the front door.

Frowning, I got up from my seat and put my book down.

"Where are you going?" Valda asked.

"Just checking up on our guest," I replied vaguely.

Knowing full well I ran the risk of being followed by my siblings or mother, I cast furtive glances behind me as I made my way to the mansion's front door. A gentle breeze caressed my face when I stepped outside, and I was just in time to see a dark figure disappearing behind the corner. Upping my pace, I followed, and caught up with Oleander on the cliffs behind our mansion.

The sight was worthy of a painting. The moon illuminated Oleander's silhouette on the ridge. His ponytail blew in the wind like liquid silver, against a backdrop of a star-filled sky and a faint mist rolling over the waves.

If I'd been a wiser man, I would've concluded Oleander wasn't doing anything unusual. Many guests had stared at the ocean in wonder during their first night in the mansion. There was no reason for me to be out here; I could return to my family by the fire.

Instead, I walked closer.

As if he'd felt my presence, Oleander turned to face me. His eyes shone brightly as he smiled, but his words came out hesitant. "Lord Montbow?"

I stepped beside Oleander, crossing my arms. "Wanted some fresh air?" I asked.

"Yes, I think I am used to being outside," Oleander replied. "I was more at ease during our journey than I am in a mansion's room. Lovely as it is, of course. I mean no offence."

"Being outside is not helping you remember anything, though, is it?"

Oleander was quiet for a moment. "No, but it's strange," he said. "I don't know, but I feel. Herbs and plants hold no secrets for me. I know their uses, their taste and smell, but I don't know how I know."

"That's still a useful skill to have," I offered. "Maybe you are a herbalist or a scholar. Even if your memory never returns, you can make a good living with that at home."

Oleander's face fell at my mention of his memory never returning and I quickly amended, "I mean, it may yet return. It's only been a few days since we found you."

"Yes," Oleander said, but the flicker of sadness in his eyes remained. "I suppose I could start over, unburdened by the past. A freedom, in a way. But I think I would prefer a clear path. Like you, knowing you were already handfasted, and have a future as the heir of a family."

I laughed. "I think you're overestimating the advantages of being promised to someone from the day your storm-touched powers awakened. I haven't seen my betrothed in years. She's part of the queen's court in Wildewall, and yet still didn't come to see me when I went to the queen for her blessing for my dragon hunt."

Oleander tilted his head to the side. "Why would she not want to see her beloved?"

"Beloved?" I repeated, snorting loudly at the thought of Ariane, my betrothed on paper, genuinely calling me her beloved. "She wants nothing to do with me as a marriage partner or person until I'm a knight and the Montbow house is restored to its former glory."

Oleander's confusion only seemed to grow at my explanation. "She won't love you until you're standing tall?"

I shrugged. "Love has nothing to do with marriage. Even if I, against knowing better, hope differently for my sisters and brothers."

"That is a real shame." Oleander bit his lip. "I would wish for everyone to experience a true love."

"Yeah, well, burning passion is not in the cards for me," I said, wondering why I was still speaking. The elf didn't need to know this about my life. It was better if he didn't know, and if he stopped looking at me so intently. I had to turn away. My gaze fell on the ocean. "The only burns I'll get are from Endris' remarks, or a dragon's fiery breath."

"I see," Oleander said. It appeared he had picked up on my unease because changed the subject. "Is it customary to go to the queen for a blessing before a dragon hunt? How does that blessing go? Is it a magical blessing?"

"No," I replied quickly. "It's just a ceremony. The queen has a staff and will briefly touch your shoulder with it for luck. A remnant of an older, more elaborate tradition, I presume."

Oleander blinked. "What kind of staff?"

"Oh, at first sight, it's just a wooden staff. But it has a blood-red diamond sphere embedded in the wood. It was a gift from..." I fell quiet for a moment and grimaced as I remembered the history behind the staff. "From an elven man named Sage Farun to king Betram. They were close before... Anyway, the royal family kept the staff, despite what happened after. It's all a long time ago now."

"Yet, not long enough for you to permit yourself to see me as anything other than an elf you must rid yourself of," Oleander replied softly. "Even if you saved my life."

Somehow, somewhere during our talk, Oleander had slipped closer to me. He looked deeply into my eyes, and my heart pounded in my throat. He wanted to remain at my side for reasons I didn't understand. Then again, maybe I did. I did understand. Because despite barely knowing him, my cheeks turned red whenever I saw him looking at me. Right now, I was struck by an overwhelming urge to climb down to the beach and lay with Oleander in the sand until sunrise, and bathe in sun-warmed water.

It would be a breath of fresh air to have someone who was outside of my family and outside of the court in the mansion. Someone who didn't have a stake in my knighthood, and didn't care about the storm god blessing me. Even if all we ever did was talk and lay in the sand, I did want him to stay longer.

I couldn't do this. I took a deep breath and steeled myself for more disappointment.

"Oleander, I found you through sheer luck," I said. "It's only common decency to put a cloak around a freezing person and not leaving them to die. Endris has already chosen to pay your debt for you by offering his services to the Montbow family. If you want to repay me as well, do it by not wasting your life. Go to the Starcross woods. Find your people on the other side and live well."

Oleander stared at me. Until now, he had been an open book, his curiosity and kindness always easily read. Now, I couldn't tell what he was thinking.

After enduring a silence that felt like ages, Oleander finally opened his mouth. "I understand. I will perform the task lady Montbow asks of me in the morning, then I will go," he murmured. "If we never meet again, which is likely, I wish you and your future wife much happiness. May you find a passionate love in your life, be it for another person or for something you do, and may you find a path to save your family without killing a creature that has done nothing to you."

Oleander bowed, then walked closer to the edge of the cliff, his back now facing me. I would have worried about it being dangerous, if I hadn't known how nimble he was. "I would like to stay out a little while longer, lord Montbow."

I felt like I needed to say goodbye. I likely wouldn't get another chance to speak with Oleander alone. Why wasn't I like Gisela, with needle-sharp words she knew exactly how to use? Then again, there was little to be said, regardless.

I swallowed thickly. "Very well," I said. "Be careful. If you see any-one approaching the mansion, go inside."

When Oleander didn't respond, I turned on my heels and fled.

Luck truly wasn't on my side tonight. As I snuck back into the mansion, Endris caught me at the door.

I flinched when our eyes met, and Endris looked at me in that deeply judgemental way only he could. Just like I didn't need to speak to look guilty, Endris didn't need to speak to scold me.

"Don't say a word," I ordered him regardless, stressing every word with flushed cheeks.

Endris shook his head with a sigh and brushed past me. "...Wasn't going to."

Debts to Repay

I had always believed elves were long gone from the world. If you paid attention, however, like I did now, they had left their mark far and wide. Long-standing traces of their presence still hid themselves all across the Thundercoast, Wildewall, and beyond.

Here in the Thundercoast, a plant with glossy, pointed leaves and a potent poison grew in the hills nearby the Marchpass ruins. In autumn when its flowers bloomed, the breeze carried a deceptively sweet scent to highest peaks and lowest valleys. The official name of this deadly plant was Bleeding Ivy. But nobody used that name—the common folk called it Elvenear for its sleek appearance and sharp leaves.

Elves were the villain in children's stories involving kidnapping and men being lured into swamps by beautiful women that turned into monsters. Implying elves had raised you was an insult for a conniving, selfish person. Those who were wither-touched, notoriously an elven gift and a dangerous one, were still often found dead of 'natural causes' outside of their villages. These deaths getting a fair investigation was questionable at best.

Despite king Betram's war being long forgotten and elves all but diminished into legend, the hatred was alive and seeped into many things without us questioning it. The longer I stared up at my bedroom ceiling while laying awake, the more examples I could think of.

I was not entirely above the superstitions either. Even now, after Oleander and I had already traveled several days together, I still told my family to lock their doors before they retired to their bedroom. Maybe it wasn't fair, but I didn't know Oleander and I hadn't told my family what he was. I had to protect them somehow from elves who... who were impossibly beautiful and said things that made my head and heart hurt.

"May I find something I'm passionate about," I muttered into the darkness.

I was not passionate about becoming a knight, or being the heir of the Montbow family. Oleander's words, him wishing me a happy rest of my life, ran through my mind over and over. So much that when I finally drifted off into an uneasy sleep, I dreamt of the beach and Oleander ankle-deep in the waves. He smiled at me. His lips moved, but I couldn't hear what he said. I walked closer to him.

"..k...u..."

"...ake up."

"Wake up!"

I woke with a start.

Endris' frantic face hovered over mine and he shook my shoulders violently. The panic in Endris' eyes instantly rendered me wide awake. It was dark in my room, the only source of light being the candle Endris carried in his hand.

"What?" I asked. "What's going on?"

"Oleander's not in the mansion."

"What?" I repeated, shooting upright in my bed. I kicked the sheets off my legs. "Where did he go? Did Mother make him go on the errand already?"

"No," Endris said impatiently. "Lady Montbow is not awake yet, and has not even handed him the letter she wants him to deliver!"

Swearing under my breath, I jumped up from my bed, crossed the room, and snatched my shirt from the chair. There was a stab of guilt in my chest. I'd repeatedly told him to leave. What if he had felt so unwelcome he left early? "Did he go on his own then? Where did he go?"

"If I knew, I would be there, not here," Endris snapped. "But yes, he seemed to have left on his own... And a short man with long silvery hair like him will not go unnoticed outside."

"Thanks for your sharp observation," I snapped back, matching Endris' annoyed tone. After throwing my shirt on, I moved on to my trousers, hopping as I pulled the fabric over one leg before stepping into the other trouser leg. "Why would he even risk leaving on his own? And why were you in his room this early?"

Endris didn't reply. He placed the candle on my nightstand and marched out of my room while I sat on my bed to put my shoes on.

Briefly, I considered waking my parents or Gisela or Conrad. Would they make this situation better, however? I didn't particularly want them to have an opinion about something they didn't understand. My family, especially Mother, would be upset I left without notifying anyone, but I'd deal with the noses wrinkling in disappointment later. I had plenty of experience with that, after all.

Endris paced the hall until I finished getting dressed. When we stepped outside, the sun peeked at us from behind waves, casting a reddish glow on the water's surface. We didn't stop to admire the sunrise. We hurried to the stables to fetch the horses and galloped to town.

By the time we reached the first thatch-roofed building, the inn, the sun was slowly rising into the sky. I spotted a ruddy, blond man crouching down on the path leading to his building. He pulled at the weeds sprouting in the crevices between stones.

Anyone who followed the road south would have to pass the inn. If Oleander went this way, the innkeeper was our best shot of getting information. Our chances were still slim if he had left at night or didn't even go this way, but it was better than sitting on our hands or searching the Thundercoast at random. I steered my horse onto the man's property.

The man had clearly not expected to be disturbed in his work this early. He jolted and looked up as I halted my horse right beside him. Resting a hand against his forehead to shield his squinty blue eyes from the sun, the innkeeper stood.

"Good morning, pardon us for disturbing you," I greeted the man hastily but polite. "Did a man with long, silvery hair pass here? Can't really miss him."

I could pinpoint the exact moment the innkeeper recognised me as a Montbow. His gaze fell on the emblem stitched onto my shirt, and his startled expression soured. "Lord Montbow. How pleasant of you to grace me with your presence," he said with a mocking bow. "Maybe I've seen a silver-haired man. I'm not sure. That sounds like a pretty rare sigh. Just like a Montbow visiting us peasants in town. Also a most rare sight."

I sighed and looked up to the heavens, as if I'd find answers to why people kept blaming me for my uncle's deeds there. Most days, I preferred deflecting sneers with lighthearted jokes. Today, however, I didn't have that sort of patience. Narrowing my eyes, I balled my fist. Sparks flashed from my hand and struck the ground, instantly turning the weeds into black ash. The man leapt back with a yelp. I was taught not to rely on intimidation, nor did I want to. I felt bad, but only for a moment.

"Where is he?" I demanded. "If you have seen something, this is the time to talk."

The innkeeper stared at me with a mixture of indigence and fear. After a few moments, the man spat on the ground. "A man with long silvery hair passed here just before dawn, my lord," he said, acid lacing his tone. "He asked for directions to the Marchpass ruins. I told him not go there, place is haunted, it is. But did he listen? No."

Endris and I exchanged a glance. We didn't speak. We simply took off again.

The place the innkeeper mentioned wasn't far from town. Gisela favoured the Marchpass ruins as a target practice range for archery, considering the townsfolk were superstitious and thought it was bad luck to go there. Apparently, folktales said it was haunted by souls of soldiers that perished when the Marchpass bridge collapsed. Gisela called their superstition nonsense—she had never seen a ghost. I was pretty sure the ghosts were just hiding from her. If my bellicose sister saw them, she would only kill them again.

Endris and I sped up the hills and I already saw the ruins looming in the distance. The Marchpass castle and adjacent bridge were once meant as a traveling route between the Thundercoast and Wildewall. Now, all that remained was crumbling towers and steeply archways leading to a brackish marsh. Crows had made their nests in the few sharp spires that remained standing, and circled around in the sky. The birds were usually the only company we had when Gisela and I practiced our shooting, but today, the ruins were crowded.

A group of around ten men were gathered near the old brick walls. Each of them carried a bow or a sword, and they were clothed in brown, with a fur lining. I recognised a few of their faces and surely Endris had to as well. They were Ytel's men. And sitting on the ground in their midst was one smaller man with silvery hair.

Oleander seemed to see me the same moment I saw him. "Help!" he called out at us.

Most of the men turned our way as Oleander's voice rang out. I saw eyes narrowing and hands reaching for pommels. Endris took out his bow as well. He drew an arrow while his horse danced in place nervously.

"Step away from him!" Endris boomed.

"Endris wait, don't shoot," I hissed. "You're not telling me I have to be the patient, tactful one here, right? You realise those are Ytel's men?"

"So?" Endris snapped.

"Just put that away," I said, pointing at Endris' bow before dismounting my horse.

I walked towards the group with my hands up. It was mostly an empty gesture. They likely knew who I was as well, and I didn't need weapons to harm them. All I needed was a snap of my fingers. Judging from their wary faces and the way none of them sheathed their sword, they knew.

Oleander's eyes were red. I saw mud on his knees and a scratch on his cheek, but his hair was safely tied and he seemed unharmed. Unharmed but scared. With his elbows pressed into his sides, he made himself as small as possible. Likely, Ytel's men had thought him an easy target to rob on the road. My veins pulsed with magic, ready to unleash a rain of thunder on them. It would be so easy, but I had to control myself.

"Lord Montbow." One older, greying man, seemingly the leader of this group, stepped to the front with an unpleasant grin. Scarred skin peeked from below his sleeves as he raised a hand in greeting, showing he'd seen plenty of duels and battle. "You are exactly the man we wanted to see. We bring word from Wildewall, and knight commander Ytel. He is seeking to collect the full payment, with interest, on the loan Harold Montbow took out from his family several years ago. Valued at fifty diamonds."

My throat tightened, and my heart thumped in my chest. Scum of the earth. Ytel had never told me about any loan. He knew the dragon hunt had failed and that I didn't have money or gems. For his men to arrive here this soon, he must've already had them waiting near the Thundercoast. He must've been betting on me to fail to spring his trap. Now I understood why he'd insisted on being the one to travel with me to the Serpentine mountains, despite obviously disliking me. He'd often spoken of wanting a mansion on the cliffs some day too.

"I see," I replied, keeping my voice as steady as I could. "Then I would have expected to see you at the mansion. I nodded at Oleander. "Not threatening a lone man in the hills."

"Threatening? We only stopped to ask why he was here alone!" the ringleader said with obviously feigned innocence. Some of the other man chuckled and smirked, while Oleander now wore an indignant expression. It was a more likely tale they were trying to rob him.

"How kind of you," I said dryly. "Then surely you don't mind if we take our guest home now." I stretched out a hand to Oleander and gestured him to come to my side.

Oleander shoulders rose and fell as he took a deep breath. Then unfolded his legs and cautiously got to his feet. Ytel's men turned to their ringleader for instructions. He pressed his lips to a tight line, stared me down for a few moments, then gave his men a subtle nod. They let Oleander pass, and the elf ran to my side, hiding himself behind me.

I willed myself to stay still as a statue and not respond to Oleander. Right now I was lord Montbow, not Laurence, and I had to act like it. "When can we expect a visit from you at the mansion?" I asked.

The ringleader snorted. "We have other business at the Thundercoast first. But rest assured: we won't forget about you. The first payment will need to be made today. If you can't, we can also accept the mansion and the land itself as payment, of course."

"Of course," I replied, smiling through gritted teeth. "We will see you there. Good day."

Part of me expected an arrow to strike my back the moment I turned to walk to my horse, but it didn't come. Ytel's men left us alone and relief flooded me once it became clear they were really retreating.

"Thank you," Oleander breathed. His voice was quiet like he was scared Ytel's men would return if he spoke too loud. He had shuffled after me to my horse and stayed very close, even if he was careful not to touch me. It made me want to wrap an arm around him in comfort, but I refrained.

"Did they hurt you?" Endris asked gruffly.

Oleander shook his head. "No, they only shoved me around a little. When I told them I was staying at the Montbow mansion they wanted my coin for the knight commander, but I didn't have any."

Endris groaned. "Why did you go to these abandoned ruins? You are safe in the Montbow mansion until you can leave for the woods, and you shouldn't just leave."

"I'm sorry," Oleander apologised softly. "Sometimes, I remember flashes of the past. I only wanted to go to these hills because I remembered a useful plant that might grow here. I wanted to collect some and return before you would miss me. I hoped it would make me remember more."

"Yeah, well, I understand," I said. "But don't run off without telling anyone, will you? I think I lost five years of my life this morning."

"I'm truly sorry," Oleander apologised again. Then a small smile tugged at his lips. "I am grateful, however, that you care about me enough to worry."

"I—" I opened and closed my mouth while Oleander's eyes sparkled and his smile grew wider.

"I didn't say that!" I sputtered, abruptly turning away from Oleander and Endris so they couldn't see my face growing beet-red. I gladly occupied myself with my horse instead. "Anyway, lovely as this scuffle has been, we need to go back home and warn everyone there's some friendly folks coming to steal even more years of our life in one day. Shall we then?"

The Elven Antidote

T he ride back to the mansion was filled with a charged silence. It was a light morning with glaring sunlight and glaring towns-folk who murmured among themselves as we rode through town. Oleander and Endris hadn't spoken with each other since their argument in the hills. Oleander dipped his head, seemingly very aware that he had done something wrong. Endris grumbled like an upset father or older brother, sour and disappointed in Oleander's poor decisions.

I had other worries. Like how in the thunder god's name was I going to tell my parents and siblings that Ytel had screwed me over? That I had blindly stepped into the trap he'd been orchestrating ever since he'd volunteered to accompany me to the Serpentine mountains? He had ensured he'd be the first to know whether I'd succeeded or failed, and that information served him well now.

While Ytel and I had travelled together, I'd been a little preoccupied with my upcoming battle with a dragon. Shame on me for being passionate about not ending up as ashes scattered across the peaks of

Mount Serpentine, or dragon dung. After that, I'd found Oleander and my full attention had shifted to not getting him killed. I wasn't exactly looking for conspiracy plots in the mountains, but my family wouldn't accept that excuse. Conspiracies were everywhere, and I had to see them. I should have seen Ytel scheming, not have my gaze misdirected at a scared elf who wasn't a threat and had only tried to help. As misguided as his help was.

When we arrived at the cliffs and approached the stables behind the mansion by foot, Oleander turned to me. "Lord Montbow, may I speak with you in private before we go inside, please?" he asked softly.

I glanced at Endris. He shot me a blank stare. Then he reached out, snatched my horse's reins from my hands without a word, and started walking towards the stables alone.

"Do you really need to speak with me now?" I asked Oleander, gesturing at my home. "In case you didn't realise, we have a serious problem on our hands and I need to warn my parents about Ytel's men."

"Yes," Oleander replied. "I'm sorry for taking up your time, but what I want to say is related to Ytel's men."

Oleander glided to the walls of the mansion and gingerly brushed his fingers against the climbing plants growing in the cracks between stones. "Yesterday, I noticed a rare flower blooming on the walls of the mansion. If you look closely, there are little specks of yellow woven into the green of the Ocove vines. These flowers only show if the plant is healthy and old. It thrives in briny sea air."

"Huh." I squinted at the twisting vines, and sure enough, after a few moments, I saw the little specks of yellow Oleander spoke about. I had never bothered learning the plant's name. It'd always just been an eyesore to me, like the cracked clay roof tiles and moss.

"In combination with a few other herbs I have found," Oleander continued, unclasping his bag and folding it open to showing me the plants he'd gathered, "And, counterintuitively, a small drop of the poison itself, they will form an antidote to Bleeding Ivy that would likely be of use to people in town. I wanted to prepare it and sell it in Wildewall where people surely have the coin if the queen's court is there."

I shook my head at Oleander's story. My stomach tightened at the thought of him traveling to Wildewall on his own. "Now, wait a moment," I said. "Last time I checked, nobody had ever found a cure for the Bleeding Ivy's sting—all you can do is wait it out and hope you live. And traveling to Wildewall? That would be an insanely risky journey for you. Look at what happened on the hills! Let alone if you try to venture off on your own to the queen's court!"

"Yes, I know that now." Oleander raised his hand to touch the scratch on his face. "I hadn't realised how much you and Endris had been protecting me during our journey here. Even stepping outside alone is dangerous."

"Yeah, well, we all get hurt sometimes. Conrad can look at that cut," I offered sheepishly. "He's usually the one patching us up and scolding us after we get hurt."

"Thank you," Oleander murmured.

Whenever Oleander and I didn't fill the silences and only looked at each other, I turned into an overripe tomato, so I quickly tilted my chin up and nodded at the climbing vines on the wall. "Never knew those pesky vines were doing anything but slowly eating the mansion... But like I said, no herbalist or doctor has ever found a cure for the Bleeding Ivy's sting. Are you absolutely certain?"

"Yes, I'm certain I can prepare an antidote."

Oleander spoke with such confidence it made me chuckle. I looked at him. "I don't think I have ever heard you this certain of anything before."

A bashful smile spread on Oleander's lips. "I don't know a lot," he admitted. "But yes, I am really sure about this. I just wanted to help, so please let me help."

"I already said you don't need to thank me, and Endris will pay off your debt," I reminded him. "Why do you want to help the Montbows this much, anyway? You hardly know us."

Oleander bit his lip. "It is not for your family. I want to help you. If I must leave, I would leave knowing you will remember me fondly."

Oleander stood there, awkwardly fiddling with his bag, and I didn't have words. If I opened my mouth, only dust would fly out. What was I supposed to say to that? That I already thought more of him a lot than I should? That he had even appeared in a dream last night?

After a few moments, Oleander shyly averted his gaze. "Endris told me what humans believe about magic," he said. "That there are gods, and the people chosen by magic are older souls, reborn from courageous heroes who gave their life in battle in a past life. We must honour them."

I let out an awkward laugh. "Please, no, don't. The attention will go straight to my head and I'll become an obnoxiously arrogant brat. Nobody wants that."

Oleander smiled. "I don't believe that you would."

"Besides," I quickly went on before Oleander would give me more compliments, "You're the one out there taking risks and getting hurt to help me. Who is the real hero here?"

"I needed you and Endris to get me out of trouble." Oleander's smile faded. He hesitated for a moment. "Lord Montbow," he then said. "Can I... can I at least return here if there's nothing waiting for me beyond the Starcross woods?"

"Endris seems convinced there will be something for you there," I deflected.

Oleander's face fell. "Endris hopes, but he doesn't know. His vision narrows if he thinks he knows the solution. Too much, perhaps. He wants me safe, but forgets to consider what I want. He doesn't want dragon hunts, but sees no other way to make coin. But the way I see it, it's not safe for me anywhere while I am alone. At least I know you won't hurt me."

If Oleander's people weren't across the Starcross woods, or wouldn't take him back, he was right. Then I might as well have left him in the valley, freezing to death. If there was nothing for him there, as the heir, I would have the leverage to make my family leave him alone. I wouldn't be easy, but still less difficult than living with the knowledge I'd turned Oleander away, knowing he likely wouldn't survive on his own.

"I'm going to regret this, aren't I?" I smiled wryly. "Fine. If there's nothing for you out there, you can return."

"Thank you!" Relief flooded Oleander's face. He leapt forward and flung his arms around my waist. I stiffened as his grip toughened and his silvery hair tickled my chin. Butterflies flitted in my stomach.

I should have pushed him away and told him this was inappropriate. I didn't, and I got punished for my perversion immediately.

A sharp thwacking sounded behind me and drew nearer. Oleander sprung back wide-eyed while I whirled around. Father limped towards us, leaning heavily on his cane with his good arm. The other arm dangled at his side. Amber hawkish eyes above heavy eye bags studied Oleander, then me.

A sense of doom seemed to drape itself over any space my father occupied. My throat went dry and felt like someone was squeezing it. "Father, I—" I started, my voice ragged.

"Bring that man inside," my father interrupted, nodding at Oleander. Without awaiting a response, he hobbled away from us, his cane striking the ground with each step.

I sighed, dragging hand down my forehead. Oleander looked apprehensive about the whole situation, but came with me when I reluctantly gestured for him to come along.

We had to walk slowly because my father walked slowly. He wouldn't accept any help, aside from the cane that he had carved and crafted himself. Nobody took being injured by bandits well, but there were people who took it extraordinarily badly; those who couldn't accept help, and those were proud. Father was both.

We walked to the living quarters where father sat down heavily in his favourite chair near the black marble mantel, which nowadays was often used by Conrad when my father was ill in bed. Father rested his hand on top of his cane and narrowed his eyes at Oleander, his face set and grim. Oleander shuffled nervously under his gaze.

"Do you have magic?" Father asked abruptly. "That you feel you are worthy enough of dallying with a storm-touched?"

"No sir," Oleander replied quietly.

I grimaced. Oleander already sounded like he struggled to keep his voice from cracking.

Father grumbled something incoherent under his breath. "What are your skills, then? Why should you have been allowed to stay the night here and eat our food?"

"He doesn't have his memory—" I started explaining, but my father's icy stare, which could make blood grow solid in veins, made my voice die out quickly. He'd clearly been told about my failure.

Oleander's shoulders drew up. He darted a glance my way. "I think I might've been a herbalist, sir. In another life."

Father grunted. With his good hand, he reached into his pocket. I opened my mouth to speak again. Before I could, father drew his hand out of his pocket and threw something Oleander's way.

With the inhuman grace I already knew Oleander possessed, equal parts wild and delicate in his movements, he ducked. His fingers shot to his waist, reaching for a weapon that should have been in a scabbard at his belt. His fingers found air instead. The small pebble father had thrown rebounded off the wall and landed on the stone floor with a thud. Oleander stood and looked over his shoulder with his eyes spread wide.

"You were no herbalist," my father stated.

Oleander gaze drifted down to his own hand, the one that had reached for his belt, shock clear in his expression.

"Father, we have more urgent problems than Oleander's worth," I interrupted, dodging my father's eyes. "We ran into Ytel's men, and they will come here later today to collect payment on a loan our uncle took out. He travelled with me to Mount Serpentine. It was a setup."

"A setup for if you didn't complete the dragon hunt," Father bitingly remarked.

I didn't need to look my father's face to vividly imagine the way he'd hardened. I'd felt the shame and dread the moment I left the mountains, but it twisted in my guts in an even more painful manner now. I'd already known how important the dragon was. Now the consequences of failure were becoming real.

"I can tell Endris we're going back to the mountains today, I—"

"Still wouldn't be in time," Father cut me off.

"If I may?" Oleander spoke meekly. "I have something that could be of use. It is worth money to these men."

Father blinked at Oleander and stayed quiet, which was the largest sign of approval I'd seen him give anyone since our uncle's betrayal.

Oleander correctly interpreted the silent approval and went on. "I wondered if people were willing to pay for a cure for Bleeding Ivy's sting?"

Father breathed in and out audibly as he leaned forward, closer to Oleander. The chair creaked. "Such a recipe is worth nothing," he said flatly. "Here at the Thundercoast, we don't pay for fairytales."

"I really think—" I started.

"What are you still standing around for?" Father gave me a dismissive wave. "Laurence, prepare the horses for the market for Ytel's men. And get this man out of my sight. I want him gone by nightfall."

I would have almost laughed at my father's dismissive bitterness. I had to laugh, else I'd lament that he no longer had any faith in the world, in people, and in anything new. And people used to say my father, and I were alike. It was hard to believe that was true.

I bowed my head. "Yes, father."

Oleander and I left the room side by side.

"I will make the antidote regardless," Oleander told me once we were out of my father's earshot. The determined shine in his eye was undiminished from when he first mentioned the antidote. "Perhaps he will change his mind, or you can convince Ytel's men to take it?"

I didn't have it in me to argue with him, but my father was right: Ytel's men wouldn't believe Oleander had an antidote to Bleeding Ivy. They would call it an old wives' tale and laugh before shoving Oleander aside into the mud. I believed Oleander thought he could make the antidote, but whether he could was another matter.

"Thank you, Oleander," I said. "You go ahead and do that."

After a curtsy, Oleander sped down the corridor towards the kitchen, presumably to make his antidote. I sighed at the walls, preparing myself for my little brother's wailing and tears when I told him we had sold his favourite animals.

Sweet Poison

When I walked to the stables, Endris was still there outside the building. He had put a halter on one of the horses, and tethered the rope to a steel ring screwed into the wall. With long strokes he brushed through the horse's coat. The horse's eyelids drooped, and she looked utterly content with this arrangement.

I walked up to Endris. "Thanks for brushing her, Endris," I said. "You'll make her look pretty for Ytel's men, who will be taking this horse later today."

Endris glanced at me over his shoulder, then returned to his brushing work. "You will bow to Ytel's men that easily? Why not have them prove their claim first with a contract? Anyone can come to you and say you owe them a sum of fifty diamonds."

I drew a breath and expelled it through my mouth. "I know you're more of a wilderness man, so let me explain. If you're not picky about who you steal from or borrow money from, like dear uncle Harold, the richer duped parties will be out for your blood. And at some point it doesn't matter whether you truly owe them. Everyone at the queen's court will believe you do. Ytel isn't a noble but he is a knight with a mostly unblemished reputation. He will more likely be believed than a family of disgraced merchant frauds."

Endris didn't seem impressed. He didn't stop currycombing the horse, nor did he spare me another glance. "Very well," he answered simply. "You are indeed better aware of noble politics than I am."

Letting out a frustrated growl, I started pacing. "Endris, I don't want you to agree with me. Can't you argue like usual?" I asked, only half-joking. "Oleander says he has another way. He claims he can make an antidote to the Bleeding Ivy's sting. But Ytel's men won't buy a fairytale, as Father eloquently put it."

Now, Endris did stop brushing and turned to me. His dark eyes bored into mine. "And what if one of Ytel's men happens to get stung on their way here?"

I blinked, then started laughing. Endris continued staring at me in his usual grave manner, quickly making my laughter die out.

I opened and closed my mouth. "You're serious," I stated. "You want to poison one of them? Right, that will surely make this easier if he dies a gruesomely painful death and we get blamed for that too."

"Or it will prove the antidote works right in front of their eyes," Endris countered.

"We don't know if it does!"

"Give Ytel's men the horses then. You're right about it being the safest solution."

Endris shrugged and went back to work. I balled my fists, then unclenched then. With a sigh, I gave up and walked away. Why did

I expect Endris could help me with this decision? At least the horses would be ready when Ytel's men arrived. There was not much else for me to do now but wait.

I went to the front door of the mansion, and that was when my eye fell on movement at the foot of the cliffs. There were men on horses climbing the winding paths. Men with brown clothes with fur lining. I cursed under my breath. It appeared the foreman was making good on his threat immediately, giving us as little time as possible to prepare for their arrival.

I wasn't the only one who had noticed enemies coming. Mother came running outside. She clamped my arm, digging her fingers into the fabric of my shirt.

"They are not above you," she reminded me quietly. "Keep your back straight. You are storm-touched, chosen by the god of thunder."

"I am?" I asked with feigned surprise. "Nobody told me about it in the past two or so minutes."

Mother shot me a stern look, but we didn't have time to bicker. Ytel's men had fast horses and they came galloping onto our land within a few moments. I wished Valda and Gisela were already awake and here. They were much better at bargaining with these kind of men than I was. Unfortunately, in order to ensure their involvement I had to pretend I wasn't home and hide in the house, as we often did. Once they saw me, it was my duty as the heir to meet them and speak with them.

The foreman of Ytel's group moved his horse to the front. He didn't dismount, so he literally looked down on me. "Hello, Lord

Montbow," he said with the same contemptuous tone Ytel often liked to use when addressing me. His voice was grating and unpleasant to listen to, like scraping on a chalkboard. "We are here for knight commander Ytel's payment. Do you have it prepared?"

"Hello," I replied through a gritted-teeth smile. "We have prepared our first payment. Will one horse do for today?"

The foreman chuckled. "I'm sorry my lord, but no. One horse is not enough. Now, if there were two..."

My jaw clenched. Unfortunately, the dim-witted vulture could count. He'd seen two horses this morning, so I could've known he'd demand all the horses he'd seen.

There was movement behind me. I recognised the thwacking of father's cane, Conrad's heavy footsteps, and Gisela's quick, light ones. It seemed more of my family members had seen the men coming. Having an audience ranked up the pressure. I felt the eyes of my family members prickling on my back.

"One horse sounds like it should be enough for a first payment," I tried again.

The foreman raised a brow, an arrogant smirk dangling on his lips. "We can also go back to Wildewall and tell the court the Montbows will not cooperate and pay their debts."

My stomach sank. That was an end-all argument. I wished their threats were empty. We had little to stand on with the queen's court. They'd have no mercy on us, and the vultures would continue to circle until we no longer had any choice but to give up everything as we no longer had any land and valuables to give.

"Agreed, then," I begrudgingly said. "Two horses."

Then, a blur with long silver hair shot past me.

"Wait!" Oleander called out urgently, and all heads turned his way.

"Oleander," I hissed. "Not now!"

Oleander ignored me. He stood in front of me and addressed Ytel's men. "What about a healing balm for Bleeding Ivy?"

The foreman looked at Oleander like he was less than a piece of shit stuck under his boot. "Lord Montbow, control your servants," he spat.

"He's not my servant, I—"

Oleander faced me, and looked at me with unshakable faith in me written all over his face. "I assure you it works," he said.

To break his trust hurt me too, but I shook my head. "Oleander, not now," I repeated sternly. "Go back inside."

Despite my rejection, not once did Oleander's confidence falter. With his head held high, and without breaking eye-contact, Oleander reached into his bag. Behind Oleander, I saw hands moving to pommels and resting there.

Oleander pulled his hand out of his bag. Clenched firmly between his index finger and thumb was a leaf of Bleeding Ivy. With the way he held the leaf and his burning determination to prove the antidote worked, I instantly realised what he was going to do.

"Oleander, no!"

I stepped forward and made a grab for Oleander's wrist, but he easily dodged out of my reach. Without a moment of hesitation, Oleander raised his hand and stung himself in the neck with the leaf.

A ripple of shock travelled through everyone on the cliffs, even Ytel's men. I heard gasps, and even yelling.

The poison of the Bleeding Ivy worked exceptionally fast, especially when inserted in a large vein like in the neck. Its largest downside, according to assassins at least, was that the effects weren't subtle. Already, Oleander's neck started swelling and the skin surrounding the sting turned red. Blood seeped out of the wound, and I was barely fast enough to catch Oleander as his legs gave away and he collapsed.

"Oleander!" I called out, gently lowered him to the ground and cradling him in my arms. Oleander breathed hard. His gaze glazed over but he moved his eyes down to his bag. His lips tried to form words, but no sound came out.

"The antidote must be in his bag." Endris, who must've heard the commotion, popped up out of nowhere and knelt down beside me.

"Right."

With trembling fingers, I opened the bag. There was only one item left in the otherwise empty compartments; a single vial holding a watery green paste. I hastily removed the cork and tilted the glass to let the paste glide onto my finger. A stinging sensation spread where my skin touched the strange paste, which would have given me pause in another situation. But here I had no choice, so I smeared it on the wound immediately.

For a moment it seemed like the paste did nothing. Then I noticed Oleander's breathing gradually slowed. The swelling on his neck stayed, but within a few moments Oleander shifted, now able to sit up on his own and support his upper body with his arms.

"It works," he said softly, between heavy breaths. "And it should be worth a lot."

Oleander achieved what I hadn't been able to do today: he made hesitation flicker in the foreman's eyes. It was rather hard to deny an antidote was real if you saw it work in front of you, and it was even harder to deny it would be worth a lot on the market.

Squinting at Oleander, the foreman eventually nodded. "Very well, we would take this," he said, though, I had a feeling he wouldn't bring the antidote to Ytel.

"No, you're getting the horses," I firmly stated, forcing my voice to stay even. "We had already agreed on that. Are you men of your word or not?"

The foreman spat on the ground and narrowed his eyes at me. "The debt is larger than two horses," he reminded me. "I want your most valuable possession."

He wasn't going to let go without a fight, but neither was my family. Being stubborn was how we had survived so far.

Gisela was the one to step in this time. "Nobody will miss a few mercenaries if they don't return to Wildewall," she said. "Except perhaps knight commander Ytel, but I'm sure we can arrange a deal with him after we start selling this antidote. We will have plenty of coin to make him forget about you."

"Take your horses and go. The payments will follow," my father added gruffly.

I was not as quick a thinker as Gisela, who'd already realised we had everything we needed to scare these men away now, but I did understand this was my moment to remind Ytel's men of my mark.

Giving my shirt a firm tug so the upper branches of the mark would show at my collar bones, I stood. The political consequences of slaying a knight's mercenary would be messy, and I was forever leashed by the queen's court, but Ytel's men had to understand I could murder them with no more than a flick of my wrist.

The foreman didn't speak. He didn't openly admit defeat, but only shot us dirty looks while Endris marched to the stables to fetch the two horses. I sat next to Oleander while we waited for his return, just in case anyone got any ideas about kidnapping Oleander for his knowledge.

Only when the clopping of hooves faded into the distance and Ytel's men were truly gone, did any of us dare to breathe.

"I... uh, I'm sorry, I don't think I can walk," Oleander told me softly. "Could you let me lay down for a bit?"

"Of course, let me help you," I replied, carefully lifting Oleander off the ground. "That was beyond reckless!" I scolded him while he rested his head against my chest and closed his eyes.

"Only if you thought the antidote wouldn't work," Endris said.

I didn't respond, nor did I care to stay around and listen to anything else my family or Endris had to say. Oleander needed my attention. I carried him inside and brought him to his room. There, I gently placed him on the bed and took off his shoes.

"Don't worry, I will be fine," Oleander told me. "With the antidote, the poison will no longer spread. I just need a moment to recover."

"And once you do, I will scold you for your recklessness further," I joked, making a small smile appear on Oleander's lips.

"But it worked, did it not?" he argued.

I shook my head, bemused. I couldn't say he was wrong, so I simply walked to the door. "I will get you some water."

When I walked outside, most of my family members were still there. From the words I caught, Conrad, Gisela, and my father were discussing the possibilities of selling the antidote. I didn't want a part in such conversations. We desperately needed a source of income, but this was Oleander's antidote. Only if he agreed to sharing, would I start making plans.

I walked on to the well to get some water for Oleander. When I returned inside with a full bucket, my mother was waiting for me in the lobby.

"Will Oleander recover?" she asked.

"I think so," I said. "He told me the poison won't spread after the antidote is applied." I pointed at the bucket. "I'm just bringing him some water."

"Good." Mother nodded. Then she placed a hand on my shoulder. "I also just wanted to remind you... It's alright to enjoy your life before you fulfilled your duties and marry for political ties."

"Sorry, what?" I asked, genuinely confused.

Mother smiled ruefully. "It's still a better life in a mansion with a man like you, than it is out there for someone like Oleander," she clarified.

I finally caught on where my mother was going with this. My cheeks burned and I cleared my throat. "I suppose it is better for most people to live in the mansion, yes," I said, still pretending I didn't know what she meant.

"... I know you suffer under the weight of your responsibilities." Mother patted my shoulder. "So take your pleasures where you can find them. Oleander wants to stay here and I can see want him here too. We'll ask him to stay willingly, as your friend."

The way my mother emphasised friend almost made me writhe in pure discomfort and embarrassment. I couldn't hide from my mother's gaze either, it appeared. It was not like my family didn't know I wasn't looking at women. We had a silent understanding I'd marry a woman regardless, have children, and have lovers on the side if my wife tolerated it. I'd gladly give her the same privileges.

"Yes, alright, fine. If you don't mind, I have to bring Oleander water now," I stammered. The water in the bucket sloshed as I hurried away from this conversation.

"Do whatever you need to succeed, Laurence," Mother called after me. "History and our family will only remember what you accomplished, not the details of how."

Guileful

After what my mother said in the foyer, I couldn't stop blood from flooding my cheeks as I entered Oleander's room and brought him water. I felt Oleander's eyes resting on me, but I didn't look at him as I placed the pitcher and a glass on his nightstand. It didn't feel appropriate to stay beside Oleander while he rested, so I didn't linger near the bed.

I turned towards to the door. "I'll leave you so you can rest."

"Wait," Oleander called out after I'd already stepped into the hallway.

Taking a deep breath, I peeked into the room. "Yes?"

"...Lord Montbow, won't you sit with me for a while?"

Oleander's eyes glistened as he looked up at me. The sight of him holding back tears welling up didn't just tug, but ripped at my heart-strings. Poor guy must've been keeping a brave face before, pretending he felt better than he did. I couldn't say no to him. Not after he had just saved my family. I could hardly ever no to him, if I was honest.

"Of course," I muttered.

I re-entered the room. I grabbed the chair from behind the desk, placed it next to the bed, and took a seat.

"Is my neck looking better, lord Montbow?" Oleander asked. He tilted his head to the side, letting his cheek rest on the pillow.

"Uh..." I leaned in and peered at the wound. I wasn't the best judge of skin abnormalities, but the swelling seemed to be less severe than it had been outside. There was a froth of blood and greenish paste on Oleander's neck, but it wasn't bubbling or expanding. "I think you're alright."

"Thank you." Oleander turned back to me.

I still read unconditional trust in his gaze, even after I'd betrayed him by letting Ytel's men insult him. A stone settled in my stomach. I'd even told him to stand down.

"I'm sorry I didn't believe you," I blurted. "About the antidote, I mean."

A small smile appeared on Oleander's lips. "It was difficult to believe, I realise that," he said. "Don't feel bad."

Oleander looked at my right hand. After a brief hesitation, he reached for it. I shivered as his fingers brushed against mine. Oleander's palm felt warm and dry, and as if on its own, my wrist turned so our fingers could entwine. Oleander tightened his grip. I didn't let go either, despite my cheeks burning. If my mother or Endris or anyone walked in right now, this would be very incriminating.

"If this is too bold, please let me know," Oleander said softly.

I was about to open my mouth and tell him holding hands was fine since he was ill, but that didn't seem to be what he meant.

"If I may ask..." Oleander paused. "What happened to you family? Why are these men after you this way? You and Ytel seemed on good terms earlier when we met at the Last Stop."

I snorted. "That looked like on good terms to you?"

"You aren't? He calls you lord."

Oleander looked genuinely surprised, reminding me of his innocence in matters of the court despite being a brilliant herbalist. I shook my head with a smile. "Oleander, whenever someone from the knights or nobility smiles at you, remember, it may not actually be a kind gesture."

Oleander's eyes grew wide as he stared at me.

"No, not my smiles," I hastily added. "Those are real. I'm not trying to trick you."

Oleander gave my hand a small squeeze. "Alright. I would be sad if you weren't honest with me."

"I am honest with you," I promised, and I was, mostly. I didn't tell him everything. I didn't let Oleander know that my heart was pounding, and that I would hold his hand even if he wasn't ill and in need of support.

"Anyway, your question. I suppose it's better if you hear it from me than from the people in town." I let out a mirthless chuckle. Already, I felt my throat dry up thinking of uncle Harold. It wasn't easy to talk about this, but Oleander had just saved all of us. He deserved to know.

"The Montbows were originally merchants, as I've already told you before," I said. "We were so good at setting up trading posts that my ancestors were elevated to nobility over a hundred years ago. For being the first merchants successful in setting up a trade route with port Richris on the other side of the sea."

I sighed. "After my grandfather passed away, our uncle Harold took over and ran the Montbow locations overseas in port Richris. He was wildly successful, or so it seemed. We trusted in him since the coin kept flowing. But my uncle was rash in his decision taking, and a swindler and a thief. He had been racking up debt and conning investors, rich and poor. His workers finally revolted on the islands, and it got bloody."

Oleander nodded in understanding. "Your father trusted his brother, who turned out to be a bad person."

"Yes," I said. "And Father's signature is also underneath many contracts uncle Harold made. My father is a warrior, not a bookkeeper. He signed, trusting his older brother blindly. Now, we can't show our faces on the Richris islands because any Montbow will get shot on sight by the sailors. The townsfolk here at the Thundercoast are mad because they suffer under our ruined reputation, too. They can no longer trade, and unsavoury debt collectors travel through town to come to us. When there's trouble or unrest in this region, it's always tied to our family."

"Yes, but that is not your fault," Oleander protested. "You must have been but a child when this happened. You did nothing wrong!"

"Maybe I didn't personally, but try explaining that to the folks in town," I said. "They are right that debt collectors come here because uncle Harold is gone now. Killed in the fray with revolting sailors. That bastard. We are the only ones left now. The only door debt collectors can knock on to demand their money back."

Oleander was silent for a moment. His eyes travelled to our entwined fingers. "Your sister Gisela mentioned selling the Bleeding Ivy antidote in town."

"Yes, she did," I said. "And I apologise for that, too. Gisela can be rather forward. She thinks five steps ahead, but she doesn't consider what other people think about those steps, nor that what she wants may not be possible. It's not our antidote. It's yours."

Oleander bit his lip. He raised his eyes to meet mine. "If giving it to you means I can stay with you, the recipe to the antidote is yours."

There was that same unyielding determination edged in Oleander's face again. The iridescent green of his irises almost seemed to radiate in the dim light and mesmerised me. "Oleander, you don't have to gift me anything," I breathed. "The Montbows made their own problems, and we should find solutions to them ourselves. You should sell your antidote yourself. It's your knowledge."

"Perhaps, but I can't do that anyway, can I?" Oleander replied. "The moment I leave the Montbow mansion to become a merchant, I will be alone. Ytel's men, or other people who hear that I can make antidotes, will try to capture me and force me to share the recipe before killing me."

I grimaced. "Well, at least you learned fast. I suppose that's true. They know your worth now. I can't say they won't try to take you if they find you on the road."

"And if I travel with Endris, I would put him in danger too," Oleander pointed out with a sad frown.

"Yes, you're right," I had to admit again. "But you don't have to give me the antidote."

"Your father was right, however. Your family needs the extra mouth they feed to be useful," Oleander pointed out. "If that's my use... The way to convince your family that I am worthy of staying beside a storm-touched, so be it."

What my mother had said in the foyer implied she had a whole other 'use' for Oleander in mind. She wanted him to be my friend, which absolutely didn't mean he'd be my friend. I fought the urge to hide my face in sheer embarrassment.

"Besides," Oleander continued, "there is one more reason for me to be here. I would hope the antidote sells and word spreads all the way to Wildewall. If I received an invitation to visit Wildewall, I would want to see the elven artefact in the queen's staff. It's all I know of my people. I can't go alone, but I could travel with your family."

"Oleander..." I trailed off. Everything he said hinted at him wanting to stay without attempting to reach the Starcross woods first. My eyes darted to the ajar door. "Wait one moment."

As I stood, I gently freed my hand from Oleander's grasp. I walked to the door, checked if there was nobody in the hall, then closed it and turned the key in the lock.

Oleander shot me a quizzical look from the bed. I sat back down, and he immediately reached for my hand again. A moment of silence fell. Oleander watched me intently, clearly waiting for me to speak.

I leaned a little closer to him and lowered my voice. "You realise that if you stay by my side, you will have to hide who you are from everyone but Endris and me?" I whispered. "And that if they see your ears, they may not look kindly upon you anymore, no matter what you did for them. No matter how much you helped."

Oleander's gaze went distant and dull for a moment. Then he nodded. "I realise," he said. "But perhaps there will be a moment that I can tell them in the future. You accepted me for who I am."

"Yes, but few people are as smart as I am," I joked. "I know a good person when I see one."

Though, I couldn't say Oleander's sparkling eyes, the curve of his lips, and his long hair and beautiful face hadn't steered that decision. And saving him hadn't meant he had my trust from the beginning. I had mistrusted him for being an elf. Had.

Oleander freed his hand from my grasp. He propped himself up on his elbows before shifting himself upright. Suddenly, Oleander's face was very close to mine, and he kept leaning in until I felt his breath from his parted lips. Tension coiled in my body. My pulse drummed in my throat. I should stop him... but why should I? I wasn't married. Everyone knew my tastes. I shut my eyes and allowed Oleander to briefly press his lips to mine. A feather light touch.

Immediately after, Oleander leaned back. The sheets rustled. When I opened my eyes, I saw Oleander had moved to the other side of the bed. He bit his bottom lip with wide eyes. "Sorry," he apologised. It's hard to stop myself when you look at me. You are very handsome. I know you find this inappropriate."

"It is." I said. The only thing that stopped me from grinning like a fool was the fact that Oleander looked genuinely scared he'd offended me. I placed my palms on the sheets and shifted my weight forward so I could press another peck to Oleander's lips. When our lips brushed together again, Oleander sucked in a sharp breath.

"Very inappropriate," I said.

Oleander smiled sheepishly at me, which also made me smile.

"Get some sleep. I'll inform the rest of the family about your decision to stay here and help us sell the antidote. I'll come back later."

"Alright," Oleander murmured.

I floated to the door, pulled on the handle, and when it didn't open, realised I forgot I had locked it. From behind me, Oleander laughed quietly. I shot him a sheepish smile over my shoulder, then unlocked the door and left the room.

The moment I was out of sight, I staggered and pressed my back against the wall with a wide grin. I raised my fingers to my tingling lips, knowing my mind would be reeling for a while. But I also couldn't remember the last time I felt this good.

Once my face no longer felt beet-red, I went downstairs to find my family members. Thankfully, my mother was no longer in the foyer. Father was nowhere to be found either, but Gisela and Conrad were still in front of the mansion.

I approached my brother and sister, jutting a thumb over my shoulder. "Before you start selling something you don't own, Oleander is willing to share the antidote with us," I informed them. "In case you forgot that was actually an important aspect of being able to sell this too."

"Great, then at least you did something useful today," Conrad retorted.

I rolled my eyes.

Gisela acknowledged my words with a curt nod and moved on to the next topic. "How did Oleander learn of this antidote?" she asked. "Father said he wasn't a herbalist."

"He lost his memory. How is he supposed to know how he knows?" I said, while making an eye sweep of the cliffs. "And where did Endris go? I had expected him to come see Oleander."

"Running the errands meant for Oleander," Conrad said. "Antidote boy is no longer leaving our protection, as per mother's orders. He's been promoted from an errand runner to someone important." Conrad shrugged." And now that we have his blessing, we need a plan how to get the materials needed for this antidote without being followed or have it be stolen."

"Without horses, it will be difficult to gather herbs fast and safely," Gisela said. "We should divide our tasks as soon as possible and spend our first profit buying new horses." She looked at me. "Laurence, I suggest you stay with Oleander and guard him. Oleander will provide a list of what he needs, and the rest of us can forage at night or in the early morning before dawn."

Conrad folded his arms in front of his chest. "I'm not foraging. I'm going to town with the remains of the antidote. I already have a few contacts in town who will be most interested in this."

My eyes fell on Oleander's bag, which was now at Conrad's waist. "How will you convince them it's real?" I asked.

There was a dark glint in Conrad's mismatched eyes. "I would say Oleander has also provided us with an excellent way of proving it, wouldn't you?"

Without awaiting our response, Conrad started walking toward the stables. He'd vanish for a few hours, then return. Conrad often travelled to town that way, allowing no one to come with him. I had no idea what he did there, but he always came back in one piece, and he loathed uncle Harold more than any of us did. I didn't believe he was out gambling or swindling like Valda had sometimes whispered in my ear.

"Laurence," Gisela addressed me. "Let us share our plan with the rest of the family, shall we? There's much work to do."

Hidden Intentions

C onrad took one of the few horses left in our stables and went on his way with the antidote tucked safely into his bag. Gisela and I watched him go down the path leading to town. Neither of us I asked questions. I didn't because Conrad wouldn't give me truthful answers, and I supposed Gisela cared not how Conrad convinced the town this antidote was real, as long as he did.

"Laurence! Gisela!" Valda's voice rang out behind me.

When I turned, a very indignant-looking Valda came storming out the front door with little Fynn on her heels. He had to run to keep up with her.

A frown was etched onto Valda's face. Her black hair, which was usually neatly braided, was now a disheveled mop. I would've teased my sister that she wouldn't want a future husband to see her like this, if she didn't look like she was about to spit fire like a dragon.

"Mother told me what happened," Valda said, her cheeks red with rage. "You faced Ytel's men in here at the mansion without me? I cannot believe it."

I held up my hands in defence. "We didn't exactly face them without you here. You were just in your bed."

"Honestly, Valda. You would sleep straight through a ball organised by the queen herself in Wildewall's court if it was held too early in the morning," Gisela said with her hands on her hips.

"I would not!" Valda huffed. "And that's not even all! You also let Oleander get hurt?"

"And you gave them Spot?" Fynn sniffled. A tear rolled down his cheek.

Shit, I had already almost forgotten about Ytel's men taking two of our horses. One of the two, a speckled horse, was Fynn's favourite. He had called her Spot. In all the commotion, I hadn't had the time to wake Fynn and warn him so he could say goodbye to Spot.

"Oh, Fynn, I'm sorry." I walked over to my little brother and kneeled to give him a hug. "Maybe we will be able to buy Spot back from Ytel's men. We have something of value to sell in town now, thanks to Oleander."

Fynn threw his arms around me. "Really?" he asked in a small voice.

"Yes, we can see what we can do," I tried my best to reassure Fynn without lying. I couldn't guarantee that we could get our horses back. Ytel's men would surely be suspicious as to why I wanted those horses back in particular, and be purposely unaccommodating.

Fynn kept clinging to me, so I scooped him up as I stood. "However, we need to prepare and sell antidotes on the market first. After that, we will have the coin to get Ytel's men off our back for good and to reclaim our property."

"Yes, well, Oleander will need to recover before all that, won't he? He's the only one who can make the antidotes." Valda clacked her tongue. "Laurence, I cannot believe you of all people would let him stab himself with vile Elvenear."

I felt a clenching in my chest. "Don't call it Elvenear. It's Bleeding Ivy," I said. "And I didn't let Oleander stab himself, alright? He made that choice and I didn't agree with it."

Both Valda and Gisela stared at me, clearly taken aback by my sudden protest against the use of the word Elvenear. It was a common folk term, after all. Used interchangeably with Bleeding Ivy. It just didn't sit well with me anymore to use that word now that Oleander was in our household.

"I will bring Fynn to his room now," I said, giving Fynn's back a rub. "Then I will be back to align our plans."

"Very well," Gisela said. "We will wait for you."

Valda looked like she wanted to ask me why I didn't want her to say Elvenear. I was grateful that Gisela placed her hand on Valda's back and took her along. It didn't stop my younger sister from shooting me curious glances over her shoulder, but it did stop her from asking questions.

I turned the other way and started ascending the stairs with Fynn in my arms.

"Laurence, when will I be old enough to join you when you talk about things in the living quarters?" Fynn asked. "You always keep me away when you talk to our mother and father. I want to help get Spot back, too!"

I brushed my fingers through Fynn's unruly hair. "You will be able to help," I promised. "Just let the adults speak first. It's all boring meetings, anyway. I wish I could stay in your room and play with your toy animals instead."

"Let's trade then!" Fynn immediately suggested. "I will be the head of the house, and you can play in my room."

I chuckled. "I will think about it."

We walked past Oleander's room. The door was ajar and I couldn't help but take a peek inside. I caught a flash of Oleander on the bed. His eyes were open, and he smiled when he saw me. I smiled back, but hurried on.

Fynn craned his neck to catch another glimpse of Oleander. "Mother told me he was going to stay here, but not as a servant," he said. "She says he's your friend. But... he's not your friend, is he?"

My ears grew hot and I hushed Fynn. "Of course he's my friend. He's a friend to all of us."

"You and mother both think I don't know, but I do," Fynn went on in a whisper. "You're going to lie together in a bed like in the books."

I nearly choked on my own spit. "What books?"

"The one at the back of Gisela's closet," Fynn replied. "It's called A Dalliance with the Duke."

I opened and closed my mouth. "By the thunder god's wrath, you're far too young to be reading those kinds of books, Fynn," I scolded him. "Stay out of Gisela's closet. I'm going to pretend I don't know that about her, and if you value your life, you will do the same."

"Alright, the book was kind of boring anyway." Fynn easily agreed. Then he leaned his head a little closer to my ear. "But I have to tell you a secret. I like Oleander much better than Ariane. She never even talks to me when she's here. I hope you marry Oleander instead."

My face grew even hotter and my skin prickled. How did one talk about such matters with a little brother who was far too inquisitive for his age? I decided to keep it simple. "For many reasons, it's difficult to break a betrothal," I said. "If it weren't difficult, Ariane Seydal would have already broken ours the moment house Montbow was ruined."

"Is it not that easy?" Fynn was silent for a moment. "Laurence, can you marry a man?"

"I, uh. Well, it has happened," I sputtered. "The north and west of Wyndmore was eventually reunited by a marriage between two women, Sonia and Katharine, because there was no son in either ruling family. The entire country might've been dragged into a bloody war if they couldn't settle their dispute, so they agreed on the union."

We arrived at Fynn's room, and I opened the door. "Such a situation is rare, however. And like Gisela's books, wanting me to marry Oleander is another secret you best keep to yourself, alright? I am already promised to Ariane, and that is final."

Fynn pouted as I set him down on the ground, but nodded.

"Good. Those are our little secrets, then." I pressed my index finger to my lips. "Now, you go play. I'll go to my dull adult meeting."

"Alright," Fynn replied listlessly. He trudged over to his wooden toy horses and soldiers on the table. He grabbed one of the horses, but there was a sadness in his eyes as he galloped it across the table. I hoped Fynn would forget about Spot in a few days, because getting mother and father to agree to going after Ytel's men for horses wouldn't be likely.

I didn't stop by Oleander's room on my way back downstairs. He had everything he needed in his room, and seeing him would only tempt me into skipping meetings and staying with him instead.

When I entered the living quarters downstairs, my family, sans Conrad and Fynn, was gathered by the fire. I saw my mother and my father standing opposite each other like two fighters in an arena. Mother was frowning, and my father's lips were pressed into a thin, resolute line. The air was thick with tension.

I might've tiptoed out of the room if my mother hadn't briefly looked up when I stepped inside and knew I was here.

After curtly nodding at me in greeting, my mother turned back to my father. "Gisela does not need to stay with Laurence and Oleander," she said. "She is much better suited to help in the fields, gathering herbs and keeping us and Valda safe."

"That boy is not a herbalist," my father bit. "And we all know it. We have no idea who he is, or when he'll show his true colours."

I cast my eyes to the ceiling, before sighing and approaching my parents. "Alright, what is going on here? What is the problem?"

"We agreed is wise to leave you here in the mansion to defend it and Oleander, who will prepare the antidotes," Gisela answered. "Where I will go, however, seems to be up for debate."

I shook my head, confused. "Because I cannot be alone with Oleander?" I asked. "You think he will harm me? Because if he wanted to harm me, he would've had far more opportunity to do so during our journey here from the Serpentine Mountains."

"Don't look at me, look at your father," my mother snapped. "I don't believe Oleander is a herbalist, but he is not here to betray us either. Why win our trust? What would he gain out of it aside from a place in our household? There are plenty more affluent families to join or try to take down for the coin. And if he wanted the last of our land and our mansion to be surrendered to Wildewall and knight commander Ytel, he could've already let that happen today."

"He could be working for another master than Ytel," my father pointed out gruffly. "He could have intentions we cannot think of because have been cut off from Wildewall, the court, and the circle of nobility for too long!"

Mother sighed deeply. "Caution is healthy. Paranoia is not. You are seeing evil intentions everywhere, Uwe. How about the most obvious explanation? The one we have been seeing all along? Oleander was abandoned by his own family and left to die. He owes Laurence. He wants to prove himself worthy and stay beside him."

"He wouldn't have offered to entrust me with the Bleeding Ivy antidote recipe if he meant to betray us," I added. "Besides, we have been alone on several occasions. I am convinced he's not after our lives."

A look of anger flashed in my father's eyes as he looked at me. "I don't trust him or his convenient 'knowledge.' You saw what I saw!

Oleander was ready to draw a sword when I tested his reflexes." My father shook his head. "I will gladly be the paranoid old man in all your minds, but Gisela will stay with you while the rest of us go out and forage. Laurence, I needn't remind you that you cannot die before you return to the Serpentine mountains and become a knight"

I almost felt myself shrink at the reminder of the dragons on mount Serpentine. I looked at Gisela, who wore a blank expression. She didn't show any emotions one way or another—you'd never know if she was glad or not with a decision unless she told you. Mother made her displeasure with my father's words more known. Without another word, she marched out of the living quarters.

I was more inclined to agree with my mother on this matter. I didn't want Gisela sitting in a corner and watching while I was with Oleander. It'd be much better to be alone with him at the mansion, with everyone else gone. It appeared my mother was done arguing, however, and I wasn't about to challenge my father on my own. All I'd get were word lashings and reminders that I needed to live because I and I alone could slay a dragon and fully win back our family honour.

I followed my mother and stepped into the hallway. With Oleander still ill in bed, there was little for me to do but practice with my bow. If I were to face a dragon again soon, I had to make sure I remained quick on the draw and ready. I could only hope my preparations this time would be enough.

On the cliffs out back, I practiced my archery without interruptions until my arms and back were sore. When the sky went grey and the sun started sinking behind cresting waves, Conrad returned to the mansion. He walked my way with his horse, as he needed to pass me to reach the stables.

"How went the outing, Conrad?" I asked the moment my brother was in earshot. I kept my gaze fixed on my shooting target.

Conrad's footsteps and the clopping of hooves stopped. "It went well," Conrad replied. "A little girl playing near the hills got stung. She is healed. The townsfolk now believe in the antidote and we can start selling."

I loosened an arrow. It struck the centre of my target. "And I suppose you had nothing to do with that incident?"

I looked at my brother, but his face was unreadable. Gisela showed little emotion, but with Conrad I truly couldn't tell what he was thinking, or what he was doing. Conrad's gaze lingered on my bow and the glowing tip of my arrow, charged with thunder magic. He scowled.

"Of course not, lord Montbow" he said. With an abrupt tug on the reins, Conrad walked on to the stables with his horse following behind him.

Cold Betrothing

G isela, ever true to her word and a stickler for her duties, rarely left Oleander and I out of her sight when we were together. She skulked outside the door while Oleander crushed herbs for the antidotes to be sold at the market. Other times she chased me outside headlong and made me shoot arrows in the storm until my fingers and arms went numb, yelling at me whenever I made mistakes.

Oleander and I hardly got a moment's peace between us. Only when a rare distraction took Gisela off of our trail, could we steal a quick kiss wherever we were. Usually, it was Oleander finding me. The elf had a talent for soundlessly moving across stone and skirting Gisela's watchful gaze, even if only for a few moments. It was never long before Gisela's voice would ring out, asking us where we were hiding this time. The most Oleander and I could do was exchange smiles, and have 'accidental' brushes of hand against hand while working.

Oleander and I weren't the only ones kept busy.

Everyone, even including my father, gathered herbs, staved off curious eyes, and collected vials for the antidotes to be sold in. Conrad's methods, while highly questionable, were effective.

The antidote sold.

The first few days, only a few vials. The antidote was a specialistic good, after all, only useful in one deadly situation. But the message of a skilled herbalist who made cures never heard of before seemed to spread like an oil stain. Many merchants loved a good story and a rare item. More and more travellers came to the Thundercoast, seeking out Oleander and his potions. Sometimes they were Conrad's friends or dark figures who were clearly up to no good with our wares, but we couldn't afford to be picky who we accepted coin from. Other guests of the Thundercoast were simply fascinated with the possibilities and existence of the antidote.

Conrad, for all his sneaking in the dark and his flaws, went and got Spot the horse back. One night, he vanished and came home with Fynn's favourite. Said he'd performed a switch trick. Fynn was overjoyed, and it seemed my cold older brother had a heart, after all. For a moment. Conrad ruined it immediately after by gruffly telling us he only did it so Fynn, who was in the bedroom next to his, would stop whimpering and sobbing at night.

A few weeks passed. With our bellies full, our coffers slowly filling, and townsfolk less bitter because of the recent interest in the Thundercoast from merchants, even my father no longer could find things other than petty complaints to grumble about. After a nice dinner with pastries from a bakery for dessert, a luxury we had not been able to afford for years, Valda stood and moved to the head of the table to address the whole family.

"I believe it's time we start sending letters to Wildewall," she stated. "We still have a few friends in the court we can address. I will let them know the Montbow house is strengthening its trading position on this side of the ocean with the help of a monopoly in rare goods. And that Laurence is traveling to the Serpentine mountains for another attempt at knighthood."

"If we write to the court, Ariane Seydal will want to visit the Thundercoast and see where we are standing," Conrad said.

"Yes, Perhaps it's soon time to invite her to stay at the mansion," my mother agreed.

Valda pulled a face, but swiftly recovered and faked a smile. "I would be most happy to see Ariane again. But Mother, you know that if we want her to visit, we need to purchase new furniture, and get rid of the vines and mould on the walls."

"No, I don't want her to come," Fynn whined. His gaze darted from Oleander to me. "She shouldn't marry Laurence."

"Fynn, hush," I told him, reaching out and pressing a hand to his mouth.

Fynn blew up his cheeks and crossed his little arms as recoiled from my hand, deeply offended. My little brother meant well, and he wasn't wrong about my interests being elsewhere, but I couldn't risk him saying this in front of Ariane as well. I couldn't even risk him saying it in front of Oleander. It was a sour subject, and I felt Oleander's eyes resting on the side of my face.

"Ariane was your... betrothed, was she not, lord Montbow?" Oleander asked quietly.

"Yes," I reluctantly admitted. "We are to be wed. Not out of love, but to unite two powerful houses. The Montbow family is a merchant family. The Seydals are warriors. Our houses could greatly benefit and compliment each other with our respective strengths. At least, that was how it was when our betrothing was decided on. Now, Ariane won't allow a wedding to happen until the Montbows are in the same standing as we once were with the court and the queen."

There was a flicker of hurt in Oleander's eyes. Then he nodded.

"I truly believe it is better if we don't invite Ariane to our mansion yet," Valda spoke. "Nothing is ever up to her standards, but our riches and our property as it is now surely will only get us scorn and complaints."

"She wouldn't be wrong," my father grumbled.

"Truly," Valda repeated, "let's not invite her. Let me write to the court instead. I will let you read the letter before I send it, Mother and Father. Surely the rumours of a rare antidote being discovered by the Montbows at the Thundercoast has already reached Wildewall. They know we speak true, and perhaps the letter will even be in time to earn us an invitation to the autumn ball."

"Don't mention the autumn ball in your letter. We are not dogs begging for scraps from the court," Gisela sharply reminded Valda. "They will invite us to the ball if they want us to attend. We will not grovel or even ask for it."

Valda pouted. "Fine." She turned to Mother and Father. "With your permission, I will write a letter."

Mother glanced at Father first. A few tense moments passed, and then my father made a dismissive hand gesture, waving Valda away. It might've seemed like a decline to an outsider, but if my father meant to say no, you would know.

Valda beamed. She curtseyed and hurried out of the dining room.

I watched her go, not able to keep myself from smiling. "You know, she's going to mention the ball in her letter," I told Gisela. "One way or another."

Gisela sighed. "I know. Valda is so clever in some ways, but her romantic ideas of courtship and balls make her blind. If she goes to the ball, all of us will be forced to come with her to protect her from herself."

"We don't decide that," Conrad spoke. "Only those who are invited will attend. If the queen doesn't mention you by name, you're not invited."

We were all quiet after that, watching the flames in the fireplace, perhaps all momentarily lost in our own thoughts about balls, romance, and court intrigue. For Gisela, Conrad, Valda, and Fynn, we still needed to find a marrying partner. Perhaps some of them would even have the fortune of enjoying their partner's company.

I was already spoken for, whether or not I liked it, since before I even knew what the word betrothed meant. A ball would have little meaning for me—my role would be to approve or disapprove matches for my siblings. I wouldn't feel like I truly deserve that honour until I'd slain a dragon and was a knight.

Still, later that night, when I was in bed, I tried to imagine all of us at the queen's autumn ball. I had never been inside the palace myself, but I knew the stories of crystal chandeliers, high ceilings, and sparkling golden corridors.

Valda would have the time of her life dancing the night away, while Gisela stayed near her to glare at the lords she deemed unworthy of attention. I estimated the chance that another man would sweep Gisela off her feet and distract her very low. Gisela would marry only if Father and Mother ordered her to, or perhaps when she was done fretting over Valda because she was wed. Fynn, if children were allowed inside the palace, would eat himself round on pastries, blatantly oblivious to all the political games going on around him. Conrad would always get attention, no matter where he was. He was handsome and charming in a brooding way. But he had never shown an interest in a woman or a man as far as I knew. All he did was sneak in the dark and go his own way, alone. I doubted he would change his behaviour, even for the queen at a ball.

And then there was Oleander.

Oleander would shine the brightest of everyone in the room. He would look elegant no matter what he wore. His movements would be most graceful, from an intricate dance to a flick of his wrist. He would have attendants of the ball, noble to servant, marvel over his mirror-like silver hair and envious of the length of his lashes. If they were so lucky to get an opportunity to speak with him, they'd melt at his wise innocence, and soft-spoken conviction.

I knew we likely weren't going to the autumn ball. Not just yet until I had gone back to the Serpentine mountains and proved myself, but I already felt a pang in my chest at knowing I wouldn't be able to dance with Oleander there. It would be very dangerous, regardless. One slip. One person seeing Oleander's ears and everything we'd built here would be over.

A soft tap on my window from outside made my eyes shoot open. I turned to the glass and gasped when I saw Oleander's silhouette painted against the starry night on the other side. He was holding onto a vine.

Throwing the sheets off of me, I dashed to the window. I slid it open and Oleander nimbly swooped into my room, landing soundlessly on the floor. After casting a hasty glance down at the cliffs, I closed the window again. Then I crossed the room and also locked my bedroom door.

"What are you doing?" I hissed at Oleander. "Well, it's obvious what you were doing: climbing vines. It is not obvious why."

Oleander bit his lip. He looked at me with wide eyes. "Pardon me. It is just that there's no easy way to have a word with you alone nowadays," he said.

"That's certainly true." I grinned. "You could have let me know sooner that you had an easy route into my bedroom, Oleander."

Oleander drew his shoulders up like I had scolded him. "I had worried you would find me asking if could come in through your window at night to be overstepping boundaries."

"Naturally. This is very inappropriate," I joked.

I would have stepped closer to steal a kiss, but refrained when Oleander didn't smile.

"My lord," he said. "There is something I have to ask of you... and something I must say to you. And I could only do it in private."

"Of course. Anything."

Frowning, I gestured at the chairs near my desk. Oleander walked there and took a seat. He looked down at the curled fists in his lap.

"I just..." he started slowly, before trailing off again. "I just wanted to you to know that I may not be a powerful noble like your betrothed, and I may not have most of my memories. But I'm not giving up your hand that easily. There must be another way than being bound to an old contract that doesn't serve you, made by your parents at another time."

Oleander raised his eyes to meet mine, and I saw the same burning determination I was intimately familiar with from him. It made me shy and heavily conscious of my awkward posture and my inability to decide what to do with my limbs. I was at a loss for words, but Oleander seemed to have plenty of them.

"Don't go to the Serpentine mountains," Oleander pleaded. "Don't slay a dragon. They have done nothing to you, and haven't you proven now that it's unnecessary to become a knight to save the house Montbow?"

I sighed. "Oleander," I started. "I can't just—"

"But you can!" Oleander protested. "You are to be the head of your family, are you not? You are the man with the blessing of the thunder god. They should listen to you, not the other way around."

"It's not only my family, Oleander," I tried to explain. "It's the court of Wildewall and the queen as well. Her reach is far and long, and if we lose her favour by not playing by the rules, it doesn't matter how well your antidotes do on the market."

Oleander frowned. He got up and stepped towards me, closer and closer until our chests almost touched. "I will still fight for you," he said, before leaning in and kissing me. "Ariane won't have you without a fight."

"It's already no competition, Oleander," I whispered to his lips as we stayed close enough to exchange breaths. "Not even close."

After a long and silent embrace, Oleander left the same way he came through the window.

At the crack of dawn, before Valda could even finish writing her friends, a letter with house Seydal's seal arrived on our doorstep with a messenger.

Invitation for Two

Ariane Seydal never failed to make an entrance, be it in person or through a messenger.

She had a habit of only employing attractive servants and wrapping them up in the latest Wildewall fashion, from stable-helps to the head of her guard. The man who arrived on our doorstep at first light could have had a lucrative existence posing as a model for sculptors. He looked as if they cut him from stone, with sharp features and alabaster skin.

We were lucky Gisela and I, while practicing archery outside in the early morning, were the ones to see the man first. Had it been Valda, she would have swooned over the young, living sculpture donned in a ruby red, well-fitted doublet. I looked too. Naturally. I wasn't blind. The young man was attractive, but he didn't hold a candle to Oleander. I accepted the letter with Seydal's seal the messenger offered me and tucked it into my bag for later.

"Good morning," Gisela said, the only one of us unimpressed by the man's looks. "How may we help you?"

The messenger's gaze traveled to the bow and arrow, which Gisela still cautiously held in her hands. Then he smiled and bowed with flair. "I am here to announce Lady Ariane Seydal is on her way to the Thundercoast and expects you and her accommodation to be ready for her arrival."

"Oh, shit," blurted out of my mouth before I could stop myself. I felt the colour draining from my face at the prospect of meeting my betrothed again. It was too soon. It was always too soon.

Gisela ignored my outburst, but I felt the anger radiating off of her in waves. She took after our mother in that sense. "Thank you for your message," she spoke crisply. "When can we expect Lady Seydal to arrive?"

The alabaster man bowed his head again. "I left a few moments ahead, Lady Montbow. She stayed in Verspetin."

I almost swore again, but bit my tongue in time. Just as we had established a steady flow of coin and a new routine at the Thundercoast, Ariane had to come and stomp all over it. "I had thought Lady Seydal would've waited until we extended an invitation to her," I said.

So I would've been ready.

"So I see," the messenger replied. "However, Lady Seydal insisted she travel here after hearing about a mysterious herbalist. She will be shortly."

"Then we best start preparing for her arrival. Laurence, let's go." Gisela jutted her arrow back into the quiver and slung her bow over her right shoulder. She didn't spare the messenger another glance as she marched into the mansion.

I nodded at the messenger and followed, but felt like there were pounds of lead in my boots weighing me down.

Ariane's visit made no sense. Ten years ago my betrothed had made it very clear she wanted nothing to do with me nor to speak with me until I was a knight and house Montbow was out of exile. Now she was here regardless. I didn't want to face her. Not until we were forced to wed.

Gisela marched up the stairs to gather everyone from their rooms. Surprisingly, Valda was the first one who made it down to the lobby. Her expression was colder than a winter storm raging on the coast as she came up to me. "Ariane Seydal is here?"

"Good morning to you too, Valda," I replied dryly. "And no, she's not. Not yet, anyway."

"Why does she want to be here?" Valda blurted.

"I suppose she's here to see firsthand if we are up to her standards now." I shrugged, hiding my discomfort behind a why smile. "She won't trust another's word. And isn't this good? If she sees we are doing well, you may even go to the autumn ball."

My head knew it was good for our family if Ariane was willing to visit and approved of us and our antidotes. But my treacherous heart was upstairs. My eyes darted up toward Oleander's room. I knew I couldn't stay hide in the Thundercoast with Oleander forever. I just hadn't realised my duty would catch up with me this soon.

"Ariane won't think we are fit for the autumn ball with the mansion looking the way it does!" Valda scolded me. "She will only complain!"

"I'm sure she doesn't expect our home to be in a perfect state after what has been going on the past decade," I replied. "If we can show her Oleander and the antidote, I am certain she sees reason and understands the rumours she must've caught at court are all true."

Valda sighed. "I hope she will listen to you. She gives you some time of day because of you are storm-touched. Not the rest of us."

"I do not, do I now? Then it's probably because you didn't deserve my attention."

Valda and I both jumped at the woman's voice at the door. We both whirled around.

In the lobby with us stood a tall, willowy woman with a flaming red mane of hair, pale skin, and dark eyes. She wore a dark blue silken dress with wide-cut skirts and tight-fitting sleeves, and around her neck dangled a pendant with a symbol of a lion. She had matured, considering the last time we saw each other she had been twelve years old, but I still easily recognised her.

Ariane Seydal had made her entrance.

"Lady Seydal," Valda stammered. She curtseyed.

Ariane rose a brow. She ignored Valda and turned to me. "Don't leave your front door open, Laurence. Not that there's anything to steal from this place." She looked around the entrance hall and hummed. "The rumours of golden halls rivalling the court's at the Thundercoast now that you are earning coin from antidotes were highly exaggerated. Disappointing."

"It's nice to see you again too after over a decade, Ariane," I muttered.

Valda claimed I would get different treatment because of my thunder god's blessing, but my greeting got ignored the same way Valda's had. Ariane's eyes slowly travelled up the steps of our stairs. "And where is this miracle herbalist you plucked off of the Serpentine mountains?"

I crossed my arms. "Considering you hardly gave the sun a chance to rise today before arriving on our doorstep, he's still asleep."

Ariane looked at me levelly and then waved at Valda like she was a servant. "Go wake him then."

Valda's jaw clenched. She and Ariane held a silent staring contest. But then Valda lifted her skirts and stomped away.

While Valda went upstairs, Ariane's servants, among which the messenger, came trickling into the mansion carrying suitcases and foods. I directed them to the right places, while Gisela and Valda woke everyone.

A few moments later, everyone was gathered in the living quarters.

We had often joked that Ariane would want to inspect her future fortunes should she ever visit, but it rang very true now. Endris wasn't allowed in the room. And us Montbows were all but lined up with Ariane in front of us, like an inspection of her guard.

Ariane's shoes clacked on the floor as she walked past. Mother and Father received a polite nod in greeting, but Valda hardly got spared a glance, and neither did Gisela. Ariane stopped at Conrad. Her gaze glided from his boots to his eyes.

"You look like you've been up to no good Conrad, as usual," she spoke crisply. "How much blood did you spill last night?"

"I never spill blood, Lady Seydal," Conrad replied without missing a beat.

Conrad and Ariane held each other's gaze for a moment longer. Perhaps I had imagined it, but I swore Ariane's lips twitched before she moved on. "And then... finally, there's the miracle herbalist."

"Lady Seydal, Lord Montbow's betrothed," Oleander replied. His voice was silk, but I saw the fierceness in his eyes and the subtle defiance in his tense posture.

I wished Ariane would walk on because the tension was already tangible, but she stayed in front of him. She was taller, and Oleander had to jut his chin up to look her in the eyes.

"What's your name?" Ariane asked.

"Oleander," Oleander replied.

Ariane snickered quietly. "A herbalist named Oleander, saved from the mountains where dragons roam by a man who was there to be a knight. Like a tale from a book." She looked at me. "Very like you to choose to save a young man rather than slay a dragon. You haven't changed."

"Thank you," I said.

"It was not a compliment, dear."

Oleander shot my betrothed a baleful glance. He was burning up, and what was even worse: he was not trying to hide it. I needed to break this exchange up, and fast.

"Anyway, we need to get to work, Ariane," I said, clapping my hands. "The antidotes won't brew themselves and we have not had the time to bring our servants back to the mansion."

Ariane smiled at me. "They should get to work, indeed. You are coming with me to your quarters, my beloved. We have much to do and discuss after not seeing each other in a decade."

I nearly choked on my own spit when she winked, and I felt her gloved fingers reaching for my hand. As Ariane took my hand in an iron grip and tugged me along, I looked at Oleander apologetically. His soulful wide eyes broke my heart, and then I got dragged into the corridor.

Once we were out of sight, Ariane instantly dropped my hand and shoved it away from her. "Outside," she ordered.

I rolled my eyes up to the ceiling. "Ah, I understand. No moving into my quarters, just you giving me no quarter. You haven't changed either."

"I simply needed to know something," Ariane replied as we walked out the front door. "And now I know."

The breeze had picked up and played with Ariane's hair as we walked to the cliffs. The rising sun made her hair glow like flames in a furnace. Her dark eyes settled on me. "Taking pretty, vulnerable young men with nowhere else to turn home to warm your bed. You are very simple in your pleasures as you are as a person, aren't you?"

I opened and closed my mouth and sputtered, "You are one to complain about taking in pretty young men. That messenger you sent wasn't taken in by you for no reason."

"I don't bed my servants."

I flushed. "I don't bed Oleander."

Ariane narrowed her eyes at me. "You would if he snuck to your room after dark. You want your arms twined warmly around him, hm?"

I stopped myself from opening my big mouth and revealing that sneaking into my room was exactly what Oleander had done last night, and nothing but a kiss and an embrace had happened. I wasn't a monster, and I wasn't unaware of the differences in power between Oleander and I. If anything were to happen between us, I would wait for him to approach me and tell me he wanted more than a stolen kiss. But speaking here would offer me the fleeting satisfaction of countering Ariane's assumptions of what happened, only to reveal that her assumptions about what I wanted to happen were right.

Ariane's mouth went to a thin line. "Laurence, do whatever you will in this desolate place. Whatever desires you have, fulfil them here and never in Wildewall. When we are wed, your lover will live in a castle separate from everyone else, and you visit him when you have no other matters to attend to. You will not ruin my reputation with rumours that you would rather touch pretty boys. Am I clear?"

I stayed quiet. Out of resentment, and out of lack of an answer. I felt Oleander's whispers from last night brush gently against my ear, reminding me I was the blessed one and that people ought to listen to me, not the other way around. To purposely scorn Ariane here, however, was to make my and Oleanders life more difficult. I chose to keep my lips together and let my gut tie in knots in silence.

Ariane averted her gaze. She pointed one gloved finger at some trees growing on an adjacent cliff near the shoreline. "Laurence, do me a favour and split one of those rocks or trees in half."

I looked at the rocks and then at the trees, which gently swayed in the wind. "Why?"

"Just do it."

"Fine."

Destroying a target at a distance took more energy and focus than simply charging an arrow point with thunder magic. I breathed in deeply and closed my eyes. At my command, I felt the branches of the tree on my chest flare up, further and wider, until it reached every vein in my body. I spread my eyes open, aimed, and with a loud thunderclap, I struck the rock. Smoke rose from the thinning grass. The only remaining evidence of my thunder strike.

I waited a few moments. When Ariane didn't offer an explanation but only stared at the smoke, I cleared my throat. "So why did I destroy an innocent rock again?" I asked.

"To remind myself there is a reason we are betrothed." Ariane crossed her arms and wrapped them around herself. "When do you leave for the Serpentine mountains?"

"When you head home, I suppose," I replied. "The court won't accept you getting injured while at the Thundercoast and will blame the Montbows, as they like to blame us for anything that goes awry in this region."

"Yes, well," Ariane said. "For once, you're not speaking complete nonsense. Especially knight commander Ytel is not happy, you know. He departed from Wildewall after me."

I swallowed some curses. "He is on his way here?"

"Perhaps." Ariane shrugged. "But even he must return to Wildewall in time for the autumn ball, and so must you."

I stared at Ariane blankly. "The autumn ball? But I'm not going there."

Ariane clacked her tongue. "Let me spell it out for you, beloved. Did you not wonder why I am here already? It's not voluntarily, and it wasn't my decision. The queen send me, and ordered me to deliver the letter that accompanied my messenger. It holds an invitation for the autumn ball. With my house's blessing."

My jaw went slack. "You are giving us your blessing to visit the court? Already? Valda will be thrilled about her invitation to the autumn ball."

"Don't get ahead of yourselves," Ariane replied flatly. "The Montbows are not in such high standing yet. A fourth child with no distinguishable features and no outstanding talents like Valda is not invited. No, the queen's invitation is extended exclusively to you." Ariane fell quiet for a moment as she turned her head, ostensibly to hide a sneer. "Well, to you and your miracle herbalist."

Ruse Upon Scheme

If I went to Wildewall, the entire court and everyone around it would know of it.

Every debt collector, every sailor and merchant who cursed the Montbows, every petty thief from the Thundercoast region who knew we had coin in our coffers now, was listening and looming in the shadows. Ariane not having a shred of compassion for our situation wasn't a surprise, but even she had to understand I couldn't take off with her and Oleander to the autumn ball.

"My family would practically be begging to get robbed. Or worse," I protested. "Especially if Ytel may be planning on coming here. I have to decline the invitation."

Ariane looked at me like I had just insulted the thunder god. "One does not decline an invitation from the queen. It's not a question. It's an order."

"If I don't decline, there may not be a house Montbow to return to!"

Leaving for the Serpentine mountains for a week had been a risk we could take. Nobody but the knight commander, a few court clerks, and my carefully chosen guide, Endris, knew I wasn't at the Thundercoast. But an event as large as the autumn ball couldn't stay hushed and hidden. I would likely be gone for at least a month.

While my heart pounded with fear, Ariane's eyes swept the coastline dispassionately.

"Yes, your enemies will certainly feel emboldened, knowing the blessed storm-touched of house Montbow isn't home and won't be able to strike them down," Ariane simply said.

"Exactly." I crossed my arms. "I am not leaving the Thundercoast unless my entire family is coming with us."

Ariane mirrored my annoyed tone. "Have you already forgotten what I said? Ytel, just like everyone else, must answer to the invitation of the queen. He will need to be back in Wildewall in time for the ball, like all of us."

I stared at her.

Ariane clacked her tongue. "Meaning, if Ytel wishes to overwhelm the Montbows, steal the land, and cover up the evidence of what he did, he will need to attack soon. Once the window of opportunity passes, everyone who has the kind of manpower to attack the Montbows must be present in Wildewall."

"That doesn't mean they can't send warriors to the Thundercoast during the ball," I pointed out.

"That remark only goes to show how little you remember of court life." Ariane sighed. "Think, Laurence. Each and every noble who is someone to this world is leaving their home to travel to Wildewall for the ball. All leaders are forced to leave their region, and nobody is risking an invasion while they are gone. Their best warriors will be home."

"So, what are you suggesting, then?" I asked. "You're saying we leave at the last possible moment and slide into the halls of the palace with a stretched leg, giving Ytel no chance to attack and then make it to Wildewall in time?"

"No," Ariane replied. "I'm saying you, me, the miracle herbalist, and our servants, if you have any, will depart from the Thundercoast at once."

"What?"

"We ride to Vespertin in the night to make it seem we left and tried to do so in secret. In reality, we return by ship."

"... What?"

"Is what the only word you can say?" Ariane asked with a smile that was stuck between amused and contemptuous. "We pretend we leave, see if Ytel takes the bait, and then we actually leave. That is all. It's plain and it's simple. I assume there are no more questions."

Ariane turned on her heels and started walking back to the mansion.

I walked beside her, speeding up my pace to keep up with her strides. "And you just arranged this already? Without consulting us?"

"I did consult you. I consulted your brother," Ariane said. "He is most capable of keeping a secret and making sure the necessary precautions are taken."

Speaking of the devil always made him appear.

As Ariane spoke, Conrad, Endris, and Valda came outside. They were going to the hills to forage for the antidotes. Ariane's dark eyes settled on Conrad, like a predator while it was hunting.

"Conrad," I said. I stared at my brother as he marched to the stables with my sister and Endris, but he didn't look up at us. "He should have mentioned what he was planning."

"There are many things he does for house Montbow that are best not mentioned." Ariane chuckled. "Do you think your storm-touched powers have been the only thing staving off the intruders all these years?"

"I didn't think that!"

I knew Valda and Gisela made debt collectors more patient with their charm or with intimidation. I'd never really known what Conrad did. Conrad went where Conrad wanted to go. Sometimes he went out to steal back a horse. Other times, I assumed he was simply visiting taverns.

Ariane smirked. "Either way, you will not have Conrad's help in Wildewall at the autumn ball. So I suggest you read your invitation and prepare yourself."

I wanted to protest purely for the sake of it, but my curiosity won. I took the letter out of my bag and swiftly read the first few lines of the invitation as we walked inside.

The lobby smelled like rising bread. Ariane's servants must have found their way to the kitchen and the rest of the mansion. The light scuff of footsteps coming from all directions was something I hadn't heard since I was little. Usually, the halls were silent.

I expected most of my family to have gone to work, but I found my mother and Oleander in the living quarters. He perked up when he saw me.

Shooting Oleander a subtle smile, I walked to my mother and handed the invitation letter to my mother. "Look at this," I said.

Mother narrowed her eyes at me, then read the first few lines, just as I had outside. I saw the exact moment the realisation of what this was dawned on her. Her dark eyes shot back up to meet mine. I read worry and excitement in equal measure in her gaze. Mother always hoped, for our sakes, that we would be welcome at the court again.

"But the invitation is only extended to Oleander and I," I muttered.

"The queen invited Oleander," my mother repeated incredulously.

Ariane shrugged. "Her majesty loves her rarities and peculiar tales. Perhaps she even wants the miracle herbalist to work in Wildewall if he pleases her."

"Oleander doesn't know the proper etiquette for such a formal event," Mother replied. "We must tell the court he fell ill and can't attend."

"You know we can't, mother," I mumbled.

Much as I didn't want to say it, Ariane was right. Unless Oleander was literally dead or had a highly contagious disease as proven by a doctor from the court, the excuse wouldn't be accepted and house Montbow would be blamed.

Oleander rose to his feet, only to bow elegantly for my mother. "I will spend all my spare time learning, lady Montbow," he promised. "Whenever I'm not making antidotes, I will study court etiquette and ensure I don't shame the Montbow family. I owe it to your son for saving my life."

"That is most diligent of you." Ariane smiled brightly and linked her arm into mine. "And we shall have my servants, my love. They'll be plenty for the both of us. Don't fret about having none of your own."

"Yes, thank you," I hastily replied. While I carefully pried Ariane's arm off of mine, Oleander's cheeks flushed with anger. He clenched his jaw and lowered his eyes. Ariane's smile widened at his rage and my discomfort.

"You can take Endris," my mother offered, gracefully ignoring the silent tug-of-war happening in front of her. "We could also summon some of our old servants back to the mansion now that we have the coin to pay them. We had been planning on that, regardless."

"They won't be in time. We need to depart tonight," Ariane said.

I opened my mouth to tell my mother of the plan, but Ariane shot me a pointed look that told me 'shut up.'

"Tonight?" Mother asked. "You had a long journey, Lady Seydal. Wouldn't you prefer to stay one night and depart at a later time?"

"No, we must leave tonight," Ariane insisted.

"If that is so, I would like to leave you with some more healing salve recipes," Oleander told my mother. "I have potent ointments that can soothe sore muscles or stop disease from taking hold of open wounds. The common folk working in the fields or at sea need them."

"They would be less expensive than the rare antidote," Mother remarked. "But good for the heart and soul of our region. I see your point. Thank you, Oleander."

Mother's smile didn't touch her eyes. I couldn't be sure, but I had an inkling that she felt what I already knew: something wasn't right.

I wanted to know why Ariane refused to tell my mother everything. Why leave everyone in the dark about Ytel and his presence at the Thundercoast, and his plan to attack? I only went with it for now because Conrad also knew. While my brother and I didn't see eye to eye and his ways were opaque like the dark, deep sea, I knew he wanted his family alive. That didn't mean I was happy with lying, however.

When I looked into my mother's eyes, I realised she was worried for me too. I'd be travelling straight into the viper's nest with an elven man and my betrothed. Thinking of it like that, I was worried about Oleander and myself too.

Conrad, Valda, and Endris returned from foraging in the hills as the sun rose to the highest point in the sky. I summoned everyone to the living quarters, and I told all my siblings and my father the news about the autumn ball. Conrad didn't bat an eye. Valda was visibly upset they did not invite her, while Gisela was visibly relieved Valda wasn't invited. Father left the room without a word and slammed the door shut behind him. Mother insisted I brought my green formal wear since I looked best in it, and gave me coin to purchase new clothes in Wildewall itself, for our wardrobe was likely horribly out-dated for capital standards. Besides that, Oleander did not even own formalwear and would have to buy it in Wildewall.

We were so unprepared, it was laughable.

My littlest brother, Fynn, didn't seem to grasp the significance of an invitation for the autumn ball yet. Born in an already disgraced house, he had never seen Wildewall's court. Besides, Fynn was get-ting attention like he had never gotten attention before, with all Ariane's servants finding him adorable and sneaking him pastries in the kitchen. There was a lot of excitement for him in one day. I was almost surprised he came up to my room while I was packing the last things for the ruse journey, after we finished dinner.

Fynn entered my room with his hands stuffed into his pockets. When he saw me, he grinned and revealed one palm with a sticky pastry on it. "I saved you one from the kitchen."

The idea of eating the half-melted pudding tart almost made me gag, so I shook my head and ruffled Fynn's dark curls. "That's sweet. You eat those yourself. I will have plenty of pastries at the autumn ball."

Fynn didn't protest. I'd hardly even finished my sentence, or he had already shoved the pastry into his own mouth. "You should take Spot when you leave for the palace," he said with a full mouth. "He will get you there safely. And back."

I smiled at Fynn's innocence and the bits of pudding on his cheeks. Him offering me his favourite horse was a big gesture, given how hard he'd cried when the horse was taken. "Thank you, Fynn. I will make sure to take Spot."

"And marry Oleander in Wildewall. In the palace of the queen."

I chuckled awkwardly. "Alright, that's enough out of you, little troublemaker. Don't let Ariane hear you. Come on, downstairs we go."

I flung my knapsack over my shoulders and picked Fynn up. We headed down the steps together.

I was late. Oleander, Endris, and Ariane already stood ready to depart, and so did all of Ariane's retainers. We said our goodbyes. I tried to push down the guilt at seeing the fear in my mother's and Valda's eyes, and the way they squeezed me as we hugged.

I mounted Spot, and we rode into the night while my family waved us goodbye. I could only imagine how worried they all were, save for Conrad. For all they knew, they were sending two utterly unprepared men to a ball that would judge them harshly for not knowing its rules. Endris, who had some understanding of the court and how it worked, could only guide us so much.

For a moment, I worried about Oleander on his horse too. I'd never seen him ride on his own, but it appeared my concerns were unwarranted. Like he moved with grace on his own two feet, he also rode a horse like a natural. He had no trouble staying in the saddle or leaning the right way to help his horse during its descent down the cliffs.

I waited until we were out of the mountain passages and in the woods leading to town before speaking up. "Are you going to tell me why you didn't share the whole story, Ariane?"

Ariane pursed her lips. "I said all I needed to say."

I glanced at Oleander and Endris, who both looked at me for answers about what was going on. "They will find out once we lead them to a ship, you know," I said. "Why the secrecy?"

Oleander's eyes went round. "We're going to a boat?"

Ariane ignored Oleander. "You will see what the plan is soon enough, Laurence. Just be patient, and don't break your pretty little head over it."

Ariane led us deeper into the woods where the vegetation grew thicker. There, three of her retainers wordlessly dismounted their horses and opened the saddlebags.

I lowered myself from Spot's back as well. Then I watched, perplexed, as the most beautiful robes and dresses emerged from simple bags. In front of my eyes, one woman and two men started changing and swiftly made a transformation from simple servants to haughty nobles.

"Ariane, why are your servants dressing up like nobles?" I asked, politely averting my gaze when the woman started disrobing in front of me, seemingly without shame.

Ariane snorted. "Think very hard, Laurence, I know you can do it," she patronised me. "What are we trying to do here? Where do we want to go, and what do we want our enemies to think?"

"We are creating a diversion," Endris spoke up. His dark eyes glided from the servants' faces to Ariane, Oleander, and finally to me. "These men and woman will pretend they are you, Lady Seydal, and Oleander... While we go elsewhere?"

"At least one of you has a brain," Ariane said.

"Damn," I muttered.

I looked at the three servants again. With this new information, I suddenly realised their complexions and stature seemed to correspond with mine, Ariane's, and Oleander's. The woman was a tall redhead like Ariane. One man had brown skin, black hair, and dark eyes like me. And the walking sculpture, who also worked as Ariane's messenger, was most like Oleander. His hair wasn't silvery, his nose not freckled, but I suppose it was hard to find someone who looked like Oleander. Nobody did. The alabaster man at least had the elf's fair skin.

"We go to the boa- ship," I said. "To wait and see if Ytel makes an appearance."

"Yes," Ariane replied. "We will circle behind the cliffs and board the ship Conrad arranged. We will see an attack coming from that position, but they won't see us coming." A smile spread on Ariane's lips. "And if they do attack, Laurence, you wiggle your fingers and burn them to a crisp with your thunder."

Caught Between

Living close to a harbour meant I saw boats and ships from a distance all the time, but it had been ages since I was last on board of one. I valued my life, which meant I didn't go near the docks that lined the waterfront. That territory belonged to merchants, sailors, and pirates, who wouldn't hesitate to plunge a knife between my ribs the moment I turned my back. Not even the thunder of the gods could protect me from all of them.

The Thundercoast's docks used to bustle with life and trade, back when us Montbows ruled the seas. It'd been better times, when my father wasn't broken beyond recognition in more than one way, and we thought uncle Harold could be trusted. I remembered little of sailing now, safe for my father lifting me into his arms and showing me the muscular men rowing below deck. He would point at the stars at night, explaining how they guided us to the Richris islands.

All the Montbow ships that weren't sunken during the revolt on the islands were sold first. The sailors had warned us to never set sail on the trading route between Richris and the Thundercoast ever again, so we had no use of ships. They would rot in the harbour, falling into decay along with our family.

We rode our horses to the shore, where a sleek galley-like craft was moored to a makeshift wharf. While I couldn't remember how to sail, some of my knowledge of seafare still remained with me. I recognised it immediately as a ship from Richris. One with a heavy ram and a plank with spikes, favoured for warfare or protection of large merchant vessels. The flag was the flag of Richris; white with a blue dragon, but soaked in old, brown blood. Pirates. This ship must've belonged to pirates. Father had always warned me to never believe people sailing under that flag. They'd speak about sparing you if you cooperated. They wouldn't. Crack the hull with your thunder. Kill them.

"Is that a pirate ship?" I asked, nodding at the ship gently swaying in the water.

"Perhaps," Ariane replied with a lopsided smile. "Does it matter? It's my ship now."

"I hope the pirates it belongs to agree with that too," I said.

Ariane no longer humoured me with a response. She handed the reins of her horse to a male servant and walked onto the wharf. The planks moaned and creaked under her feet but didn't break. Ariane boarded the ship first, with some of her retainers hurrying after her.

If Conrad had arranged this ship, I was willing to bet the pirates were food for the bottom feeders in the ocean. In pieces. I tried not to dwell on the fate of the previous owners as I boarded the ship myself.

I thought I'd feel some kind of way when standing on deck, given our family's history. But I pressed my palm to the boat mast rising into the sky, listened to the waves slapping against the hull, and felt nothing. Until my eyes fell on brownish stains on the planks below my feet. Old blood.

Since we left the mansion, Oleander had been staying very close to me. He was standing beside me now, too. I hoped he hadn't noticed the smears under his feet. I remembered he didn't like Ytel even mentioning violence, let alone seeing blood.

"Look at the sunlight on the water," I distracted Oleander, pointing at the ocean. "Isn't it beautiful?"

I walked to the railing, and Oleander followed. He peeked down over the edge and smiled. "It is," he agreed.

We watched the waves together as Ariane's servants coiled ropes and lifted the anchor. After a few moments, the boat rocked, and we were off, heading for open water. I assumed we would slowly circle around at the cliffs near my family's mansion, waiting for an attack.

I leaned towards Oleander. "If it comes to a fight tonight, stay aboard this ship," I told him quietly.

Oleander's eyes went round as he turned to me. "But I don't want you to go alone."

I thought we were speaking quietly, but apparently, not quietly enough.

"He is right, Oleander," Endris inserted himself into the conversation from behind. He crossed his arms as his dark eyes settled on me.

"You don't want to be in the range of fire when lord Laurence rains thunder on Ytel's men."

"Right. Promise me you'll stay on this ship, Oleander," I said.

Oleander's jaw clenched. He looked like he wanted to protest, but eventually he nodded.

"Very touching this. Truly. "Ariane stepped next to Endris. "But you better spend the limited time you still have preparing for Wildewall. The court isn't like the Thundercoast, dear: forgiving with a mild climate."

"Oh, I'm aware," I muttered. Ariane wouldn't have wanted to live in Wildewall if it wasn't cutthroat. I was pretty certain about that.

"If you are aware, you aren't acting like it," Ariane retorted. "Stop slouching and stand up straight. That's lesson one, Laurence. In Wildewall, you are a storm-touched before you are a man. Pay mind to that. Here you are lord Montbow. There, you are somebody embodying the will of a god and there are expectations tied to the status."

I grimaced, but straightened my back when I noticed I was indeed slouching. Expectations tied to my status? They could certainly expect me to be tied. Tongue-tied. "I am aware of that too," I said.

I had been in the capital after the mark had manifested itself on my chest and abdomen. Mother and Father had paraded me around, but we had never entered the queen's palace. Like sailing, I had few memories of Wildewall. But I remembered the stares and people looking at me a certain way. Some of them had bowed. Some of them had gifted me trinkets representing the thunder god. I didn't get in trouble for not understanding rules back then, but people are far more forgiving of children. Now, they would expect me to behave as if I'd been at the court all along. Even if that wasn't fair, as the Montbows had lived in exile.

"Oleander and I should practice our manners if we are to be presented to the queen indeed," I said. "We'll move into a cabin, and I will share with him what I know."

"You two together in a cabin? I'm certain you have a lot you would want to teach him there," Ariane said with a smirk. "But there are people present on this ship who can explain Wildewall's court a lot better than you can."

Ariane gestured at a plump woman to come over. She had large breasts emphasised by her tight dress, golden ringlets of hair that framed her heart-shaped face, and piercing blue eyes. Another one of Ariane's servants that was, like the others, gorgeous.

"She's going to teach us?" I asked.

"No." Ariane snorted. "Nele, take over for me here, my dear. I have two gentlemen to teach the ways of Wildewall."

Nele curtsied for Ariane. "Yes, Lady Seydal," she replied in a hoarse voice.

"I will sit in the crow's nest and look out over the shoreline," Endris offered.

"We all know of your eagle-eyes, Endris." Nele smiled at him. "That is a great idea."

Endris wasted no time nimbly climbing up, and I was envious of him already. The sea was calm, the breeze cold but not freezing, and most of all Endris wouldn't have to listen to court rules from up there.

"Let me guess: you're the one who is going to teach Oleander and I then," I asked Ariane rhetorically.

"Of course, who better than me?" Ariane replied with a flick of her wrist. "I will lead the way."

"Right you will," I said with a sigh.

I didn't even dare to look at Oleander's face as he and I were led below deck. The look in his eyes would likely be more destructive than my lightning.

Ariane brought us to a cabin. Judging from the size and the interior, it was likely the captain's cabin. There were large windows, a bookcase, and a table with a map where one could decide a route. Ariane had us sit but stayed on her feet herself, like a strict school teacher standing over a bunch of children.

"I feel the need to emphasise again that this ball can't be taken lightly," she said, staring directly at me. "As a grown man with a branch of the thunder god on his chest, everyone will ask you for the story of your mark. It is most important that the story you tell about your mark is entertaining, so I suggest you start writing down a tale to tell them. It doesn't have to be true. Just make sure you don't bore anyone, especially the queen. And you must ask others like you about their mark as well. You will be required to recognise other god-touched."

Ariane's gaze shifted to Oleander. "And you, the miracle herbalist, will attend as an oddity that attracted the attention of some nobles. Since you are low-born, you will only speak when spoken to."

"Lucky you," I muttered to Oleander, because only speaking when spoken to sounded a lot easier than what I was supposed to do upon meeting people: recognise they were special somehow, and repeat the same made up fantastic story over and over.

Oleander's lips twitched as he looked at my absolutely miserable expression, but when he turned to Ariane, his eyes were cold and hard. He immediately put the information he was given to use and only nodded at her, not opening his mouth.

"Good." Ariane sniffed. "It seems you already understand your place. Seen but not heard. I believe you know enough. You can leave now."

"Ariane," I warned her. "People will surely want to speak with Oleander. He saved the Montbow family and made a cure for a poison that was, until now, a death sentence."

"Lord Montbow, you praise me far too highly," Oleander replied in a low, almost seductive tone I had never heard him use before and sent jolts straight to my groin.

Ariane's eyes narrowed while Oleander gave me a sultry look. His antics were clearly meant to piss Ariane off. I sputtered helplessly, caught between two roaring fires. My ears grew hot. "You, uh, you did all the things I just mentioned though," I eventually brought out.

"Yes," Oleander replied in his normal voice, seemingly sensing that he shouldn't cross the line too far. "And I have been reading the books about etiquette you have graciously provided me with in my room."

I gaped at Oleander. "You read those? Voluntarily? How did you not fall asleep?"

"Apparently, because your herbalist is more interested in drama and far better at playing court games than you are by nature, Laurence," Ariane said, her gaze lingering on Oleander. "The way you joke shows me you don't understand yet. You have very limited time to learn many rules. Grace and subtlety in conversation can't be taught in two weeks, but rules can."

Ariane turned abruptly and pulled two books out of the bookcase behind her. Together, the books were so thick she needed two hands to carry them. She slammed them onto the table in front of me and Oleander. "Laurence, you will read the chapters on those blessed by the gods in Wildewall. I will interrogate you tomorrow to see if you have learned. Oleander, I believe you would benefit more from learning the servant's rules in Wildewall." Ariane smiled kindly. "That is all you will ever be. A servant to us, the high-born."

I thought the silent struggle between Ariane and Oleander was over, but that seemed to be far from the truth. Oleander had fire in his eyes, but quelled it before he spoke. He took the book Ariane offered and started reading.

I breathed out through my mouth in relief, and then groaned when I looked at the absolute monster of a tome I knew so well already. I recognised it as the authority on court etiquette. We had two copies of it at home as well. It was literally heavy enough to use as a murder weapon.

Ariane raised a brow at my sounds of discomfort. "Is there a problem, my beloved? I assume this particular information is only a refresher for you. You have already read this at your estate before."

"I have," I confirmed. "It has been a while, that's all."

Until I was twelve, learning about behaviour at court was extremely important. Then our house collapsed, and I had to help and guard our home along with everyone else in our household. I didn't have time to read when I was fishing, or striking trees down with my thunder for in the fireplace, or learning how to shoot my bow. My priority was to learn how to kill dragons with crackling arrows so I could become a knight, not reading how to act in court. The Montbows were a far distance away from court. Still were.

Exhaling heavily, I opened the book and looked through the table of contents to find the chapters on god-touched. While searching, I wondered if Conrad was so mad at me because he too had to learn all this dry shit by heart until he was thirteen. Only to then find out he no longer would be required as an heir. I'd be angry, too.

Both Ariane and Oleander were reading now, and I had little else to do but join them. Some parts I could skim. Nobody needed to tell me where the whither-touched, or bleeders, fell in the court hierarchy, after all. Those who could manipulate blood and flesh and raised people from the dead or killed them for power would not be welcome in Wildewall. The elves had almost brought a human kingdom to their knees with this power in the Starcross woods, and so it was a forbidden. Wielders would mysteriously die.

I learned that in Wildewall, as an element master, I was a decent third on the list of most desirable. My thunder god blessing was only seen as below healers and diviners, respectively called light-touched, fate-touched. On the off chance I met one of those, considering maybe one of them was chosen every three-hundred years, I'd need to greet them with a deep bow. If I could believe the book, they would always leave their mark visible on their body so we could recognise them. That would be required of me as well.

There were illustrations of the distinct patterns that signified different blessings. I tried to commit them to memory, but it didn't take long for the symbols to dance in front of my eyes. I decided to only concentrate on learning the two marks I'd have to bow to when in Wildewall; a sun and an eye.

By the time we had to light the oil lanterns as the sky behind the windows grew darker, I was no longer able to absorb more words. Oleander and Ariane were still immersed in their studies, but I was staring at the ocean. My thoughts wandered to my family. They had to be worried sick, while I worried about them and Ytel's men.

I had faith in Endris, whose eyes were much sharper than mine, to see if they were in trouble. But now that it was dusk and nearing the most likely moment an assault would take place, I should be up deck watching over my family.

I was about to stand and excuse myself when there was a rapid knock on the door. Ariane stood, but the door already burst open. Endris barged into the cabin.

"Pardon the intrusion, lord Laurence," he said.

"I smell fire in the breeze."

Like Smoke in the Night

"There's a fire?"

I slammed the etiquette book shut and rose to my feet. A sinking feeling settled in my stomach as I left Oleander and Ariane in the cabin and marched after Endris, who was already on his way up to the deck again. We climbed the stairs, and I immediately went to the railing and looked up at the cliffs. I didn't see nor smell anything. Around me, Ariane's servants were calmly doing their tasks or standing guard. It appeared Endris had warned no one besides me.

I turned to Endris. "Was that a way to save me from the Wildewall etiquette lessons? Because if that is the case, thank you so much."

"This is no time for jokes." Endris glared at me. "Breathe in deeply! There is smoke coming from the shore."

Oleander stepped beside me, and I nearly jumped. His footsteps were so quiet, I hadn't noticed he had also followed us. "I also smell serpentine powder," Oleander murmured, lowering his tone so only Endris and I could hear him.

I squinted at the shore but saw no fire nor smoke rising. Then I did as Endris suggested and breathed as deeply as I could. The wind gusted into my face, that was when I caught a whiff of what Endris meant, the faintest scent of smoke.

Endris' face darkened. He grabbed my arm. "I don't smell it, but if Oleander is right and there is serpentine powder, this is very dangerous," he said.

I glanced at Endris, then at Oleander, and finally settled my gaze on the Montbow mansion resting on top of the cliffs again. "What is serpentine powder?" I asked quietly. "Why is that dangerous?"

"It's used to blow up buildings, like the mansion, with a single spark," Endris hastily replied. "If you make the mistake of accidentally igniting that powder with your thunder..." Endris trailed off, letting the heavy end of his sentence hang in the air.

"Blow up buildings?" I repeated. A chill ran down my spine.

Endris' and Oleander's faces lit dimly by the sinking sun looked tense but certain. They both seemed convinced we needed to go. Behind Endris, I saw Ariane climbed up, looking annoyed at my and Oleander's sudden departure. It was for a good cause, however, as she would soon see.

I nodded at Oleander and Endris. "Very well," I said. I stepped away from the railing and faced the crew of the ship. "We need to go!" I boomed. "To the shore!"

Nearly all the men and women looked up from their work, but they didn't otherwise react. I stared at a bunch of blank expressions. "What are you waiting for?" I asked. "Do it."

Ariane chuckled and patted my shoulder. "Dear beloved, you have to understand these are my servants, not yours. They answer to me. And so, if you want to go to the shore, you answer to me too." Ariane's eyes travelled to Endris and Oleander. "You're going to tell me what you boys were whispering about in the corner?"

"They smell smoke. And Oleander smelled serpentine powder," I hissed. "Faintly, but surely. I believe them. We have to go."

Ariane looked at the shore, just like I had. "I smell nothing," she said. "And I see nothing either."

"It's there, lady Seydal," Endris insisted.

"If so, if you smell the powder, that means the powder was lit," Ariane replied. "We would have seen and heard the effects of serpentine powder being lit, don't you think?"

"Ytel's men having a weapon like that is already dangerous," I protested.

"It is not fully dark yet. If someone was approaching the mansion, Nele would have seen them move from the crow's nest," Ariane countered, pointing up at the woman sitting in the nest.

"Not if they are climbing the steep side of the cliffs rather than using the paths," Oleander protested quietly.

Ariane raised a brow. "Ytel's men in full armour with heavy weaponry climbing the cliffs? They ride horses, dear, not mountain goats."

"What do we have to lose by going now, Ariane?" I pressed. "I need to be at the mansion to defend it, regardless. Why not now? Why are we waiting out here in the sea in the first place?"

Ariane pressed her lips tightly together. For a moment I thought I wouldn't get answers, but then she reluctantly spoke. "Conrad and I agreed on a sign. He will ensure everyone is inside, give the sign, and once we see it, you are to spark lightning all across the mansion. From the ship, not the shore. Your life would never be in danger that way."

I raised and dropped my arms with an exasperated sigh. "Great, and when were you planning on telling me about this?"

"Since you are expecting Lord Montbow to play a crucial role in this plan, it would have been courteous to tell him what was going on," Oleander agreed.

Ariane narrowed her eyes. Oleander jutted his chin and stared back at her. I felt the thunder crackling already without me ever lifting a finger.

Without breaking eye-contact with Oleander, Ariane addressed me. "Do you let your servants speak to me in this manner, Laurence?"

"No, stop it. Both of you," I said. "My family could be in danger, and it's clear we can't follow the original plan now. What if I try to light up the cliffs with thunder while there's serpentine powder all over it? Ytel's men will die, sure, but there also won't be cliffs anymore for the mansion to stand on."

I looked down at the pale glimmer playing over the dark water. There were no big waves tonight, and I knew the direction of the currents was in my favour. If I wanted to, I could swim to the shore.

"If I can't use my thunder, then I still have Stormbringer, my bow, to fight," I said.

"Don't be ridiculous, Laurence," Ariane warned me. "One person allegedly smelled a trace of this powder. I would have known if Ytel had been smuggling serpentine powder, and Conrad and I have already agreed on a sign. He will warn us if our help is needed."

"If I may ask, what is the sign you agreed on, Lady Seydal?" Endris asked politely.

Ariane didn't reply. She crossed her arms.

"Fine. If you still want to keep me in the dark after all this, I will follow my own plan," I said. I climbed on the railing of the boat. It was slippery, and I almost lost my balance and toppled over the edge. My heart sped up in my throat as I looked down. The water's surface was suddenly quite a distance away when knowing you have to jump down.

"Laurence, stop this!" Ariane hissed, taking a step towards me.

"No, you stop this!" I retorted without turning. "Stop with the secrecy and the scheming behind my back. If you'd rather arrange all your plans with Conrad, why don't you just wed him instead?"

A brief, charged silence fell. "A flare," Ariane finally spoke, quietly. "The sign is a flare."

"A flare," Endris repeated. "One that requires powder to light, by any chance?"

I looked over my shoulder. Ariane's eyes spread wide at the same time Endris' did.

"Yes," Ariane breathed. She regained her composure fast, but the flicker of fear in her eyes had been clear as day.

"You mean Conrad tried to give the sign already?" I cursed and hopped down from the railing. "We need to go to the shore!"

"If our theory is right, they will already know Conrad wanted to alert someone," Endris said. "They will be on the lookout for us."

"So what?" I called out. "We have to help them!"

Endris dipped his head. "Yes, we do. But if they don't see us coming..."

"We gain an advantage back," Ariane finished Endris' sentence. "They think they prevented the flare from going off. They don't expect reinforcements." Ariane placed her hand on the railing. "This boat is too large," she said. "It can't go to the shore unseen fast enough if there are people on the lookout."

"So, we swim," I said, pointing at the dark ocean. "We can reach the shore in a few moments without being seen in the dark."

Ariane still hesitated. Her eyes shifted to Oleander and narrowed. "We would base a lot on a hunch and theories," she said. "And the claim from a servant that he, and he alone, smelled serpentine powder."

"I did smell the powder," Oleander defended himself with an indignant frown. "It's there."

Ariane ignored him and turned to me. "Do we have any reason to doubt his word, Laurence?" she asked. "He is... a relatively fresh addition to your household, is he not? Has he ever been alone with Ytel, or vanishing without an explanation?"

I shook my head. We were wasting time. Oleander was nimble and able to move in and out of my bedroom without getting caught. He was smart and a talented herbalist. But he had never moved against us. I'd doubted Oleander in the beginning, but it wouldn't make sense for him to lie now.

Plus, when I looked into Oleander's soulful, pleading eyes, I found my answer there. He feared for my family as well.

"We have no reason to doubt his word," I said.

Oleander offered me a tiny smile. He had the most beautiful smile, and I couldn't help but hold his gaze a little while longer.

Ariane made a disgusted sound. "Enough. It is time to go then."

Ariane turned to her crew. She didn't speak, but only made a gesture with her hand. A few of the stronger-looking men and women stepped forward and gathered with her, including Nele. She was now dressed in leather armour, thankfully. Swimming with steel or in a dress would not go well.

"Lord Montbow will lead you to the shore," Ariane told her warriors.

I stared at her, flabbergasted. "You're not protesting me swimming there?"

"Would it make a difference?" Ariane shot back.

"No."

"Then go." Ariane spun on her heels and marched away towards the stairs leading below deck. She stopped before climbing down. "Don't die," she said. "Or I will have to dig you up and kill you again."

"Got it."

I grinned, then took a deep breath to steel myself before facing Ariane's warriors on the deck. At least they seemed much more willing to listen to me now. "We're going into the water," I said. "The currents are in our favour. It'll be a short swim. When we reach the shore, we have to be quiet. Endris will be at the front, and we follow."

Endris nodded at me.

"Be prepared for the use of serpentine powder," was my last warning to Ariane's warriors. Then I strapped my quiver closed tightly so I wouldn't lose all my arrows on the way, and made sure my knife was secured.

While I checked my equipment, Oleander approached me. "Be careful, Laurence," he mumbled.

I smiled, but didn't speak. I couldn't promise I'd be careful, after all. Going to the shore wasn't being careful.

"Whatever happens, stay on board, Oleander," I said. "If there is fire, hide below deck."

"But Laurence, that's not fair," Oleander protested. He grabbed my hand and tugged on it. "It's also dangerous for you."

"Yes, but you're not a fighter, Oleander," I replied, giving his hand a squeeze before gently prying myself free. "Stay here on the ship."

Oleander eyes glistened. He blinked rapidly. "Alright."

I had to walk away from him. We couldn't embrace here on the deck. I would have to return so we could do so later in the privacy of my chambers.

After taking a few deep breaths, I stepped over the railing and leapt off the deck. As I hit the water, the cold engulfed me and the briny water stung my eyes. I rose back to the surface and started swimming.

Behind me, more shadows plunged into the water, three at a time. I didn't look back after that. I kept my eyes fixated on the cliffs and cleaved my way through the waves as fast as I could. Thankfully, I was right about the currents carrying us to the sand.

I stepped onto solid ground, water dripping off of me. The splashing behind me indicated the others were close behind. Endris was the first to step onto the beach beside me. It had grown dark enough, so he looked like a mere silhouette to me, but I saw how he pressed a finger to his lips.

Endris crouched and stayed low, so I followed his lead. Ariane's warriors did the same. We shuffled forward, somewhat spread out. Once we left the sandy banks, Endris led us onto a path that meandered through the cliffs.

I kept taking deep breaths, but I didn't smell more whiffs of serpentine powder. I didn't see enemies either, but after we'd climbed a few feet further, Endris suddenly held up his hand. We all came to an abrupt halt, pressing our backs to the cliffs or taking cover behind jagged rocks.

A moment later, I found out why Endris told us to hide. Light danced in the dark, coming from a turn up ahead where the path ascended beyond our sight. The flame moved our way. Endris reached for his dagger and snuck forward while the rest of us hid with hammering hearts.

Footsteps drew near and the moment the man turned the corner, Endris jumped him, knocking the man to the ground with an elbow digging into his chest. I couldn't see the man's face, but judging from Endris' reaction, pushing a knife to his throat, he wasn't on our side.

"You stay quiet," Endris hissed, emphasising every syllable. "You scream, you're dead."

A whimper sounded, and the man slowly shifted his hands up in surrender.

"Who is your leader?" Endris demanded first, but I didn't even need that question answered. I recognised the contours of the fur lining of his clothes.

"Ytel," I whispered.

"Y-yes," the man stammered.

"What are your plans?" Endris continued his interrogation.

The man shook his head. Scared as he was, he wasn't betraying his leader that easily.

Endris brought the knife closer to the man's neck. "Do you have serpentine powder?"

"No, no!" he breathed. "We do—"

The man's voice drowned out by an ear-splitting explosion coming from the cliffs. A flare of light burst up into the sky. My ears rang, and it disoriented me for a moment. I had to lean against the cliffs to stay standing.

"Serpentine powder!" Nele yelled behind me.

Endris slit the throat of the man and sprung to his feet. He sheathed his dagger, pulled out his bow, and started running.

"Mom, Dad!" I yelled. I ran after Endris, calling out my siblings' names in a blind panic.

We arrived at the top of the cliffs and the mansion was burning. Several columns had already collapsed at the front. The stench of rotten egg was unbearable, and thick smoke made it hard to see and breathe. I covered my mouth with my sleeve and searched for my family.

Nele dashed past me towards a man. Swords clashing, they disappeared in a blanket of smog that was rapidly swallowing the entire cliffs. Then another man popped up in front of me. He charged me with his weapon raised, and the flash of steel made me react on an instinct. I spread my fingers and lightning erupted from my palm. My enemy fell at my feet, dead. I didn't ignite more powder.

I looked down at my palm, and almost released another thunderbolt when someone yanked on my arm. I was able to refrain at the last moment when I saw it was Endris.

"To the mansion's back door!" he ordered. "We must go inside and climb to the top floor!"

Endris kept a tight grip on my arm as I ran with him. "Why?" I yelled back.

"Because you're going to rain thunder on them from up there!"

I coughed. My lungs felt like they were burning. "I can't see anything. I can't aim with this smoke! I will hit everyone!"

"I have a plan," Endris promised as we reached the back door of the mansion, leading to the kitchens. His dark eyes bore into mine. "Trust me, Laurence."

A Missing Knife

- -

E ndris threw the door to the mansion open and ran inside. I went after him, despite it seeming like an awful idea to enter a burning building. The kitchen was empty but there was already a thin layer of smoke floating in the room. Whatever Endris wanted to do, it would have to be fast.

"Valda! Conrad!" I called out as we hurried through the kitchen and into the hall. "Gisela!"

I didn't receive a response. Endris' fingers dug into my arm as he dragged me along. The smoke grew thicker the closer we came to the stairs, and my eyes stung. In the lobby, the flames had spread to the carpet. I felt the blistering heat on my skin.

"Up!" Endris bellowed. "Wait on the balcony!"

Endris let go of my arm and turned to the living quarters. "What are you going to do?" I asked.

"I will set the trap."

I wanted to ask what trap, but Endris ran like the wind and vanished into the living quarters before I could utter a single world. For a moment, I hesitated. If the fire spread, I'd be trapped inside. Burning alive wasn't appealing, but neither was yielding to Ytel's men.

Endris better have a good plan.

Cursing under my breath, I ran up the stairs two steps at a time. On the second floor I called out for my family again with no response, and then I dashed on to the third floor. There was a balcony in the master bedroom. My parents' bedroom. It looked out over the road leading to our mansion, the nearby woods, and beyond that, the town. I assumed that was the place Endris meant for me to go.

I burst through the door, hoping to find my parents holed up in their chambers, but it was empty. The bed was unmade and my father's cane was gone, however, indicating they had left in a hurry. Swiftly crossing the room, I stepped outside onto the balcony. Above me, I saw muddled pinpricks of light in a dark sky. Below me, figures with weapons moved in the smoke. It wasn't safe for them to stay in there much longer. The smoke and serpentine powder burned in my lungs with every breath, and I wasn't even in the thick of it.

I had done as Endris said, but after a few moments of waiting, doubt gnawed at the back of my mind. I couldn't just sit here forever. What was he planning on doing? I paced, and another few moments later, I grew impatient and wanted to go outside to find Endris. That was when someone stumbled onto the balcony behind me.

Valda's hair was tangled, and black smears were smudged all over her face and ripped dress. Her eyes filled with tears when she saw me, and she let out a strangled sob as she pulled me into an embrace.

"Laurence," she cried out, "I thought you had left. How are you here?"

"Don't worry about that right now," I replied, squeezing my sister tightly. "Are you alright? Where are the others?"

"I don't know. I only found Endris, and he told me to find you on the balcony." Valda sniffled. "And he told me to tell you that you need to aim for the woods."

"Aim for the woods?" I repeated. I stared into the distance at the black silhouettes of the trees. "With my thunder? Why would I do that?"

"I don't know. Wait for the horn and aim for the woods. That's all he said."

I shook my head in confusion. "I have no idea what Endris wants, but we can't stay here much longer. The mansion is burning. We need to get out."

"No, wait, look," Valda said, pointing at the ground below.

I squinted, and then I saw what she meant. A lone figure on horseback moved towards the woods. It was a mere shadow crossing the landscape—if you didn't look carefully, you'd miss it. Then the deep sound of a horn echoed across the cliffs.

A moment later, I heard men yelling: "retreat!" A dozen more figures ran from the mansion after the person on horseback. The horn had to symbolise an order to retreat. The men ran for the woods.

"That must be them!" Valda called out. "The men who attacked us."

"I can't tell from here," I protested. "And neither can you. What if they're not? What if they're Ariane's warriors?"

Valda frowned at me in disbelief. "Why would Endris tell you to strike the woods if they're not Ytel's men?"

Because both Endris and Ytel lived in Wildewall, and my only real tie to Endris was Oleander. But Endris and Ytel had never truly seen eye to eye either.

"Laurence, please," Valda pleaded. "Stop them. They will return to Wildewall and spread lies about what happened. You know they will!"

I released a shuddering breath. If we were wrong... I looked at the figures heading for the woods, the ones I'd soon kill, and muttered a soft prayer to the thunder god asking for forgiveness.

Then I closed my eyes. I drew all my power to my mark until it burned brighter than the flames consuming the mansion. Sounds faded. All I heard was my heart thundering. All I felt was sweat running down my neck and raw energy coursing through my body like the unstoppable currents of the sea. I balled my fists and gathered more magic until my chest was about to burst. Then I opened my fingers and released my magic.

The heavens tore as I sent bolt after bolt crashing down near the woods where men ran. When my rain of thunder ended, nothing moved anymore in the dark. The strength left my body soon after and I slumped to the ground despite my attempts to hold on to the railing of the balcony.

"Laurence? Laurence!" Valda's muffled cries rang in my ears. I felt her hand pressing on my back and then I passed out.

The next time I blinked my eyes open, light flooded my vision. With a groan, I shielded my face from the sun with my arm. When my eyes adjusted, I realised I was downstairs in the kitchen, covered in blankets and sore from neck to hips. The room was silent; I didn't hear fighting and everything in the kitchen looked normal. The only evidence I had that I hadn't only dreamt of a fight and the mansion in flames was the pain in my lungs and upper body. I coughed and swatted the heavy blankets off of me.

Hasty, light footsteps instantly came my way. "Lord Montbow!" Oleander called out, before his worried face hovered over mine.

My mother and Valda soon joined him. Under their watchful gaze, I sat up slowly. Not that I had any choice in the matter. Every moment I made sent searing jolts of pain through my mark.

Mother rested her hand on my shoulder. "How are you feeling, Laurence? Don't move too fast."

"I'm alright," I replied through gritted teeth. I had gone through this before. After using my god's blessing to its fullest strength, my magic always silenced in me for a while, but it would return.

"Where is everyone? Did we all make it out?" I asked as I tried to stand. Oleander helped me by putting my arm across his shoulders and pushing me up.

"We're all here, Laurence," my mother replied. "Also, thanks to you. Rest easy."

"No, I want to see everyone," I protested.

"Can we please take him to the living quarters, Lady Montbow?" Oleander asked quietly. "I don't think Lord Montbow will rest unless he sees everyone alive."

"You're probably right," Mother said with a sigh. She gestured me and Oleander to come along.

We walked to the living quarters together, with Oleander supporting me. On the way, I saw the lobby had all but collapsed. The staircases looked like the fire touched them as well, and I wasn't sure if they were even usable anymore. Large buckets stood orderly in a row adjacent to the stairs.

Before my mother opened the door leading to the living quarters, I heard agitated voices arguing inside. They abruptly stopped when Oleander, my mom, and I stepped inside the room. All eyes shot my way. My entire family was there, and Ariane and Endris, too.

"Thank you," I muttered under my breath to the thunder god as relief flooded me. Then I grinned widely at the occupants of the room. "Please, don't stop talking on my behalf."

"Laurence!" Fynn immediately jumped up and ran at me with wide open arms. I didn't have the heart to tell my little brother to be careful, so I bit on my lip to stop a groan in pain from spilling from my lips as I bent down to hug him.

"We all thought you were gone, but you weren't! I knew you'd never let us down," Fynn said, burying his head into the crook of my neck.

I chuckled, grateful there was still at least one family member with absolute faith in me. Everyone else seemed to keep their plans secret.

I looked around the room and found only tense and serious faces. Especially my dad and Conrad had never frowned deeper. Mother had also seemed troubled on the way here, and I wondered what in the thunder god's name was going on.

Oleander helped me to a chair, and I sat down heavily with a moan. "I see everyone's alive," I said. "I'm very glad to see it."

"Yes," Ariane replied. "It's all very fortunate. Endris knew Ytel's commander uses a horn to communicate with his men. By killing the commander and blowing the horn, he could trick them into leaving the battlefield, turning them into sitting ducks for you to zap."

"I see," I said. "What's with the long faces then? The mansion is damaged, sure, and the plan didn't go according to, well, plan. But we won, right?"

"If you believe killing everyone is a victory," Ariane replied.

I raised a brow. "What do you mean? Killing everyone was your plan all along. You wanted me to, I quote, rain my thunder down on Ytel's men if they tried to attack."

"Ytel is dead, Laurence," Ariane deadpanned.

"What?" I frowned, then looked down at my open palm. "Did I...?"

"No, he wasn't struck by your lightning," Gisela replied. "He was further away inside the woods, hidden... but not well enough."

"It was a knife," my father added. "Multiple stabbing wounds inflicted to make it hurt, to make it hard to breathe, before he would finally die."

I hastily covered Fynn's ears as father went into the details. The little tyke squirmed in my grasp until he broke free. He looked at me indignantly.

"Endris and Fynn, could you check up on the horses?" my mom asked. "The poor beasts had quite a scare last night. Especially Spot needs you."

My mother knew exactly how to appeal to Fynn, the animal friend who was always eager to make himself useful. Fynn stood up straighter. "Yes, Mom," he said without arguing.

Endris also stood without a word and walked out with my little brother.

When they were gone, Gisela took out a piece of cloth from underneath the table and unwrapped it, revealing a knife with blood still clinging to the sharp side. "This is the knife we found on Ytel's body."

I recognised the knife. It had Montbow's signature on it. "This comes from our kitchen," I said.

Mother pressed a hand to her forehead and squeezed her eyes shut. "Killing Ytel's men because they attacked us is one thing. Killing a knight another. That will send tongues wagging in Wildewall. By the thunder god, just as we thought better times were coming."

"So? He attacked us first," I said. "He blew our front door out of its sockets with his special powder."

"That wasn't Ytel's powder," Valda said, side-eying Conrad. "That was our powder. For a flare. Most of us just didn't know we had it."

Conrad didn't respond to Valda's accusations.

"It's all in the past now," Gisela dismissed Valda's words. "We need to look forward. We have a dead knight in our woods, a barely liveable home, and Laurence's departure to handle now."

"Did anyone confess?" I asked. "To killing Ytel?"

"No," Father replied flatly. "And anyone who is smart wouldn't come forward now. They would immediately be under arrest for killing a knight of the queen, and on their way to Wildewall to rot in the dungeons for the rest of their days if they are not executed."

"Wait a moment, a knight like Ytel isn't entirely above the law either," I protested again. "Ytel died a warrior's death, and it happened during a clear assault on a noble family. Wildewall's laws are clear about this."

"You would be right if the Montbows were a noble family," Ariane said. "Less so as long as you live in exile." Ariane looked me up and down. "But if you go to Wildewall's ball and dazzle them, you may be reinstated in the court and have your word count as more than a mere disgraced merchant. Your storm-touched status helps with that. You will at least get a hearing and a chance to plead not guilty."

I knew I had to attend a hearing in Wildewall if a knight died in our territory. But did we truly have no guilt in this matter? I glanced at Conrad. He and Ariane had been keeping so many secrets I didn't know if he didn't.

As a matter of fact, several people in this room would have the knowledge to pull a murder like this off, and literally everyone in this room had a motive.

To all my family members, Ytel was a thorn in our side which kept trying to dig its way in deeper and deeper and had tried to bleed us dry several times. To Endris, Ytel was an arrogant knight and the personification of the worst nobles offered; on a power trip and perpetually hungry for more than he should want. Perhaps it wasn't something he held a grudge over, but I could never be sure about Endris. Even to Oleander, Ytel was a man who had murdered a dragon. Something he repeatedly cautioned against. Then there was Ariane, who could have ordered one of her servants to do it. Maybe the warrior who stabbed Ytel was dead already. I couldn't tell; we'd all gotten scrambled and split up in the panic and nobody saw everything that happened because of the smoke. Everyone with access to our kitchen could have done this, except for little Fynn and me.

"Perhaps it is better this way," Ariane offered with a shrug. "You sent a clear message to others who are after the Montbow family with this kill. You Montbows have been too soft and careful, anyway." Ariane hummed. Either way, it's even more crucial now that Laurence departs for Wildewall as soon as possible."

"Wouldn't it be dangerous to leave my family and the mansion undefended now?" I asked. "They will know."

"It will be more dangerous if you don't go to the capital and form the narrative before others make up stories in their heads themselves," Conrad said. "You can decide what people believe."

Conrad stared intently at me with mismatched eyes. Forming the narrative is what he would do. He'd spin the story in his favour with ease, saying little, but saying just enough to make people doubt.

I sighed. "What am I supposed to sell them then? What narrative?"

"Do we need to decide everything for you?" Conrad mocked. "You tell them it was a tragic fate for Ytel, but such is the risk if you get greedy and try to claim land that doesn't belong to you. It shouldn't be hard. Ytel is not there to defend himself, after all."

"People in Wildewall knew what he set out to do," Ariane agreed. "All you have to do is act as Conrad says and make the Montbow family look honourable and upstanding, and Ytel, the villain for trying to take advantage of your misfortune."

I swallowed thickly. "He must have allies. Ytel," I said. "Someone will take revenge while I'm gone."

"We can't exclude that possibility," Gisela admitted.

Valda offered me a small smile. "It's a risk, like sending you to the mountains was a risk, but if it pays off... maybe we will get to dance at next year's autumn ball as well. And at least we now have a boat to escape in."

"I will also write more of our old, loyal guards," Mother said. "Some of them may return now that we can pay them. Leonardo even offered to stay for free, remember?"

I smiled, remembering the blond, zany swordsman who used to bounce around here. He was an orphan, incapable of sitting still and barely an adult, but damn, that guy could make swordplay look like art.

Mother grabbed my hand and squeezed it. "You will go Wildewall's autumn ball with Endris and Oleander. Then you travel to the mountains to kill a dragon and become a knight."

My gut twisted. I wanted to tell my mother no. I didn't want to leave my family behind undefended, but Ariane and Conrad also had a point. I would help my family more if I did what was suggested: spin the narrative and do everything within my power to get the Montbow family in good standing so we would have protection from the court.

"Very well," I caved. "We'll go to Wildewall as planned."

"Good, I'm glad you finally see reason," Ariane spoke crisply. "My servants are on their way back with our traveling supplies. My surviving warriors are resting now and will be ready tomorrow. The wounded stay here and join Montbow's guard when they recover."

I snorted at Ariane's confidence. "Looks like your plan paid off in the end, huh?"

Ariane smiled at me like a satisfied cat. "Of course my plans paid off. They always do, beloved."

The Star-crossed Lovers

The scars of last night's battle were carved into the landscape. Cracks in the rock where thunder struck weaved through the charred remains of what had once been green moss and creeping thyme. The fire in the woods nearby reeked of burning flesh. I imagined bodies piled up in the same large clearing where my sisters and I used to play robbers.

"Did it have to happen this way?" I asked Gisela, who was standing with me at the foot of the cliffs. I gestured at the smoke circling up into grey clouds above the woods.

Gisela followed my gaze. "No," she replied curtly. "You could have let them overrun us, surrender the mansion, and end the Montbow bloodline."

"Gisela."

"See it this way then: the woods will flourish as their ashes fertilise the soil and provide us and the town with more fruit to eat," Gisela stated. "They serve a noble purpose now. That is more than they could say in life."

I just shook my head. Gisela and I had these discussions before. She saw it as wasteful to not use the bodies and had little regard for funeral rites. I was unconscious when Ytel's dead men were moved to the clearing in the woods and set on fire. Ariane's servants did it, maybe, or my family members. But I was the one who had killed all of them. The least I could have done was burn them myself.

I also wished I had time to help rebuild. Leaving the Thundercoast with the memory of a collapsed mansion and blood soaking the ground left a sour taste in my mouth. I also didn't want to make my family explain to the townsfolk what transpired here last night.

Gisela put her hand on my shoulder. A rare, sympathetic gesture. "It's time to say goodbye, Laurence."

"Yes..."

"But I have one last thing to say to you," Gisela said, squeezing my shoulder. Her eyes bored into mine. "Father's warning still stands, Laurence. Don't give your trust too easily. Especially not to beautiful men with long hair and soulful eyes. Remember that you don't know him, and you know nothing of him."

"I need to fear long-haired men? I don't think Endris is dangerous, Gisela," I joked.

Gisela narrowed her eyes. She didn't laugh.

I sighed. "If Oleander meant me or us harm, he would've already made his move by now. He had plenty of opportunities. You should listen to Mother instead of Father."

"Perhaps," Gisela replied. "But I believe it wise to pretend like you have no allies in Wildewall. Not truly. The capital is very different from the Thundercoast. We're on the outskirts of palace society, and there you will be in the thick of it. Remember that."

"I understand."

"Then let us go back."

Gisela turned on her heels, and we headed up the cliffs together. Guilt stabbed at my chest as I saw everyone waiting for me in front of the battered mansion. I would be leaving my parents and siblings for much longer this time. I couldn't help them if something happened.

Oleander, Endris, and Ariane and her servants looked ready for travel. My horse, Spot (as Fynn insisted), was saddled as well. Fynn was holding the reins, but when I approached, he offered them to me.

"Spot will keep you safe," Fynn said as if repeating the words often enough could manifest it as a truth.

I brushed my hand through Fynn's hair and pressed a kiss to his forehead. "Thanks, kid."

Valda came up to me with a tense smile and pulled me into a hug. "I'm so jealous you get to travel to Wildewall. Bring me a gift when you return."

"I will, Valda," I promised.

Mother was next to say goodbye with a kiss pressed to my cheek. "Stay safe, Laurence," she said. "Remember that you're blessed."

"Make the Montbow family proud," my father added, gravely serious. I nodded, quickly moving past him with Spot before the shame of already failing once by returning from the mountains empty-handed caught up to me.

Conrad leaned against the wall with crossed arms a little distance away from the others. He only stared at me when I nodded at him. I expected little else in terms of a goodbye from my older brother, and got on my horse.

As we rode off and I watched my family disappear into the distance, I wondered if Ariane had another trick up her sleeve. It seemed we were truly leaving the Thundercoast until I noticed we were bending off in the wrong direction. We weren't on the route to Wildewall that I knew.

"Are we going somewhere else again, Ariane?" I asked. "This is not the way to Sunmere valley."

"How very observant of you, Laurence," Ariane replied. "That is because we're not traveling through the valley. There is a faster route."

I thought about it for a moment. "What, you don't mean...?"

"Through the Starcross woods," Ariane replied.

My eyes shot to Oleander.

Ariane noticed. She looked over her shoulder at Oleander, who was riding behind us with the other servants. "Ah, yes," she said. "We're traveling to your home, aren't we?"

Oleander's eyes went wide. I subtly nodded at him to just go along with it. Following my instructions, Oleander nodded, too. "Yes," he said. "I'm from the Starcross woods."

Ariane hummed. "Interesting. I though the old Lord Montbow said you had no memories of who you are."

"He doesn't," I defended Oleander. "We assume he's from this region because of his accent."

"Naturally," Ariane said. She tugged on her horse's reins and slowed down until she rode next to Oleander. "Since you don't remember, do you want a history lesson about your home?"

"Ariane," I protested.

Ariane didn't listen and turned to her servant, Nele. "Nele, tell us the story of prince Malte and Sage, the blood traitor."

"Ariane, this isn't necessary. Stop," I protested again, mostly because I was very familiar with the tale. Everyone in the human world was familiar with the history of the Starcross woods, and I didn't want Oleander to hear it. My stomach sank at the thought of the expression on his face when he heard Sage's fate.

Nele shot Ariane a questioning look. When Ariane waved my concerns away, she started her story regardless.

"When elves roamed these woods before the war, prince Helmold, called Malte by the people, travelled to the Starcross woods to lead a charge in the name of his father, king Bertram," she said. "He was to kill the elves who had attacked a band of merchants traveling through the woods and stole their blood to use in their dark rituals. When prince Malte rode into the woods, something glimmering between the trees spooked his horse. It ran, separating prince Malte from his guards, and threw him off of his back. When prince Malte woke up, he had an arrow trained on his face. An elf named Sage Farun had found him. But, enchanted by his handsome face, the elf didn't shoot. Instead, Sage treated Malte's wounds and kept him hidden from the others. Eventually, prince Malte healed from his injuries and travelled home, but he kept meeting with Sage in secret. They became lovers... until king Bertram declared a war on the elves, and they were on opposite sides."

"That is where the woods got their name," I quickly told Oleander. "The Starcross woods for star-crossed lovers. That's the whole story."

Ariane smirked. "That's not the whole story, Laurence. I know you pay little attention to history classes, but even you know this. Continue, Nele."

There was a brief silence, and then Nele went on.

"Prince Malte and Sage wanted to find a way to prevent this war. They made a plan to separate the elven woods and the human cities with an elven artefact and a blessed human who could energise it and create a barrier with it. Sage would steal the artefact from their holy temple, and prince Malte would arrange a god-touched blessed human to help them. They would meet at the edge of the woods."

"If we are travelling through these woods now, I suppose no barrier was raised?" Oleander asked through gritted teeth.

"No," Nele replied. "Sage forgot his loyalty to his people and stole the artefact, dooming the elves. But prince Malte remembered in the end that his people were more important than his love for one man. He killed Sage and took the artefact to present to his father, the king. Without their powerful artefact, fed by years of accumulated life force and blood collected from unfortunate humans who travelled through the woods, the elves could no longer fight the humans."

"Sage Farun chose, and so did king Bertram's son. A treacherous elven man, and a human man loyal to his people and a hero," Ariane said.

Oleander's expression was blank, his eyes icy cold in a way I'd never seen. It sent shivers down my spine. "You call Sage Farun a traitor," Oleander spoke after a short silence. "I hear a loyal lover who trusted his human lover to help him prevent a war from ever happening. The only mistake I hear is on Sage's side. For believing prince Malte could be trusted."

Oleander dug his heels into his horse's flanks and galloped ahead of us. Ariane let it happen with an amused smile. "Touchy," she said. "And rude. Have you not been teaching him how to behave like a servant, Laurence?" She glanced at me. "Get him in line, or I will."

I pressed my lips to a line. Then I made Spot gallop and followed Oleander to the front of the line.

"Hey, are you alright?" I asked, riding beside Oleander.

Oleander didn't immediately respond. He kept his eyes trained on the road for a few moments longer before he turned to me. "Who do you say the traitor in this tale is?" he asked. "Sage or Malte?"

"I..." I trailed off.

I had heard the stories about the Starcross woods, but I had never given it much deeper thought. It was simply history. A past event. Nele told the story in a relatively kind manner compared to some history books. Most depicted Sage Farun as a perverted, ugly man, and prince Malte as a handsome hero who saw the perversion of the elven man for wanting to sleep with him and took advantage of it. He was the reason lessons in how to charm people became part of a knight's required skills.

"I personally like to think they truly loved each other," I said. "That it wasn't only a trick played by prince Malte to get the artefact. That he took his decision because in the end he didn't believe that Sage was sincere or that their plan could work. Prince Malte never actually became a part of the court, you know? He vanished after killing Sage and giving the king the artefact."

"And what if Sage was sincere? Bloodshed could have been prevented. " Oleander's eyes were sad as he stared into the distance. He lowered his voice. "I do not wish to be like Sage Farun. Will you not be like prince Malte and turn me in to the queen when we arrive?"

"Never," I said promptly.

Oleander briefly closed his eyes. "Don't say never too lightly, Laurence."

"Never," I emphasised. "But I can't speak for others. The danger is there. A lot more danger than there was at the Thundercoast." I swallowed and glanced back over my shoulder. "Would you not rather stay in the Starcross woods when we get there? And if there's nobody there, you can go back to the Thundercoast."

Oleander blinked. "Would the queen not be upset with you if you don't take everyone who was invited with you to meet her?"

"Perhaps," I admitted. "But I'm willing to risk that."

"Then I am willing to risk entering Wildewall. If you're with me," Oleander replied. "I just hope I will find my memories there. Perhaps I will remember something when I see the elven artefact of the queen, or read more of the past in the library."

"Yes," I said vaguely. Oleander wouldn't find kind tales about elves in human libraries, but I knew I couldn't keep him away from them. I would only have to make sure I was with him when he went. "But for now, please come to the back of the line with me and ride with the servants."

"Lady Seydal told you to come get me, didn't she?" Oleander pulled a face. "I don't like her."

"I know," I said with a sigh. "But we can't afford to have her get suspicious, Oleander."

Oleander showed his distaste with a wrinkled nose. "Fine," he said. "For you."

Oleander turned his horse around. I followed him, and we went back to our respective places in the line. Oleander in the back with Endris, Nele, and the other servants who weren't guards. And I rode next to Ariane.

"Good," Ariane said. "Glad to see you remember he is a servant."

I clenched my jaw and kept my mouth shut.

Ariane and I had little to discuss, so we rode mostly in silence until we reached the first larger town on the way. Brittleton was nested between lush fields of green, surrounded by cows and sheep. Due to its location and the abundance of wildlife, it was a constant battle for these shepherds to protect their animals from predators. I'd never seen shepherds carrying broadswords and bows outside of Brittleton.

Ariane had arranged a stay at a nearby castle that belonged to her aunt and uncle. It had been a long ride, so after a quiet dinner, I immediately retired to my assigned chambers. The steward had told me I could take the room to the far right, the last door in the hallway.

I yawned as I reached for the doorknob, eager to go to sleep. All my tiredness instantly vanished, however, when I opened the door and there was already someone in there.

Oleander sat on my bed and smiled apologetically when he noticed he'd startled me. "My apologies," he said. "Is it alright that I'm in here?"

I exhaled through my mouth and locked the door behind me. "Of course," I said. "But you have to go back to your room, Oleander. All Ariane's servants are here and if they find you with me we're in a world of trouble."

"I know," Oleander said. "I will only be here for a moment. I just wanted a moment alone with you. Just for a little while."

Slowly, Oleander reached for his ponytail. He untied the ribbon on his hair and a waterfall of silver cascaded down his shoulders. Then he patted the sheets, inviting me to sit with him.

My heart was beating wildly in my chest as I did as he asked and sat, sinking into the soft sheets and mattress. With a smile, Oleander leaned in and softly pressed his lips to my neck. The palm of his hand gingerly grazed my knee, before slowly starting a slow ascend to my thigh.

I released a shuddering breath as blood rushed to my groin. "I thought you didn't remember anything."

Oleander laughed quietly, his breath fanning my neck. "I don't need memories to know how I want to touch you. But... I suppose could use some reminders."

Leaning back, Oleander looked at me through half-lidded eyes. I breathed in sharply as his nimble fingers travelled further up and he touched me through my pants.

"What's this?" Oleander asked with purposeful innocent eyes. "You'll have to tell me. I have no memories."

I wanted him to go on. Desperately so. But, with a jolt, I remembered where we were. There was a large risk of getting caught and I didn't want to risk Ariane's ire for sleeping with Oleander under her family's roof. "We're not alone in here," I breathed. "They will notice you missing."

Oleander hummed. "That depends on how fast we are done."

We would be done very fast if Oleander kept his hand where it was now and rubbed. "Oleander, we can't. Not in here," I urged him but already regretted my words the moment Oleander listened and retracted his hand.

"Alright, I understand," Oleander said with a pout. "Could we be alone in the city, away from prying eyes, then?"

"It's a big city, Oleander. I think we can manage there."

"Good." Oleander offered me a smile before turning more serious again. He slid his hands up to my shoulders and pressed a kiss to my lips. Then, he playfully pushed me down onto my back with surprising strength. I stayed sprawled out on the bed with a throbbing groin, while Oleander moved to the window. He tied his hair and then climbed out of the window, disappearing into the dark with a playful sparkle in his iridescent green eyes.

City of Wonders

Brittleton castle was only a taste of what was waiting for me at Wildewall, and it was already far too strong for me to stomach.

My morning started with me jolting upright in my bed at the sound of rustling fabric. The servant standing in my room stammered he'd only entered to wake me and help me get dressed, and almost literally crawled out with his nose pressed to the floor when I told him I didn't need help. The look on his face before he closed the door left me feeling like I'd insulted his ancestors and kicked his horse, too.

The servants at the Thundercoast had never behaved like this. It left me wondering if it was simply the result of the Seydal family running a tight ship, or if all servants of the richer families of the court were like this.

If I ever had people working for me again, I'd teach them to not crawl for me or buy me clothes that cost a fortune. The shirt and pants the man had left in my room were smooth but sturdy. They were the most comfortable garments I'd worn in a long time, but my skin crawled thinking of how they could probably pay for all the labourers needed to repair our mansion.

After getting dressed, I did my best to avoid people as I strode past the stained glass windows. Oleander would be proud of me, because I managed to sneak outside of Brittleton's castle unseen. Only the unblinking eyes of the portraits dotted across the corridor walls saw me leave.

I thought the horses would make for pleasant company in the early morning, and it seemed there was another person who shared my sentiments. When I walked into the stables, Endris was already with the horses. He often seemed to prefer being with animals whenever he wasn't out in the mountains guiding people to dragons. Perhaps I would feel the same way if I lived in Wildewall.

Spot came to the front of the fence with her ears perked, and I gave her neck a soft pat in the passing. She snorted, making Endris look up at me.

"Endris. You're up early," I greeted him.

Endris crossed his arms. "The servants are whispering about you."

"Oh no." I groaned, flicking my gaze upward to the wooden ceiling. "It wasn't about wanting to get dressed on my own, right? Because I swear—"

"They're saying you killed Ytel."

I shot Endris an incredulous look. "I didn't."

"You don't need to convince me," Endris said. "To be more specific, they think you gave the order."

I turned to the entrance of the stables with a sigh, placing my hands on my hips. "I'm not giving orders to anyone. I'm not even the head of house Montbow yet."

We'd had little time to solve murder mysteries before we were forced to depart or risk being late to the queen's ball. While on the road, however, I had pondered about this stabbing incident. By now I was pretty convinced it was Conrad and Ariane scheming again. They were awfully fast with pointing out how I could get my family out of this accusation by attending a hearing in the capital. It was dangerous to point fingers, however. If they found my brother guilty of Ytel's death, it would play out as my father had said: he'd hang in Wildewall. Ariane could probably get out of that morbid fate, but her name would be tarnished, too.

I turned back to Endris. "Who do you think did it?"

"I don't know," Endris replied with irritation lacing his voice. "I was too busy stealing the horn and making them retreat."

"Yes, but who do you think did it?"

Endris shrugged. "Does it matter? The kill will be attributed to the Montbow family, which means it'll be attributed to the most prominent member of that family, which is you."

"Great," I said with a wry smile. "Now I'm going to Wildewall as a knight killer and a boorish, disgraced coastal merchant. They're just going to love me, aren't they?"

"They might, if you walked around bare-chested and kept your mouth shut."

"Bare-chested, huh?" I raised a suggestive eyebrow, knowing full well that Endris was talking about my mark and not my upper body. But I still enjoying watching the vein pop out on his forehead.

With a huff, Endris marched past me and left the stables. I jogged after him with a chuckle, and caught up to him on the long, winding stone path leading to the castle.

"How can you stand it, anyway?" I asked. "Living in the capital? Wildewall sounds like the last place someone like you would be."

Endris glanced at me. "It's a place with many possibilities."

"Like what? Having five-hundred ridiculous social rules and if you accidentally sneeze wrong, you have now gravely offended someone's mother?" I snorted at my own joke.

Endris frowned at me. "To have influence. Wildewall is the beating heart of the court. It's the place where decisions affecting an entire country are made."

"What do you want to change then?"

"Many things," Endris replied vaguely. "But most of all, our knight's trial."

I shook my head. "Endris, I've told you this before: you're in the wrong trade. You guide people up that mountain for a living. That doesn't sound like something you should do if you're so against the trials."

Endris avoided my eyes. "It's complicated."

"I'm sure it is," I said. "And you never told me why you want to protect Oleander so badly, either. Why?"

"I did tell you. I protect him because he has done nothing wrong. He doesn't deserve scorn for the crime of being an elf in human lands."

We had almost reached the castle. Endris' gaze rested on a few servants scurrying about. He stopped walking, grabbed my arm, and pulled me to the side, out of sight of the servants.

"If you want what's best for Oleander too, make him cross the woods," Endris told me in a hushed voice. "Now is the perfect time for him to disappear. Convince him. The city is no place for him."

"I already offered," I said with a shrug. "But Oleander is quite determined to learn about his past, and he thinks he will be able to in the city. He is willing to risk it."

A pained expression crossed Endris' face. "He's walking into the dragon's den. Only cruelty awaits him if he gets caught as an elf inside Wildewall."

"Have you told him?"

"Repeatedly. But he won't listen to me. Or to you, apparently."

"Maybe if I didn't go, he wouldn't either, but..."

"You can't refuse an invitation from the queen," Endris finished my sentence. "Regardless, if we are all going to Wildewall, you and Oleander need this." Endris reached into his bag and handed me a thick envelope, and a green, wool brimmed hat.

I raised a brow, but accepted both items and put the hat on my head. "Alright. Why do I need a hat? Is this Wildewall fashion?"

Endris pressed a hand to his forehead and sighed. "That's not for you. It's for Oleander. To ensure his ears stay hidden."

"Oh. Right." I plucked the hat off with a sheepish smile. "And the papers?"

"A written speech for your hearing regarding knight commander Ytel's death. Read through it and memorize it when you have the chance."

I glanced at the envelope and tucked it into my bag. "Fine. And I will try to convince Oleander one final time," I said. "But let's get out of here as soon as possible first. This place gives me the creeps."

It wasn't the building itself that made my skin crawl. The castle was well-maintained and the stained glass beautiful. It was definitely built for Seydal family, with itbeing extravagant, big, and manned by servants who were scared of a noble's shadow.

I was glad to leave Brittleton and the Seydal castle behind me, even while knowing I was heading for a similar place. We travelled on roads wide and narrow until the sun went down, and I studied the text Endris had given me by candlelight in my tent at night. It blamed Ytel for his own death, which didn't sound like my words, but that was likely the point. I was kept busy studying at night. But while the sun shone, and we rode our horses, my thoughts often wandered to home and I prayed there hadn't been more attacks.

Days passed this way until we entered the only woodlands of the north. I knew immediately where we were. The Starcross woods.

I had expected to feel something as we entered and rode in the shadows cast by tall trees, but felt nothing. I stopped to pay tribute to the god of thunder by carving their sign into a tree and asking for them to continue lending me their strength, and still felt nothing.

When I'd thought of the Starcross woods, I had imagined sensing echoes of an ancient magic. A reminiscence of the powerful artefact these lands used to house. I'd imagined feeling a certain sadness left by the bloodiest war that had ever taken place in our history. But there was nothing. Aside from birds chirping overhead, the woods were empty and silent. The trees were the same as the ones at the Thundercoast, and there was no one here.

While I was disappointed, Oleander stared wistfully into the distance. We were never alone during the day, so I couldn't ask him what was on his mind nor touch him like my hands were itching to do. Given Oleander's reaction to this place, I decided to make my last attempt to persuade him to go across the border and bring himself to safety here. I was running out of time to do it. Wildewall was close to the woods.

When we ended our journey for the day and the servants set up our camp, I thought of ways to sneak to Oleander's tent. He shared with others, so it would be difficult to go there unseen. Then I realised I didn't need to go unseen. The rules were different away from the Thundercoast. To the people here, Oleander was my servant. He wasn't, and I refused to call him such, but nobody knew about that in this encampment.

I was lord Montbow, a man with an invitation to the queen's ball, Ariane's betrothed, and a storm-touched soon to be a knight. I had my rights, and I could simply march up the servant tents and demand for my 'servants' to walk with me outside.

As I straightened my back, tilted my chin up, and marched to the servant area, I already hated every moment of acting like a lord. There was a young man standing guard in front of the tent. He froze when I caught his gaze.

"You. Get Oleander and Endris. Bring them here," I ordered. The command was strange to my tongue, but the young man bowed and all but dashed past the tent flaps to do as I told him.

A few moments later, Oleander and Endris stepped outside and looked at me in question.

"We're going for a walk," I said.

"Yes, lord Montbow," Oleander replied meekly, darting a glance at the young man who'd retrieved him and Endris.

I lit a torch and led Oleander and Endris away from prying eyes until the campfire was only a small dot of light. After Endris checked and gave me a curt nod, indicating we weren't followed, I took a deep breath.

"It's not too late. You can still leave, Oleander," I said. "I would come find after the entire ordeal in Wildewall is done."

"You also don't have to worry about finding the lands across the border empty," Endris now offered. "I have seen the people who live there."

I turned to Endris, shocked. "And is there a reason you've failed to mention that sooner?"

"Because," Endris started slowly, narrowing his eyes at me, "I have brought people there myself. Men and women from Wildewall with elven blood, and wither-touched who would have likely ended up dead or facing made-up trials for having a hated gift."

"Endris, you smuggle people?" My jaw dropped. "Is that why you live in Wildewall?"

Endris pressed his lips into a thin line. "If this comes out, you kill me. Do you understand?"

"Yes," I mumbled, my mind still reeling from this revelation. "I understand."

After letting his gaze linger on me for a moment longer in warning, Endris turned to Oleander. "And you are squandering the second chance you've been given. Do you understand how incredibly lucky you are that Laurence is from the far southern coast and not a northerner who feels much more strongly about elves? Everyone on this side of the country lost someone in that war. Everyone on this side of the country will cut you down where you stand if they find out who you are."

Oleander's eyes were wide and watery. He looked at Endris, and then at me. "But... I want to stay with you," he told me. "We were going to be together in Wildewall."

"I know," I said. "But—"

"Lord Montbow? Lord Montbow!"

Oleander, Endris and I all jolted and whirled around when a female voice suddenly interrupted me. It came from the direction of the camp. Twigs snapped underneath boots, and a few moments later, Nele appeared in front of us. She bowed for me.

"Forgive me, lord Montbow, but you and your servants musn't leave the camp. It's simply not safe out here."

"Of course, I understand," I said. "I believe we are done here, regardless."

Oleander dodged my gaze, but there was nothing I could do or say about it. Nele escorted us back to our respective tents, and I already knew I wouldn't have a chance to talk to Endris or Oleander alone before we'd reach the city. I could still hardly wrap my mind around Endris being a smuggler, but making Oleander vanish was truly the safest option. If he just waited for me across the Starcross woods, I would happily bring him any book or knowledge I could find in Wildewall's library.

I hoped with all my might that Oleander would be gone by dawn, even if my chest hurt at the thought of possibly not seeing him for several weeks. But when the sun rose after a restless night, Oleander was still with us. Endris hid his disappointment well, not giving a single outward sign of what he had to be thinking. I had not quite mastered the same skills, so I kept my distance from Endris and Oleander as we packed up and left the Starcross woods.

Within a few hours, the land flattened, and the trees thinned, until we reached golden plains. Soon after, I saw large city walls looming in the distance, surrounded by a wide canal with glittering water. Behind the tall walls, even higher spiralling towers made of blinding white stone rose into the sky. They reminded me of Oleander. Even if the sparks coming from the stone were only the sun playing tricks on my eyes, they looked like flares of magic, just like his eyes. At the centre of the walls, there were two massive red stone gates. As we got closer, I recognised the gate's arched emblazoned symbols as god-touched signs. Mine, a branching bolt of lightning, was there too.

I was nervous for many reasons. Part of it was of course worry for Oleander's safety, but I was nervous for myself too. The city walls stretched as far as I could see, and the towers overlooking the city were so tall they made me feel tiny like an ant.

"You see how large those towers are, do you?" Ariane asked when she noticed me looking up. "Welcome to the city of wonders, which is not only the queen's home, but also the magical capital of the entire world. Widely admired by people for the splendour of our houses of worship."

"Yes, I have read about that," I replied vaguely.

Ariane didn't mention it, but the 'houses of worship' were part of a past competition that ended in tragedy. The larger your temple was, the higher your status. Priests of various gods, in a quest to show they worshipped their god more than any other, no longer paid mind to safety and whether their structures were actually strong enough not to collapse under the weight of a higher and higher towers.

The books about Wildewall I'd read said some of the collapsed buildings still lay in ruins in the temple district. Since then, beliefs had reformed into emphasising honouring gods equally and thanking all of them for the gifts they share with a few of us. Naturally, people still had their favourites in secret.

I snorted. "Well, at least the people of Wildewall eventually grew past the urge to compare temple-sizes."

Ariane ignored my remark. "Open your shirt," she stated flatly as we approached the stone bridge crossing over clear, glimmering water.

"My, you also want to see my bare chest?" I asked. "It's in very high demand these days."

"Don't flatter yourself. Reveal your mark," Ariane amended with a shake of her head.

"Fine." I opened a few buttons on my shirt to reveal the mark carved into my skin. "But now I wonder: what do people who have their mark on their lower stomach or leg do? Do they simply cut a piece of fabric from their pants or wear a shirt three sizes too small to show off their mark?"

Ariane just glared at me. I didn't get an answer while I genuinely wanted to know.

I received little time to mope or ponder about it further. As our horses stepped onto the bridge, hooves clopping on stone, there was movement up ahead. With a loud rumble that vibrated in my chest, the gates of Wildewall opened for us. I saw several stone-faced guards in blue uniforms behind the gates. The sides of the bridge had carvings of ferocious-looking dragons spitting fire on a swordsman.

Nothing about this was threatening. Not at all. My stomach lurched with nerves. I rolled my shoulders back and undid one more button of my shirt to show more of my mark. I had a creeping suspicion I was going to rely on it a lot in the coming few days to carry me and Oleander through this city and the queen's ball safely.

No Good Deed

- -

I had never seen so many people gathered in once place. Wilde-wall's streets were bustling with life. They made the Thunder-coast's docks, which used to be the largest marketplace I knew, seem tiny in comparison. I marvelled at the tall stone buildings, the foun-tains with dragon statues, and the countless of stands selling fresh fish, bread, pelts, jewellery, oils, and more. I didn't even recognise all the goods for sale or what their purpose was. Later, when we were out of Ariane's judgemental earshot, I'd ask Endris about them.

Despite the crowds, our passage was unhindered. As we rode our horses across the plaza, people hastily stepped aside like waves parting for frigates. Left and right, I felt eyes trained on my exposed chest. I did my best to ignore the stares until a woman up ahead shrieked. A loud thud followed her cry as her cart with wares toppled over. Apples, oranges, and other round fruits rolled our way across the ground.

My body reacted before my mind could catch up and question if what I was about to do meshed with Wildewall's etiquette. When I glimpsed the woman's horrified expression, I immediately brought Spot to a halt, dismounted, and started collecting pieces of fruit to bring back to the cart.

People leapt out of my way as I walked to the woman with my arms full of fruit. She had managed to push her cart upright, and I gently placed her wares back where they belonged. I didn't expect a thank you or a smile from the woman—people at the Thundercoast certainly never offered any acknowledgement. If I ever helped them, they ducked their heads and walked away before they were seen with a Montbow and got side-eyed by their neighbours. But I had also not expect the reaction I got here. When I turned to the woman, she had eyes like saucers and watery with tears. Her lips were parted in a silent scream. We made eye-contact for only a moment and then she dropped to her knees and pressed her forehead to the ground.

"Thunder god's chosen one. Please, don't punish me," she pleaded. "Please don't hurt me. I have children to feed."

I gaped at the woman. "What? No. Stand up. Why would I hurt you or punish you?"

Behind me, Ariane cleared her throat. "Laurence, my beloved, please, we must hurry. We have a long day ahead and we haven't time to punish merchants for their unsightly behaviour. Let us resume our journey."

Ariane put on a high-pitched, chirpy voice, making her sound every bit like a doting betrothed. I stared up at her in surprise, and she smiled softly at me. "Get back on your horse now, my sweet and leave the merchants to their business."

I opened my mouth to protest, but when I made an eye sweep of the street, I only found fear in the people's eyes. Some visibly flinched as I looked their way and lowered their gaze. Now I realised what Ariane meant. It was probably no use trying to talk to them while they seemed to be so scared. I quickly mounted Spot with a beet-red face.

Ariane's expression hardened as she turned to the merchant woman who had pressed herself against the ground. "You are in luck today, woman," she said. "Spread the news that Laurence Montbow, storm-touched, has arrived in Wildewall and we will spare you your punishment for slowing us down with your graceless presence."

"Y-yes, my lady," the woman stammered.

"Now, get out of our sight."

The woman scrambled to her feet. She ran to her cart and pulled it after her as she fled the scene, half running, half sliding down the road, leaving behind most of the fruit that had fallen on the ground. The bolder people surrounding us dove on the grapes, oranges, and apples like vultures, picking up the free treats as fast as they could. Nimbly, they danced out of the way of our horses' hooves as we started moving again.

The moment we were out of sight, Ariane glared at me. Already, there was nothing left of the adoring betrothed act she'd put up in front of the merchants."Laurence, for the love of the thunder god, could you please stop embarrassing yourself in every single place you enter?"

"I was only trying to help her!" I protested. "The poor woman lost most of her wares. How will she feed her children?"

Ariane clacked her tongue. "The only thing you just did is scare that poor women needlessly. When a noble, or even worse, a storm-touched, gets off their horse, it means you messed up and you will get punished. If you wanted to help that merchant, you would have ignored her to show her and the others that you're graciously giving her a pass for inconveniencing you."

I shot Ariane an incredulous look. "That's not helping. That's rude. The people of the Thundercoast never behave like this. They're not scared of us, and they shouldn't be."

Ariane responded with a shrug, "All I'm hearing is what I already knew: you Montbows have been soft. You're allowing them to sneer at you. Even disgraced, you can still reduce anyone to a fried blood smear on the walkway, but you allowed them to forget about your power by crawling for them. The people of Wildewall, on the other hand, still understand how easily you could snuff out every life in this street, should you so please."

"Yes, because waving your sword at all who oppose you has worked out so well for my uncle Harold," I retorted. "Fear-mongering and tyrannising definitely work. Until the people finally had enough and rise, which is the reason house Montbow is in the mess it is in now."

Ariane raised a brow. "There is middle ground to be found between being a tyrant like your uncle and rolling over like the rest of your family seems to want you to, my dear," she said. "Regardless, enough about that public embarrassment. We have future embarrassment to prevent. Let us head to the inn so we can change you into more appropriate garments for the city. You'll also need to get fitted for more outfits after the hearing tomorrow. Oh, but try not to talk to the tailor if you're going to behave like you're from the southern coast."

"I am from the southern coast," I replied. "Proudly so."

Ariane didn't respond. She only sighed deeply, and I didn't feel like arguing further, either. Even I realised it was probably a good idea to keep my mouth shut while there were so many eyes on me.

Ariane wasn't lying when she said people of Wildewall worshipped god-touched and that it would shock me how different things were in the capital. Oleander was also right when he said I was probably going to be in more trouble than he would be inside the city walls.

Ariane guided us away from the marketplace, and I was glad to leave my embarrassment behind. Crowds thinned, and we passed an arched bridge with more dragon engravings. The difference between the marketplace and the district on the other side of the bridge was night and day.

It was like stepping into an idyllic world. Lush green bushes with flowers in all the colours of the rainbow grew in orderly rows on the sides of the road, and the road itself ended in a sparkling, clear lake. A waterfall cascaded down from cliffs that formed a natural barrier around this part of the city. The walls, which were built up against the cliffs, continued further ahead.

Only the wealthy seemed to come to this part of town. I saw men and women dressed in frilly clothes and with many expensive-looking pieces of jewellery worn around fingers and necks. Many of them had servants shuffling after them with heavy bags. I still felt eyes resting on me, but the well-born people reacted in a whole different manner than the merchants and the commoners did. Instead of fear, I received double-takes with raised brows, followed by a curtsy or a bow. This response was a lot easier to deal with, especially since remembered from the etiquette book that I was to give these people a nod but to not acknowledge them further if they didn't have a mark.

Through a miracle that had to be the thunder god's work, we arrived at the inn without further incidents. Ariane steered towards a stone archway with a nameplate above it that read, in golden swirly letters, 'Prince Malte's Honour.' Through the archway, we entered a courtyard with fragrant flowerbeds. A building that was worthy of being named after a prince came into view.

Like the temples, the 'Prince Malte's Honour' inn was carved out of bright, white stone that lit up in the sun. The shape and style also reminded me of the spiralling towers in the gods worship area, but with flatter and wider towers, which I assumed were bedrooms for guests.

Beautiful as this inn was, staying at a place named after the prince who won humans the bloody elven war gave me a sense of foreboding. I didn't dare look at Oleander to see how he felt, but a stone settled in my stomach as we dismounted to head inside.

Five stable boys who somehow seemed to know exactly when we'd arrive appeared out of nowhere to take our horses. All the other inn staff seemed to be highly trained and even stealthy. The hostess welcomed us with a bright smile and a deep bow. We didn't have to wait a single moment before being escorted up the stairs, yet all my bags were already in my rooms before I reached my room myself. I hadn't seen a single person in the hallway bringing anything upstairs, making me sincerely wonder if the inn had trapdoors that allowed the servants to slip silently through the building.

The woman who'd showed me my room curtseyed and closed the door behind me. Before I knew it, I was standing in a luxurious inn room alone. My arrival at Wildewall had been a blur. I already missed my family, even Conrad and my dad, terribly. Valda would know how to act. Gisela wouldn't be daft enough to get off her horse to help a random woman in the street. She would've stopped me, too.

The sudden silence in the room made me realise my heart was pounding and every muscle in my body was tense. I breathed in and out deeply, grateful for the moment of respite, and took in my new environment.

The entire room reminded me of Ariane. Luxurious, needlessly extravagant, but also tasteful. The carpet was cyan blue with god-touched symbols woven into it. On the round table in the corner, grapes, cheese, and a carafe of what I guessed was some sort of fruit juice were stalled out. Two curved wooden chairs stood beside the table. I also had a four-poster bed with dark blue sheets, and an outfit was neatly folded on top of it. It looked similar to what the nobles outside wore, and I figured these were the 'more appropriate garments' I was to change into before heading outside again.

I ignored the clothes for now and walked over to a set of paintings on the wall first. The men and women portrayed all looked vaguely familiar to me. War heroes from history classes which I'd mostly slept through, but I guessed the handsome raven-haired man wearing a crown with a red gem embedded in it was prince Malte.

I snickered when I noticed one of the 'war heroes', a blonde woman, had a hole in her pants at the height of her thigh. She also had a mark in the shape of a sun and it seemed I'd been right all along. People actually did cut a hole in their clothing to make sure their mark was visible. Imagine having a mark on your ass. Your god had to really hate you if they branded you there.

With a smile still lingering on my lips, I walked over to the table and poured myself a glass of fruit juice. While I drank the liquid pure sweetness, I wondered where Oleander and Endris were right now. One of the inn staff had whisked them away to another place and I probably shouldn't be leaving them alone for too long in this city, especially Oleander.

Unfortunately, leaving my room meant worming myself into the 'appropriate garments.'

"Oh, you've got to be kidding me," I grumbled as I grabbed the outfit Ariane had chosen for me off the bed and gave it a proper look. Wildewall's weather was warm compared to the Thundercoast, but that didn't mean I want to walk around in a top that had so little fabric to it I might as well walk around bare-chested. There were almost no sleeves to speak of, and I'd be showing skin down to my navel. Why the tailor had even bothered putting two buttons at the bottom of the shirt so I could 'close' it was beyond me. At least the pants were normal, and I was even more grateful now my mark wasn't on my thigh or ass.

With a deep sigh, I sucked it up and slipped into the clothes. When I caught my reflection in the mirror, however, I almost laughed. It wasn't that I looked bad. My chest was broad and strong from years of shooting arrows daily, and the green fabric complimented my brown skin tone. But wearing a sleeveless green vest-like garment made of shiny and thin material wasn't exactly my usual style.

As I turned around to check myself from the back, there was a rapid knock on the door. "Laurence, are you changed yet?" Ariane's voice sounded through the door. "Are you coming downstairs?"

"I don't want to!" I called back. "Why exactly are you making me go outside half-naked?"

"Oh, would you stop being a child? This is god-touched fashion and all the others with a mark on their chest wear it too. Just come downstairs," Ariane huffed. Then her footsteps faded into the distance.

I cursed under my breath and glanced at myself in the mirror one last time. It'd take some getting used to, like many other things in Wildewall. I'd be happy if the hearing and the ball were behind me and I could go home.

Squaring my shoulders, I resigned to my fate, left my room, and headed downstairs.

In the common room of the inn, there was an audience waiting for me. Ariane, Nele, Endris and Oleander all looked up when I entered.

I immediately noticed none of them were made to change clothes. I might've complained about it, if I hadn't made eye-contact with Oleander first.

Like many people had today, Oleander was staring at my chest. Unlike all the others, however, it clearly wasn't about my mark. Oleander's gaze slowly wandered down to my midriff and abs. He bit his lips as he lifted his eyes to meet mine and the look he gave me, combined with his radiant beauty, made my face and ears burn. If we could have, I was certain we would've moved into my room right now.

Oleander blatantly seducing me with his gaze in front of Ariane and everyone else made words catch in my throat. Thankfully, Endris stepped in and saved me from having to speak.

"Lady Seydal, the hearing is tomorrow, correct?" he asked. "The day is still young. Would lord Montbow have the rest of his time today to see the city?"

Ariane crossed her arms. "And what would my beloved be planning on seeing today?"

"I want to go to the library," I said. Standing opposite Oleander, I suddenly remembered the promise I'd made to him: we'd go looking for his past. The history of the elves.

Ariane side-eyed me. "Because you are so interested in reading?"

"I would be inside somewhere not talking to people, and I will study my speech," I lied with a shrug. "It sounds like one of the safest places to be for a boorish south-coast man to me."

"I see." I still read suspicion in Ariane's expression as to my motives, but she didn't question me out loud.

"And I will take Endris and Oleander with me," I added. "Endris lives here. He can keep me out of trouble."

"Then I insist you also take one of my servants with you," Ariane replied, gesturing at Nele. "For protection."

I struggled to keep myself from grimacing. Having Nele there as a spy for Ariane would make it a lot more difficult to learn about elven history without her finding out. Endris, Oleander, and I would have to try to lose Nele inside the library because I couldn't think of a good reason to refuse Ariane's offer right now.

"That's very nice of you," I said with a forced smile.

"Visiting Wildewall's library is an excellent choice, lord Montbow," Nele politely told me. "There are many brilliant historians and scholars who know much of the city. I noticed you had an interest in the elven wars, so I would especially recommend speaking with Ezra Dagon, the most knowledgeable historian on elven culture in this city."

"I believe we shouldn't," Endris interjected before I could open my mouth. "He's very busy."

"Surely he's not too busy for lord Montbow," Nele shot back with a smile. "It's truly not a problem."

Oleander stood hesitatingly beside me, his green eyes searching my face. A historian specialised in elven history sounded exactly like the kind of person we needed, but I'd caught Endris' reluctance to see the historian loud and clear too.

"We'll see what we'll do when we get there," I answered vaguely.

Endris' jaw clenched like he'd hoped for me to decline the offer ful-ly, but I couldn't take my words back now. Seeing Endris' suppressed frustration made me feel like I'd just made another mistake—one much worse than helping a woman in the street.

Familiar Ties

T he woman at the front desk of the library raised her hand, or-
dering us to stop without looking up from her leather-bound
book. "Names and purpose in the library?" she drawled.

Nele cleared her throat and stepped sideways so the librarian saw
me.

The elderly woman raised her eyes with a deep sigh, then
dropped her quill in the ink when her gaze landed on my chest.
"Storm-touched," she breathed, leaning over the wooden desk. She
dipped her head in submission, her grey hair dangling dangerously
close to the candle. "My apologies, I—I didn't notice. Please, head
right on in, sir. Your servants as well. We're honoured to have you at
our library."

"Uh, thank you," I replied with an awkward smile, not quite used
to the special treatment yet. I probably wouldn't be able to get used
to it even if I spent many years in Wildewall.

While I stepped past the front desk with hesitance, Nele seemed to
know her way around and strode across the entrance hall. She ges-

tured for us to follow her. Long corridors lit by candlelight stretched out in front of us. The ceiling was high, arching to what I estimated had to be at least twenty feet above us.

Nele led us to a set of wooden doors, which had stone statues in the shape of a robed man and a woman standing on each side like guardians. Endris stepped forward and opened one door for me, Oleander and Nele, and then we found ourselves in the middle of a gigantic open room.

Light poured in from windows overhead. Tall shelves filled with books were lined up as far as my eyes could see, and many scholars shuffled through the aisles. In the corners I spotted small reading desks with chairs, but on the first-floor balcony, there were more spaces which appeared to be private studying rooms. I hoped to retreat in one of those later.

"So, you people in Wildewall are just incapable of creating small, humble buildings, then?" I joked in Nele's direction.

She grinned at me. "Do it grand, or don't do it at all, lord Montbow. And if it's knowledge of the elves you seek, I would only bring you to the place with the most knowledgeable historians."

"Yes, and Ezra Dagon is most certainly the best of them all," Endris agreed, his gaze deliberately trained on me. "He knows everything there is to know of the elven war, their history... and their mannerisms."

Even after he finished speaking, Endris kept staring at me intently. He'd been making similar remarks during the ride to the library, but now that he emphasised mannerisms it suddenly hit me. What Endris had been trying to tell me all along.

Nele was bringing us straight to a historian who was the foremost authority on elves in this city. The historian would likely recognise elven characteristics in Oleander when faced with him. Shit.

The thought stopped my heart dead in my chest. I'd nearly been too late. We were already in the library. A shiver of panic and dread raced down my spine as I realised I had to come up with a reason to either dismiss Oleander without raising Nele's suspicion or to blatantly refuse seeing Ezra Dagon within the next few moments.

I chose the latter.

"I appreciate your offer, Nele," I said. "But I won't see the historian today. I want to practice for my hearing tomorrow. And Endris and Oleander will stay with me as well."

Nele's jaw went slack in surprise. Then she regained her composure and bowed curtly. "Of course, lord Montbow. I wouldn't want to impose."

I acted like the arrogant storm-touched they seemed to want me to be here and didn't react to Nele's apology. I turned away from her and looked up at the balcony. "Is there a place where I can study on my own in here, Nele?"

"Yes, naturally," Nele said. "It's on the first floor, as you had already guessed. Please, follow me."

I nearly breathed a sigh of relief, thinking I'd avoided catastrophe. Endris' face relaxed visibly as well.

And then Oleander opened his mouth.

"Excuse me, lord Montbow. I would like to spend some time reading books," he spoke up softly. "May I join you in your study room later?"

"Absolutely not," blurted out of my mouth much harsher than I'd meant it in a flash of panic.

Oleander's eyes widened, and I almost apologised to him. I wanted to explain this library was so large that losing someone in the rows of books was easy, and I couldn't risk him running into someone with evil intentions while alone. But I had to bite my tongue in front of Nele.

"I need you to stay in my sight," I continued in a calmer tone. "We can return here another time."

While I had received Endris' subtle message loud and clear, it appeared Oleander hadn't. He looked crestfallen at my sudden rejection and nodded meekly.

"If you want, I can help you find some books on elven history later, Oleander," Nele offered, seemingly feeling sorry for him.

"Find books on elven history? In here? Hah!" Behind us, a male voice chortled. I turned and saw nobody until I turned my gaze down. A very short, ancient-looking man looked back up at me with beady, sparkling eyes that reminded me of magpies. A mane of wild grey hair circled his crown with a bald hole in the middle.

"Master Dagon," Nele greeted him.

"Nele and Endris," he replied with a kind smile that nearly made his eyes disappear behind folds of skin.

"This is Ezra Dagon, the historian I told you about, lord Mont-bow," Nele said excitedly, right before her face fell as she remembered I didn't want to see him today.

I didn't want to see him for a damn good reason. I felt the colour drain from my face as Ezra glanced at Oleander and I subtly moved myself in front of him, blocking Ezra's vision. Endris did the same and helped me hide the elf in the library filled with people who hated elves. By the thunder god's wrath, what had we gotten ourselves into?

Ezra raised a curious brow, but he didn't comment on our strange behaviour. He wasn't tall nor broad enough to easily look past me and Endris without leaning to the side.

"Lord Montbow, young storm-touched, proud Southerner, I would certainly not waste my time on the trite elven propaganda you will find in here." Ezra spread his hands, gesturing at the books surrounding us. "You must know these works, if we can call them that, are full of lies."

"Are they, well—" I tried to interrupt Ezra, wanting to send Oleander and Endris away from us quickly. But the old historian didn't acknowledge my attempt at speaking.

"You must know that the elves were not hideous, like many history books like to claim," Ezra continued. "They were actually quite beautiful. Appealing to humans with large eyes, long lashes, and graceful movements. And while us people like to think they were forest-dwelling savages, most were well-groomed like nobles."

"No kidding," I muttered, sending Endris a wry glance over my shoulder. "Ezra, why don't we—"

"In fact, being so beautiful and aesthetically appealing to us humans made the elves a lot more dangerous," Ezra went on, lost in his own story. "They used the fact that we easily put our trust in beautiful people against us to make children especially walk with them into the dark Starcross woods, never to be seen again." Ezra frowned. "As a result of that strong attractiveness, there are a lot of half-elves or part-elves, too. There are no consequences from doing so. Their children could breed, too."

"Fascinating," I said, but definitely remembering to stay on my guard. Judging by what Endris said, admitting you even had a drop of elven blood in Wildewall was dangerous business. Something Ezra affirmed a moment later as well.

"If someone has elven blood, however, they best not reveal it. It won't end well for them," the old historian said with a chuckle and an amused shake of his head.

I wisely kept my mouth shut and only nodded with a tight-lipped smile. The next step would be to end the conversation and leave, shuffling forward to ensure Ezra didn't accidentally catch a good look at Oleander.

Twice now, however, Oleander didn't seem to understand he had to keep quiet.

"What happens to people who reveal it?" Oleander's voice rang out. He brushed past Endris and stood beside me, a defiant look I knew all too well on his delicate features. The last time I'd seen Oleander look like this, he had poisoned himself with a Bleeding Ivy leaf just to prove a point.

"Oleander," I warned him with my heart drumming wildly in my chest. Ezra could see his face now. "Don't talk to master Dagon. Why don't you go looking for books? You wanted to, right?"

"That's quite alright, young storm-touched," Ezra soothed me before turning to Oleander. "Oleander, was it? An interesting name choice."

I held my breath as Ezra's beady eyes narrowed for a moment. But then he smiled pleasantly. "Anyway, Oleander, if you reveal elven blood in a human town, you have a death wish. It's not against the law on paper, but people like that tend to disappear. Like them whither-touched. The elven gift that killed our children. There are many families here who have a story of the war. A grandmother or a grandfather taken by elves of perishing. It's sensitive here in the North."

I saw Oleander's nostrils flare as he breathed in and out deeply. His jaw set. "How sensitive?" he asked tersely.

With a sound somewhere between a giggle and a snort, Ezra raised his finger to the ceiling. We all looked up, but saw nothing but a roof. Then, a few moments later, temple bell chimes coming from outside entered the library through the windows.

It seemed to be the sign Ezra had been waiting for. He snapped his fingers and lowered his arm. "That is an excellent question, Oleander. And you arrived on the right day to ask it. Come." Ezra fervently gestured for us to come with him, his puff of hair bouncing on his head.

"What do the bells mean, Ezra?" I asked.

"You'll see."

Ezra started walking.

"Don't go with him, Oleander," Endris said. "You will find nothing you want to see out there. It's a trial."

Oleander glanced at Endris, but didn't hesitate a moment and promptly followed Ezra. Endris cursed under his breath and glared at me like this was all my fault. We both understood Oleander would not be stopped, however, and we rushed after him. Nele, in turn, rushed after me.

As we exited the library, the sun stung in my eyes after getting used to the warm candlelight. The chimes grew louder and faster.

"Hurry now, we're going to miss it!" Ezra called out over his shoulder. The ancient man was deceptively fast on his tiny feet and kept ahead of me despite me almost jogging. I almost lost Ezra in the commotion, because there were many people attracted by the chiming coming from the temple. These people seemed to pay my mark less mind, distracted by something up ahead.

A large crowd gathered in the square in front of one of the tall, spiralling temples. I caught sight of two men standing on a platform in front of the temple. One of them carried a sword, and one of them was masked and bound. A dozen more men in heavy armour guarded the staircase that led up to the platform.

My blood ran cold as I realised what Oleander was about to witness. This wasn't just a trial, it was also the execution of the punishment. I grabbed his arm. "We need to leave," I told him. I tugged on his arm, but Oleander yanked himself free.

"No," he said firmly.

While Ezra seemed content to wait a distance away from the platform, even if I couldn't imagine the small man being able to see anything going on from here, Oleander kept pushing forward.

"Damn it," Endris said as he started elbowing his way after Oleander. "Oleander, stop!"

Up ahead, the bells stopped chiming. The man carrying the sword ripped the mask off of his prisoner's face.

"Help, no!" the prisoner wailed, utterly terrified. "I don't have elven blood, I swear! Why won't anyone believe me?"

"Silence!" the man with the sword boomed. "We will not listen to your forked-tongued lies!"

The grim reality dawned on me fast. This was one of the 'unfair trials.' They were about to kill this man, elven-blooded or not, right in front of Oleander.

I couldn't let that happen.

While I had been uncomfortable with the attention the townsfolk gave me for my mark, now I was ready to wield the full power of it. Lifting one hand, I made thunder crackle inside my palm. Left and right, people gasped and leapt out of the way, similar to the merchants in the market district.

My path freed up as people crashed into each other to get out of my way. I rushed forward and reached the stairs before Oleander did.

"Wait!" I called out to the men on the platform.

The armoured guards in front of me seemed confused about what to do. They likely had orders to let none pass, but they weren't faced with an unfamiliar storm-touched in the crowd often. Even the armed man on the platform, who I assumed was the leader of this execution, momentarily hesitated. Then his gaze hardened. "Please, do not interfere with city justice, blessed storm-touched."

"Then tell me what this man did!" I demanded. "You talk of justice, but where's your proof that he did something wrong?"

Oleander reached my side and grabbed my arm. His fingernails dug into my skin. "Please, Laurence, help him," he pleaded quietly.

The captain narrowed his eyes and nodded at two of the guards on the staircase. They marched forward with a clear intent to intimidate me.

I straightened my back. "I asked a simple question that deserves an answer," I said through gritted teeth.

Behind me, people started booing as the crowd grew restless at the delay.

"Kill him!" a shrill woman's voice demanded. "Kill the filthy half-elf!"

A hand landed heavily on my shoulder. "It's too late," Endris hissed in my ear. "We can't help him, and you can't risk spoiling all your goodwill in this city, nor can we let Oleander stay in this crowd. Think this through!"

I turned to Endris. His dark eyes were haunted and it was clear as day he wanted to help the prisoner, whether he was actually elven or not, just as much as we did. He had the wisdom Oleander and I lacked, however; to choose our battles and to choose them wisely.

I glanced at Oleander's wide, pleading eyes, and then at Endris. I knew what the wise decision was, but I also knew I wouldn't be a blessing to live with myself it I stepped back. Instead of backing down, I stepped onto the staircase. It seemed the guards had anticipated this move, however. I groaned as a strong pain in the back of my legs made me fall down on the sharp edges of the steps. My arms were twisted on my back by a guard, and the man on the platform looked vaguely disappointed at my decision. Then he stomped the back of his prisoner's legs, so the poor man dropped to his knees with a pained whimper.

Steel flashed in the sunlight, and it was over. The half-elf prisoner hit the ground. He gurgled as the sword left his body and Oleander cried out. Endris held a tight grip on his arm and started dragging him away under only feeble protest. The guard who sat on top of me to keep me down loosened his grip and I stood with a huff, glaring at him. There was nothing I could do anymore, however. The half-elf was already dead. Then I mouthed a sorry to him, a stone sinking in my stomach as I turned away.

While the crowd cheered and celebrated, Endris led us to a back alley away from the noise. It seemed we had lost Nele for the time being.

A pregnant silence filled the air between us until Endris finally sighed. "Do you get it now?" he snapped. "This is why I don't want you in the capital, Oleander. This is what happens to people who get caught in here! Why don't you ever listen?"

Oleander looked down at the ground. He didn't respond to Endris' scolding.

Endris looked at me. "And you. You really don't know anything outside of a simple life at the Thundercoast, do you? You cannot yell at a paladin and demand for him to explain himself or bullrush him! The only reason you're not dead right now is because of that mark on your chest."

Like Oleander, I didn't respond. Endris' words stung, but not as much as seeing Oleander hurt.

Pressing a hand to his forehead, Endris paced through the alley. "I can't help you survive this city if you run amok and do whatever the hell you want. If you draw the attention of historians and expose us to—" Endris stopped abruptly in the middle of his sentence and stiffened.

"Expose us to what?" I asked.

"He means us, Laurence. As in me and Endris," Oleander said softly.

"You..." I gaped at Endris.

Endris crossed his arms. He looked behind him and above him to check nobody was there. "I am related to Sage Farun," then he curtly stated. "In a distant past, one of his sisters mingled with my grandfather."

I opened and closed my mouth, struggling to come up with what I was supposed to say to that. Endris didn't give me a chance to recover, however. He turned his back on me. "We are going back to the inn," he announced, marching off without awaiting a response.

The Fire in You

E ndris retreated into his room once we made it back to the inn.
The door slammed shut and stayed shut.

Oleander walked with me to the common room, but he sat in the
corner with his arms crossed, seemingly lost in thought. He politely
asked me to be left alone. Nele was still nowhere to be found. I felt
slightly guilt for leaving her behind in the crowd outside, but she'd
find us again, eventually.

Considering the hearing about knight commander Ytel was tomorrow, I read my notes one more time in an attempt to learn my
plea by heart. I was utterly unsuccessful. When Nele finally walked
into the inn a while later, I hadn't read a single word.

Nele's eyebrows twitched when she saw me sitting at the table. She
tried to suppress her annoyance at me abandoning her in the square,
but I easily read it in her gait as she approached.

"Lord Montbow," she greeted me. "Pardon me for losing you in the
crowd for a moment there."

"We left," I replied crisply. "We didn't know we'd be exposed to barbaric practices if we went to the square. If we had, we wouldn't have gone. We don't execute people in front of houses of worship at the Thundercoast."

"With all due respect, this isn't the Thundercoast, my lord," Nele said, only a thin layer of politeness remaining in her tone now. It seemed Wildewall locals didn't take well to it when their customs were criticised by a peasant from outside the walls. "Priest Landefort addressed me about your interruption of the trial. He wants compensation."

I sighed. "If it's coin he wants, I will pay him later. Priest Landefort can get in line."

"No, lord Montbow. He wants your servant," Nele nodded at Oleander, "to work at his temple of fate to repent. For a week."

I turned to Oleander. He planted his hands on the armrests of his chair and shot upright, visibly startled.

"No, absolutely not," I retorted immediately. "Oleander is here as a guest of the queen. He's not going into temple service or whatever the priest has planned for him." I frowned. "Why does he call himself a priest while he cuts people down with a sword, anyway? That's not what a priest does."

"In Wildewall," Nele emphasised, "a priest is an authority who may perform punishments in the name of their temple, lord Montbow."

"And he already performed his punishment," I said. "Tell him I would be happy to personally pay his temple tribute if that softens the blow to his ego, but he's not getting Oleander. He did nothing wrong."

Nele shook her head incredulously. "My lord, this is a very generous offer from priest Landefort. It would only be a few days of light service inside the temple, then Oleander would be released and they would forgive you for the interruption. And naturally, Oleander would be allowed to go to the queen if he was summoned by her."

"My answer for priest Landefort is no. Oleander is not going any-where," I repeated firmly.

A hint of annoyance passed over Nele's features as she glanced at Oleander, perhaps wondering what was so special about him that I wouldn't allow him out of my sight for even a week. Then she curtseyed. "As you wish, lord Montbow. But I feel compelled to warn you the priest won't be pleased. The temple of fate is powerful. This could have consequences for your hearing tomorrow."

"So be it," I said. "If he's looking to collect, then I will pay him or I will go into service for a week, but not Oleander."

Nele stared at me, almost horrified. I had a feeling the nobles from Wildewall would never submit themselves to servitude. But ducking my head and falling in line had been my life so far. I knew who I was and what my mark meant to people, but I truly hoped to never reach a point where my pride would impede my ability to protect my loved ones or taking responsibility for things I did. Even if the Montbows were reinstated at the court and I received all the luxuries my heart desired, I would remember what living in exile was like.

"Please let him know my decision, Nele," I said.

Nele opened her mouth, seemingly to protest, but she shut it again before a word came out. "As you wish."

Nele departed from the inn soon after, and I was left with a dull headache and a boring speech I still needed to learn for tomorrow. I glanced at Oleander to check if he was alright after this uncomfortable exchange. While the sadness in his eyes about the half-elven man lingered, Oleander smiled softly at me. Then he stood and walked to the bookcase. As he passed me, I felt his hand subtly brush against my shoulder. Even with Nele gone, we had to behave like lord and servant—we were still being watched by the inn staff. We couldn't speak entirely freely, but we could exchange looks while Oleander read, and I made notes for the hearing.

Word of what I did with priest Landefort and how I refused to hand Oleander to him would reach Ariane's ears, likely before dusk today. I had assumed I'd get a scolding into the morning when she arrived for dinner, but Ariane never came back to the inn. Nele didn't return to the common room either. When I retreated to my bedroom later, however, there was a familiar-looking man stationed in front of the door. One of Ariane's servants. The man with a face cut from marble. He stepped aside and let me enter my room without saying a word. When I looked out my bedroom's window, I saw more of Ariane's servants patrolling in the courtyard. It seemed she'd certainly left people watching me, even if she and Nele weren't here.

It was probably for the better. I hadn't exactly made myself liked in Wildewall today, and I had the hearing tomorrow and the queen's ball to look forward to. If today was an indication of how those events would go, it would end in catastrophe.

Tonight could well be the last quiet night I'd be having in a while, so I had the inn's staff draw me a bath. I could use the soothing, hot water to help me relax, and I needed a body of water nearby to pray to the thunder god. Normally, I was at the coast and near the sea. During out travels, I'd looked for a river or lake. In the city, a bathtub would have to make do.

While sighing at the sensation of hot water engulfing me, I prayed for fortune tomorrow. I prayed for my family's safety at home. I also wished I could share this luxury with Oleander, who was stuck in the servant's quarters. If I summoned Oleander to my room, however, that would certainly reach Ariane's ears, and I'd face her wrath. Even more so than I already would for my run in with the priest.

Although I had little going for me the past few days, it appeared the god of thunder was listening to at least one of my prayers tonight.

My eyes shot open when I heard a sliding window, followed by a quiet thud of someone landing gracefully on the floor inside my room. It was a familiar sound, yet, when light footsteps approached the bathroom, I had a brief moment of panic. I gripped the sides of the bathtub and pulled myself to a sitting position, preparing to channel my magic if this wasn't who I thought it was.

And then Oleander appeared at the entrance of the bathroom. His eyes widened when he saw me.

"Ah, I'm sorry!" he apologised when he saw I was in the bathtub. "I didn't know you weren't decent." Oleander turned his back on me and stepped away from the entrance, but not until after he swiftly let his eyes trail down as far as he could before the rippling water protected my modesty.

A flush crept up my cheeks as I grabbed the towel and raised myself out of the tub, sprinkling water all over the floor in my haste. "It's alright," I said. "But you have to tell me how you're able to keep entering my room like this."

Oleander chuckled. "Are you decent now?"

I glanced down at the towel around my waist. "Yes, I suppose," I said.

Oleander stepped into view. Again, he didn't hide the way his eyes glided down my chest to my navel before he settled his gaze on my face. "Nobody seems to pay attention to the servants in this city," he said. "That is how I move unseen."

"That can't be true," I replied. "You're far too beautiful to miss."

Oleander smiled. "You flatter me."

"I mean it. But..." I walked over to the window and peered down. The walls were steep and smooth, and I couldn't for the life of me figure out how Oleander had scaled them. "Those walls aren't climbable. Seriously. How did you get up here?"

"Ah, but these walls are climbable for me," Oleander said. "The smallest nooks and crannies can be used as an anchor point if you know how."

"How...do you know how? Have you started remembering more?"

Oleander was silent for a moment. His smile faded, and he turned away from me. "Flashes, fleeting memories, and dreams. Like before."

"I see." I closed the drapes and took a step away from the window. I looked at Oleander's back and his silvery ponytail. Compared to this afternoon, during which Oleander had seemed sad and faraway with his thoughts, he seemed to do better now. I didn't want to make Oleander sad again, but we had to discuss today now that we had the chance.

"Oleander, our meeting with the historian and the execution on the square showed the dangers of the city," I said carefully. "Are you sure you want to be here? Endris is right: there doesn't seem to be anything good for you to find here."

Oleander turned on his heels. He looked deeply into my eyes. "Are you sure you will walk the path of the knight, will wed Ariane, and cannot be persuaded otherwise?"

"What?" I frowned. "I don't see how those two things are related."

"Laurence, it is clear to me you never wanted your storm blessing or the consequences of it." Oleander let out a soft sigh. "But it's in you, regardless. Something larger than you chose you, and you can't turn your back on your gift and what it means. In a similar way, it's not that easy for me either."

I shook my head in confusion. "I don't understand what you mean."

Oleander swallowed. He opened and closed his mouth as he tried to find words. "I mean the life you're more attuned to, Laurence. I..." Oleander faltered. "Your heart longs for another place and time. You're not where you should be. Don't you want to be home on the coast rather than facing a hearing? To not murder innocent creatures in the mountains for an arbitrary badge of honour from a queen and a court you don't know or care for? To not wed a woman you don't love out of duty?"

For a moment, I didn't recognise the Oleander standing in front of me. He spoke louder and his voice had lost its usual soft gentleness. Even his entire demeanour seemed different. I'd never thought of Oleander as weak, but now he reminded me of the way Conrad looked when he snuck out of the mansion at night. Dangerous and sharp. The memory of Oleander in our living quarters, dodging my father's cast rock with cat-like nimbleness, came to mind.

"I do these things because I want to take care of my family," I said. "I have to."

"Yes," Oleander muttered. "And you wouldn't be you if you didn't want to help them, because you're good. You're good. But you have to choose a side in the end, Laurence. You can't help everyone."

I shook my head, confused again at what Oleander was trying to say.

"You stand up for a half-elven man you don't even know in the square," Oleander clarified. "You heard Nele. This will considerably complicate the hearing regarding Ytel's death. It lowers your standing with the court further once they catch wind of it. You can't protect both your family and every accused half-elf in this city."

Oleander sighed. "But I should tell myself those words first. You wouldn't have followed me outside if I hadn't run away. That was foolish of me. I'd let my emotions get the better of me. A potentially very costly mistake, and I'm sorry."

I just stared at Oleander. "Oleander, you're... you're very different tonight," I said. "You don't sound like yourself. It's been a long day. Perhaps you just need some rest." My eye fell on the bowl filled with fresh fruits in the corner of the room. I gestured at it. "Have something to eat and drink. I don't understand how to peel or eat half of these, but maybe you do. Oh, but be careful if you want to cut them. The knife is sharp."

Oleander followed my gaze. He looked pained. I couldn't read the look in his eyes well as he regarded the fruit and drinks I offered. Then he shook his head and turned back to me.

"I'm sorry, Laurence," he repeated.

"No, don't be. I'm the last person who is allowed to scold another for letting their emotions get the better of them in the heat of the moment." I took a step closer to Oleander. "It'll be fine. I'll sort it out with the hearing tomorrow. If not, you have already helped the Montbow family so much with ways to earn new coin. Perhaps we won't rejoin the court in the end, but we won't starve."

I opened my arms and wrapped them around Oleander. He stiffened for a moment, but then welcomed and leaned into my embrace, settling against my chest and closing his eyes. "Just tell me one thing, Laurence."

"Yes?"

"Tell me you don't want to be a knight, and that you don't want to marry Lady Seydal. Don't talk about choice or family or duty. Only tell me about what you want."

"I want..." I licked my lips nervously. It was hard admitting it, even if I'd thought about not wanting my blessing or my arranged marriage a million times. So many would have hoped to stand in my place. All my siblings would take my storm-touched gift in a heartbeat. They'd gratefully accept being head of my family, and yet, I was the one who had received the honour. The only one who wasn't suited for the role.

I breathed in and out deeply. "I don't want to be a knight, and I don't want to marry Ariane," I said, the words feeling strange to my tongue even if I'd thought them many times.

Oleander lifted his head and looked up at me. "It's a painful fate if the fire in you would never truly roar because it never had a reason to," he whispered. "Because you haven't found your passion."

Oleander had said something similar to me a while ago, while we were standing on the cliffs. I hadn't realised it at the time, but now I understood he meant us, in this room, in each other's arms.

"Oleander," I muttered.

"Yes."

Oleander titled his chin up while I leaned down, and our lips met in a passionate kiss. His hands slowly travelled down my sides to my waist, his touch leaving goosebumps on my skin. Then his thumbs hooked behind my towel, and he tugged, making it fall to the ground as our kiss grew deeper. We started moving to the bed. Oleander's hand pressed to my bare chest as he gently guided me backward.

My stomach flipped nervously. I'd hoped for this for a while now. I'd wanted this. But now that the moment seemed to be here, I was painfully aware of my lack of experience. Everyone always expected me to take the lead as the Montbow heir, but it seemed Oleander didn't.

Oleander broke our kiss as we reached the bed. Grinning darkly at me, he gave me a surprisingly hard shove, making me land on my back on the mattress. The realisation that he stood fully clothed at the end of the bed while I was completely naked made my face down to my neck grow hot with embarrassment.

Oleander didn't look at me, however. He strode over to the bowl of fruit, and brought a green fruit I didn't recognise with him back to the bed. He placed it on the nightstand.

I subtly reached for the sheets to cover myself, but Oleander was beside me in a flash, placing his hand on mine to stop my movements. "Laurence, you have no reason to blush," he said, softly kissing my cheek. "I should be the one blushing. You're impressive. And the mark of your thunder god does continue much further down. I am glad to have found out the answer to that question."

"Ah, yeah, it even dips below my..." I started replying, but I got distracted and trailed off as Oleander reached for his hair tie, undid it, and strands of silver cascaded down his shoulders.

"Navel," I breathed.

Oleander hummed. A smirk tugged at his lips as he stepped out of his pants and opened his shirt, letting it drop to the floor. I stared at his bare body and held my breath. Oleander was slender, but also lean and poised. I hadn't looked at him as closely in the mountains, but I did now. I took in the subtle curve of his hips, his flat stomach, and the wiry muscles of his arms. He looked strong as well as beautiful.

"Is it more sensitive, too?" Oleander asked.

"What?" I asked dumbly.

Oleander chuckled as he crawled beside me on the bed. "Your mark," he said. "Is it more sensitive?"

"I don't think so, only when I use—"My breath caught in my throat as Oleander leaned down and kissed the branch of my mark on my collarbone. "My magic," I finished my sentence with a sigh. "Maybe it is more sensitive."

A wicked grin appeared on Oleander's face. "A shame it didn't cover your entire manhood as well, then.

"You want me to get aroused every time I used my magic?"

"Yes," Oleander said. "And if it aroused you, I would now want to tie you up, tell you to channel your magic, and watch you squirm without a single touch."

I gaped at Oleander. The sharp contrast between his innocent, green eyes and freckled face and the words coming out of his mouth made me turn an even deeper shade of red.

When Oleander noticed he had me at a loss for words, he looked pleased with himself and scooted over to the nightstand. He grabbed the green piece of fruit he'd brought to the bed earlier. It was elongated with tapered ends.

"Did you know this fruit provides a sort of... juice that is used to lessen friction?" Oleander asked. He grabbed both ends of the fruit and snapped it in half. The insides of the fruit were hollow and white, and a bit of transparent juice dripped out.

Oleander lowered one half of the fruit down and let it hover above my manhood. He tilted his head to the side and looked at me. "May I?"

I nodded and twitched when the cool liquid poured on me. Oleander set the fruit aside on the nightstand once it was empty. When I didn't move straight away, Oleander pecked my lips. "Are you just going to lie there now, my lord?" he asked teasingly, his eyes sparkling. "I was hoping you'd finally be comfortable enough to braid my hair now."

I let out a laugh. "No, that is definitely still too inappropriate," I joked, while reaching out to brush a strand of silver behind Oleander's pointed ear. Oleander leaned into my touch, lips parting in a content sigh. Encouraged by his reaction, I let my hands wander down Oleander's shoulders to his flat stomach, admiring the smooth, freckled skin while my heart pounded in my throat.

I would have been content taking it slow and getting to know each other's body with soft touches and stolen kisses throughout the night, but Oleander was less patient. He allowed me to explore his body for a few moments longer, but then he grabbed my hands and placed them on his waist as he straddled me.

That night, I finally learned what Oleander had been trying to teach me on the cliffs. All this life was about wasn't my mark, my duty, or coin. What I needed was Oleander's gaze clouding over in pure bliss, his heavy breathing and moans in my ear, his silvery hair tickling my chest, and the fire inside both of us roaring.

Verdict

At the crack of dawn, I woke up to an empty bed, a glare in my eye, and loud banging on my door.

Groaning, I shielded my face from the sun and shifted myself upright. I looked at the nightstand and found the culprit of the glare: a fruit knife sitting innocently on the wooden surface. The rays of the sun reflecting on its blade cast light into my eyes. Half of a piece of green fruit laid next to the knife. A drop of transparent liquid clung to its edge. The memory of Oleander breaking the fruit open with an impish smirk playing on his lips brought heat to my cheeks.

I flinched as the banging on my door grew louder.

"What is it?" I called out.

"It's time to rise, lord Montbow," Endris' voice sounded on the other side of the door. "You mustn't be late for your hearing."

"Yes." I sighed. "Be right there."

I brushed a hand through my unruly hair and stared at the empty spot beside me on the bed. The sun shining into my room warmed my face but not my heart. It was cold without Oleander here. I knew he couldn't possibly have stayed the night, but I wished he had, anyway. I wished we would be here in each other's arms, rather than him in a servant's room and me facing a trial.

After stretching out, I made myself stand. The faster I would go to the courtroom, the faster this would be behind me. Then there was the queen's ball, and then I could hopefully leave Wildewall and the court behind me for the foreseeable future.

I donned myself in clothes which seemed to be made for gallivanting and showing off wealth. There was an unreasonable amount of gemstones embedded in the tunic's fabric, but at least I wasn't half-naked today.

Unfortunately, I would have to be alone. Much as I would have liked Oleander in the room for moral strength while I stood trial, I decided it was too risky to expose him to a crowd. I left him at the inn, hoping he would understand, while Ariane, Endris, Nele, and a few more of Ariane's servants escorted me to the trial court.

Last night, I was the happiest man in this city. This morning, I was in a courtroom facing a trial, on behalf of my entire family, for a crime I didn't commit. One Ytel had brought on himself by coming to the Thundercoast intending to steal Montbow land.

Also, nobody had told me trials were public events in Wildewall. Well, at least not this public.

Seemingly, they were very popular events. The trial court was a tall building consisting of one fully open room with an audience of at least two-hundred people already present. I halted at the entrance, losing my bearings for a moment at suddenly being confronted with this many people.

I was also very aware that everyone would see my hesitation should they look over their shoulder at me now. Several people did, and murmurs started echoing through the room.

"Laurence, move!" Ariane hissed in my ear. Her palm pressed against my back and she pushed me.

With my heartbeat in my throat I walked, one foot in front of the other, past stone-faced guards stationed at the entrance. I tried my best to ignore the rows of people on my left and right, all staring at me. Looking ahead wasn't much better, unfortunately. There was a judge with eyes dark like onyxes staring at me from a table positioned on a stage that towered over the crowd. A council of eight people wearing all black surrounded her, four on the left and four on the right. Hoods decorated with god-touched symbols covered half the council members' expressionless faces.

As I walked further into the room, I realised there was also a balcony above me, filled with men and women donned in fancy clothes. These had to be the noble born attendants of the trial, seated up high and always making sure they were ascended above the common folk. Priest Landefort was among them, literally looking down on me just like the judge.

I was grateful my back would be turned towards the audience as I spoke to the judge and the council. Endris had prepared me for the trial and it worked here in Wildewall. In essence, it was very simple. The judge and her council would listen while I told my story. They would have listened to Ytel's story after mine, but he was no longer here to defend himself.

I swallowed nervously. The words I said today were on behalf of my entire family, Oleander and Endris. For everyone who had been present at the Thundercoast the day Ytel died. Standing alone with a council and a judge in front of me and an audience behind me, I felt incredibly small.

I hoped sincerely that my voice would come out even as I opened my mouth. "Your honour. Highly esteemed members of the council," I spoke the words Endris had written down for me. "Knight commander Ytel's untimely death was an unfortunate event and we, too, mourn the loss of one of Wildewall's finest at the Thundercoast."

While I talked, one of the jury members took off his hood, revealing Ezra Dagon's lined face. He winked at me, leaned over to the judge, and whispered something in her ear.

A moment later, the judge held up her hand.

I didn't know what to do. Ariane nor Endris had never told me they could interrupt me in my plea. They told me the judge would let me talk. Maybe I'd be asked a few questions, to which I'd repeat parts of what I'd already said during my plea. The sign of holding up one's hand up was universal, however. I quieted down while my stomach lurched with nerves.

"Did the Montbows kill knight commander Ytel?" the judge asked me. Her voice was monotonous, her expression blank. I couldn't read her intentions with these questions.

I wetted my bottom lip. "Knight commander Ytel was killed in the thick and chaos of a battle at night. None of us have witnessed who was the culprit," I said, my mouth moving on its own because my head filled with cotton and panic. I was glad I had read Endris' words so often that, while I thought I didn't know them by heart, I could repeat them effortlessly.

The judge leaned forward, her chair creaking as she shifted. "Are you certain one of the servants, Lady Seydal's, or yours, who were all present in the mansion at the time, didn't have a grudge against the knight commander and killed him?"

I gaped at the judge.

This wasn't a question Endris had prepared an answer for. He had given me three sheets filled with beautiful words about how the Montbow family sorely regretted the situation, how I knew knight commander Ytel from our journey to the mountains, and how we all wished things would have ended differently. I would have ended my plea with an offer of fifty diamonds to Wildewall. A donation equal to the amount of coin we allegedly still owed Ytel. It was a beautiful speech, but I couldn't use any of it to answer the judge's question. I had to think of an answer on my own.

"Uh," I stammered, silently cursing myself because everyone in the room could hear my stuttering. "No, your honour. Our servants were not in the mansion nor in the woods where the knight commander was found, the night of the murder."

I swore I read a hint of surprise in the judge's expression. "Are you certain blessed storm-touched?" she asked. "Would any of your townsfolk have had the opportunity and reason to murder him?"

"Everyone would have had an opportunity in the dark," I blurted. "But no, the townsfolk wouldn't have had a motive."

"I see." The judge sat back in her chair. "Continue your plea, lord Montbow."

I cleared my throat. "Thank you." I took a deep breath and did my best to continue my plea. The words I spoke barely registered in my mind—I was numb and frantic at the same time. I didn't know what the sudden questioning from the judge meant, and I couldn't ask until after we had vacated the courtroom.

Thankfully, the judge and the council allowed me to finish my entire plea without further interruptions.

"That was all, your honour," I ended my speech with a small bow.

Much to my surprise, a lukewarm, polite applause filled the room. A trial truly seemed to be a public affair in Wildewall, almost a form of entertainment. No wonder Endris had put so much effort into crafting beautiful, lyrical sentences with more difficult words than needed.

"Thank you, lord Montbow," the judge said after the applause faded out. "You may retreat into a private room with your loved ones to await our verdict."

Two guards stepped beside me and let me into a room in the back. When I stepped inside, Ariane was already sitting on a curved armchair situated in the centre of a round room with red curtains aside the tall windows. She sipped tea from a porcelain cup. Her face wasn't a storm, so I reckon I didn't mess up too badly. Still, I was certain she had something to criticise.

I walked to the free armchair, dropped myself into it, and exhaled loudly.

Ariane kept sipping tea. "Tea?" she offered, nodding at the pot on the table. It stood on a small, iron platform with holes and a flickering flame below it.

I glanced at the pot, then turned back to Ariane. "You have nothing to say about the trial? No ridiculing, no remarks on what I did wrong according to Wildewall etiquette?"

Ariane took a sip of her tea.

"Really? Nothing?" I asked. "You have nothing to say about what happened at the half-elven execution yesterday, either?"

"I will pour you some tea," Ariane replied as if I hadn't spoken at all, before promptly doing as she said.

Confused, I accepted the cup of tea Ariane made for me. But if she didn't want to scold me, I wasn't complaining.

After a few more moments of silence, Ariane sighed. "Ezra Dagon was offering you an easy way out," she said. "You could have blamed anyone you wanted and walk away scot-free."

I didn't understand what she meant for a moment. Then I remembered Ezra whispering to the judge and my eyes widened. "So that's what he wanted," I said. "Look, I don't know who stabbed Ytel and killed him. And even if I did, I got a taste of what Wildewall's 'justice' is like yesterday, so I wouldn't tell them regardless."

"Huh," Ariane said with an arched brow. "So you're saying several people have tried to extend their hand to you, and you spat on it every time."

I frowned. "If you mean priest Landefort and Ezra Dagon, then yes. I don't want their deals."

"So it was a conscious choice then to not take their offers?" Ariane mused. "Interesting."

It wasn't. I hadn't the faintest clue what Ezra was offering me with the judge right until now, but I wasn't about to tell Ariane about that. "I don't want their deals, no," I repeated. "I am not selling out Oleander, Endris, my family, or your servants just to gain the respect of Wildewall's nobles."

A small smile played on Ariane's lips.

"What?" I asked.

"I think I feel a little bit of respect for you. What a strange feeling."

I snorted. "What would you have done in my stead?"

"I wouldn't sell out my people," Ariane said, pursing her lips. "Maybe I would sell out you or Oleander if the threat to me was large enough."

"Only me and Oleander? Thanks," I said sarcastically. "And here I was, thinking you'd throw everyone at a judge after the first misstep they took. Your servants certainly seemed scared of nobility in Brittleton's castle."

"They feared you because of your mark, Laurence," Ariane said. "Not because of anything I said to them. I know it is difficult for you to imagine." Ariane wrinkled her nose. "It is difficult for me to imagine. But I needn't remind you these people see you as someone very special. They will look away for many of your mistakes, but their goodwill will run out."

I crossed my arms. "I will keep making 'mistakes' if that means protesting against unfair trials and not blaming an innocent for a crime."

Ariane shook her head in 'disapproval', but I saw a smile tugging at her lips before she hid behind her tea.

This was probably the longest we'd ever conversed without Ariane mocking or scolding me. I wasn't about to try my luck today. I would've been content with silence, but then there was a knock on the door.

It swung open and Ezra Dagon stood in the entrance. He grinned. "Hello children," he said as he stepped inside.

"Master Dagon," Ariane politely greeted Ezra. She nodded, and Ezra bowed.

I would have felt bad for making such an old man bow, but Ezra didn't seem to suffer from his old age. He walked faster than I did, his body supple like a young man's. His eyes sparkled as he looked at me. "My, you are quite a rebellious one, aren't you, young storm-touched?"

I smiled sheepishly. "Not on purpose, I assure you."

Ezra chuckled. "Be that as it may, I'm afraid this behaviour hasn't made you many friends with the court or the temples. You stepped on many toes."

"I already had a feeling the nobles had very long toes, and they were easy to step on," I joked. "And what exactly does that mean?"

"It means you should start considering the consequences of your deeds, lord Montbow," Ezra said. "Surely, you came here knowing you had to impress Wildewall's nobility, not antagonise them?"

"I didn't mean to do that."

"Yet, you did," Ezra pointed out. "The judge and the rest of the council didn't want to rule in your favour, I'll have you know. They told me to bring you the verdict, and they want someone hanged for the crime. It doesn't particularly matter who." Ezra let out his distinct little giggle. "But fear not. I made sure the vote wasn't unanimous, and I asked for another week to reconsider the outcome of the trial."

Ezra gazed me with raised brows.

When I shot him a questioning look, Ariane released a sigh. "This is the part where you ask what he wants in return for that, Laurence."

"Oh," I said dumbly.

Ezra raised his brows even higher, wrinkling his lined forehead further.

I resisted the urge to sigh myself. It seemed like everyone wanted something for everything they did in this city, and I was beginning to feel like a puppet on a string.

"What do you want in return for that?" I asked reluctantly.

Ezra grinned. "So happy you asked, lord Montbow. My request is simple. All I want is a conversation in private with your servant. Oleander the... herbalist, is it?"

I was immediately on my guard. "Why?" I asked.

Ezra raised his hands in defence, seemingly sensing my change of tone. "I have an interest in his knowledge, young lordling. Fret not. All I want is to pick his brain about how he thinks of his antidotes and what else he knows of medicine."

"I thought you were a historian specialised in the elven human war." I crossed my arms.

"I'm a scholar, lord Montbow," Ezra corrected me with a smile. "And I am always seeking more knowledge."

"I'm certain Laurence agrees, master Dagon," Ariane said. She shot me a hard look that said I better not try to argue with her.

Ariane didn't understand what was at stake, however. Endris' warning was fresh in my mind. If anyone was going to discover what Oleander was, it was Ezra Dagon. Maybe he already suspected, and that was why he wanted to see Oleander again.

I couldn't think of a good reason to deny his request. At face value, it seemed like such a small favour to ask compared to what it would gain me. If the Montbow family was to be found guilty of murder, someone would have to hang. My hand would be forced. I'd have to point at someone innocent as Ytel's killer, or risk them choosing a culprit because someone had to be blamed.

I broke out in cold sweat. This was what Oleander meant with choosing a side, or everyone will burn. I would ruin the trial if I tried to keep everyone safe. For now, I had to agree or else I'd quickly run out of options.

I breathed in and out. "Very well," I told Ezra.

Ezra clapped his hands. "Splendid! I will ensure your verdict will be more... favourable."

Humming a cheerful tune, Ezra left the room.

I buried my head in my hands. "What have I done?"

"You made the right decision," Ariane said. "Letting master Dagon have a conversation with Oleander is the best path. I don't understand why you refuse to let him talk to anyone."

I bit my tongue. Of course, Ariane didn't understand, and I couldn't explain to her how dangerous it was. "Can master Dagon be trusted?" I asked.

Ariane thought of it for a moment. "He is good on his word, if that is what you ask. But manipulative to get what he wants."

"You say manipulative like it's a dirty word," I joked. "Why? You are constantly talking about how you want me for my mark alone. Is it only alright if you are manipulative?"

Ariane's eyes lowered down to her tea. "I was five years old too when I was promised to you, Laurence. I was a child with no say in the matter, just like you. And now we are here. Breaking betrothals is forbidden by the gods and shamed by the court, and I'm trying to make the best of that despite knowing you're in love with Oleander and everyone will see it after one blink when they see you together. Do you think I enjoy this?"

Ariane's eyes met mine again. A flame burned in them. "We will see each other again at the ball," she said, before standing, straightening out her skirts, and walking out of the room.

Back to the Wall

While I was standing trial in the court building, I had left Oleander at the Prince Malte's Honour inn. Back home at the Thundercoast, Oleander had a tendency to wander off on his own if he felt a reason to. I was grateful to see he didn't do that here, and seemed to realise how dangerous it was for him to stray inside the city walls.

As Ariane, Endris, and I walked into the common room, Oleander sat at the table nursing a glass of water. He stood abruptly when he saw me enter, almost knocking over his drink. This behaviour was uncharacteristically clumsy of Oleander, and I fought the smile tugging at my lips. I could barely stop myself from smiling regardless whenever I looked at him after last night. We had to behave properly in public, however. I didn't want to aggravate Ariane by having rumours of my indecency spreading in the streets of Wildewall. Especially not after we sort of got along for the first time inside the court building.

Oleander seemed to have the same problem I did. There was a sparkle in his eye, but he compensated for it by looking at me with a frown so deep it crinkled his forehead. "Welcome back, lord Montbow," he spoke politely. "How did the trial go?"

I glanced at the innkeeper standing behind the bar. He appeared busy dunking mugs in water and scraping leftovers off of plates, but that didn't stop him from listening at everything going on in his inn. The walls had ears here, and I was highly aware of it. "The trial went fine, Oleander, thank you," I lied. "We'll await the innocent verdict while we prepare for the queen's ball tomorrow. I wish to visit the bathhouse today."

I turned to Ariane. "Is there anything else you need of me today before I take off?"

Ariane's eyebrows twitched. Then she shook her head and smiled brightly. "No, we have discussed everything we need to discuss today, love. Oh, but do behave yourself with the gentlefolks in the bathhouse. And with anyone else you may speak with today."

Ariane's chirping may have sounded like a doting betrothed teasing her beloved to anyone listening, but I knew she was warning me. Ezra was...particular, and it was best I didn't cross him and neither should Oleander.

"I lack your effortless grace, of course. But I'll make sure we all behave," I said with a forced smile.

Ariane hummed. "Good. I will see you before the queen's ball tomorrow, Laurence," she said, twirling her red hair around a finger like a lovesick woman. "Do let me know when the judge gives her verdict."

The way Ariane could so easily alternate between loving betrothed in front of others and cynical in private would have made me laugh if it didn't frighten me in equal measure. In order to survive in Wildewall, however, it was clear to me now I had to play Wildewall's game, too. If I wanted to bring this visit to a good ending, I couldn't afford to ignore the hierarchy and rules of this place any further.

As Ariane left the inn's common room, I put what I had learned in Brittleton's castle into practice. Even if acting like a snobby god-touched who couldn't even change his own clothes made me almost physically cringe.

"I will change before heading into the city. Oleander, Endris," I said. I snapped my fingers and started walking towards the staircase.

Neither Oleander nor Endris seemed to take my sudden attitude seriously. Endris was unfazed and unblinking as he followed me. Oleander pressed his lips together. His cheeks flushed with effort as he seemed to hold back his laughter. His reaction was contagious, and I had to hold back my laughter as well, until we reached the door of my chambers. There was nobody stationed at my door; Ariane seemed to have dismissed the cavalry for now.

My room was one of the few places where Oleander, Endris, and I could hope to speak in private, but I had failed to take one thing into account. The nightstand. Immediately, Endris' dark eyes shot to the knife and the green fruit dripping on wood beside the bed. My face grew hot. Endris was no fool. He knew what that fruit was used for.

Thankfully, Endris allowed me to keep my secrets and my dignity. He only looked, but didn't speak as I hastily closed the door behind me.

"We're certain there's nobody listening in here?" I asked Endris in a hushed tone.

Endris narrowed his eyes. He searched the room, looking out of the windows, rapping his knuckles on walls, opening the large closet, and peeking into the bathing area. Once he seemed satisfied, he returned to me. "There's nobody listening," he said.

"Alright." I swallowed thickly as I looked at Oleander. "There's someone who wants to speak with you in private. Ezra Dagon. He asked if you could come see him at your first convenience." I turned to Endris. "I know what you're going to say, Endris," I said before he could open his mouth. "Master Dagon can't talk to Oleander because he'll recognise what he is."

Endris' expression darkened. "If master Dagon hasn't already noticed in the library. Knowing Oleander is an elf could well be the very reason he wants to see him. To rip off his hat and confirm what he already knows before sending him to priest Landefort for execution."

"Did master Dagon mention why he wishes to speak with me, Laurence?" Oleander asked softly. "What does he believe I can do for him?"

"Many things, if he knows you're an elf. He's a historian who dedicated his life to studying elven culture and history," Endris said through gritted teeth. "An elf who didn't vanish? You would be a dream come true for him."

"That's not what he wanted," I said. "He wants Oleander's knowledge of poisons and antidotes. Or so he claims. I don't know if those are false pretences or not."

Oleander blinked. "Well, do... you want me to tell him everything I still remember of poisons and antidotes, Laurence? I will, if you ask it of me."

Oleander looked at me for guidance, but I didn't have any to offer. If Ezra was genuine, it felt wrong to deny him knowledge on how to save lives. I had to think of my family, however. We needed Oleander's recipes, and we needed to be the only ones selling rare antidotes to keep ourselves afloat. It wasn't my decision to take, however, even if Oleander wanted me to decide.

"They're your antidotes, Oleander," I said. "Your knowledge. I'm grateful for everything you did for me and my family, but you decide who you share your recipes with. Not me. We have to act like it in within the city walls, but you're not my servant."

Endris expelled a deep sigh, pressing a hand to his forehead. "Why are we entertaining the thought of allowing master Dagon to speak with Oleander in the first place? Decline and say it's not possible to arrange a meeting."

I smiled sheepishly. "I would have done that. The problem is, master Dagon was part of the judge's council, right? He seems to have them in the bag and his demand for not selling me out and declaring the Montbow family guilty of Ytel's murder was to speak with Oleander. If I decline, one of my family members will be declared the culprit and will have to hang."

Endris cursed under his breath. "Of course he did. That's why he whispered to the judge. Shrewd old coot."

"You are familiar with his work, too, then?" I asked. "Ariane also said master Dagon had a talent for making the odds in his favour."

"Yes," Endris said. "And you never know what he wants. He climbed his way up to being the official palace historian by skullduggery and elbowing, but never quite so you could prove it."

"Master Dagon has ties to the palace?" Oleander asked, sounding surprised.

Endris nodded. "Yes. He resides in one of the towers as the court historian. He used his influence and knowledge about elves to also weasel his way into council positions for trials. Originally, he was only invited for trials involving accusations of whither-touched. A traditionally known branch of elven magic. Now, he also receives invitations to higher profile trials like lord Montbow's."

Ezra Dagon sounded dangerous. I didn't want to expose Oleander to a man like that, but what choice did I have? I sighed. "I don't want any of my family members hanged, Endris," I said. "Nor do I want Oleander executed when master Dagon finds out. I don't know what we should do."

"Is there nobody else who can sway the judge and grant you an innocent verdict?" Oleander asked. "Like the queen. Surely she outranks everyone? We could travel to the palace and try to have an audience with her first. She already summoned us to Wildewall because she wished to speak with us, no?"

"She wants to speak to you and lord Montbow, and everyone else. It's the queen's duty to speak with all her guests at a ball, Oleander," Endris replied. "She outranks everyone, yes, but they're not letting us walk into the palace and speak with her outside of the ball. The only reason we will be able to enter the palace at all today is because master Dagon expects you."

"Oh," Oleander breathed. "But is the queen present inside the castle right now? We could always get lucky."

"We won't be lucky," Endris deadpanned.

I wanted to protest and defend Oleander's idea, but realised I couldn't. Being granted an audience with the queen herself a day before her ball sounded like a highly unlikely tale. I let out a frustrated sound. "I could tell master Dagon the first possibility to speak with you is after the ball. I can tell him to wait, and hope we can convince the queen to let the Montbow family go while at the ball."

"You could, however..." Oleander bit his lip. "If master Dagon is as clever as Endris says he is, he will know what you are doing. It's alright, Laurence. I will risk speaking with him if that means I can prevent you from being accused of murder."

"But—" I started protesting. Oleander stopped me by raising a hand. "Please, let me do this for you. You have saved my life as well. Let me save your family in return."

"You have already more than repaid us by sharing your knowledge," I said. "You don't owe me."

A smile curled up the corners of Oleander's mouth. "Do you remember why I wanted to come to Wildewall?"

"Because I'd be in trouble with the court if I didn't bring you," I replied promptly.

Oleander chuckled. "Yes," he said. "To help you, like you have helped me. My second reason was because I hoped to regain some of my memories. In order to do that, I wanted to read at the library and I wanted to see the palace and meet the queen as well."

Oleander's burden was much heavier than mine. The Montbows had lost their family fortune, but Oleander had lost his entire life in the mountains. In all the commotion surrounding knight commander Ytel's death and the queen's ball, I had forgotten all about Oleander's needs. Guilt stabbed at my chest. Endris and I had dragged him out of the library, not taking his wishes into consideration much to keep him safe inside the city. If there was a chance he could regain more memories, I understood Oleander wanted to take it.

"You wanted to meet the queen because of the staff she carries, which is adorned with an elven-made gem," I thought out loud.

Oleander nodded. "You remember. I think seeing it may help me remember something of my past. I don't know if it works that way, but I remembered how to make an antidote in a flash when I saw the flowers growing in vines on the mansion walls and smelled the Bleeding Ivy's leaves. Besides..." Oleander let his gaze glide from me to Endris." I will be forced to visit the palace tomorrow for the ball. There will be many people present who could see me for who I am. Today, the palace will be much quieter. I won't garner attention. If there is a slight chance I could silently meet the queen with no additional eyes on me, and not attend the ball tomorrow, don't we need to take it?"

Endris grimaced. He didn't open his mouth, however, because Oleander had a good point. Every public appearance he made was a risk, and among the nobility visiting the ball, there would be more scholars like master Dagon.

Oleander settled his eyes back on me. "There's a guarantee they will find the Montbow family guilty of murder if we don't give master Dagon what he wants. But there is no guarantee master Dagon wants to harm me or recognised me. Perhaps he truly only wants information."

"Have you not been paying attention at all?" Endris scoffed. "Everyone in this city tries to harm elves! They cut down even people suspected of having a drop of elven blood like dogs in front of the temples!"

"Have a little faith, Endris," Oleander replied with a small smile. "Not everyone. You and Laurence have protected me. You protect all the elven blooded and undesirables."

"Don't assume master Dagon thinks the same," Endris sharply retorted. "He will just as easily turn you in, depending on what he wants. He's unpredictable."

"I understand the risks," Oleander said. "But I'll speak with him."

"I've known you longer than today, and you're not going to change your mind, are you?" I joked wryly. "I know that look in your eyes."

Oleander smiled at me.

"Let us go to master Dagon's tower then," I said.

"Wait," Oleander said as I made for the door.

I looked over my shoulder. "What?"

"Shouldn't you actually change your clothes like you said?" Oleander teased me with a wink. "What will the staff think?"

I looked down at the ridiculous clothes I wore. I'd already forgotten I looked like a walking jewellery store. Sounded like one, too. "Yes."

"Do you need my help to change into other clothes, lord Montbow?" Oleander teased me further.

Endris groaned and pulled a face. "I'm waiting downstairs. Before I lose my lunch." He abruptly marched to the door and slammed the door shut behind him.

Oleander and I looked at each other and laughed. Then Oleander's smile faded as I closed the distance between us and pressed a kiss to his lips.

"What have I done to deserve you?" I murmured to his mouth, before pulling him into a hug and burying my face in the crook of his neck.

"I don't know," Oleander muttered back.

"Whatever happens, I'm not letting master Dagon or anyone else hurt you."

Oleander didn't respond, making me lean back to look at him. His eyes were trained on the bed and nightstand behind me, but he turned his gaze to me as I searched his face. He was no longer smiling. There was a flicker of sadness in his eyes, but it was gone so fast I wondered if I'd imagined it.

"Don't make promises you can't keep, Laurence Montbow," Oleander said. "Nobody can protect everyone."

Oleander grabbed my arms and gently freed himself from my grasp. "Change your clothes. We shouldn't delay."